C-02

Books by Taylor McCafferty

Pet Peeves
Ruffled Feathers
Bed Bugs
Thin Skins

Published by POCKET BOOKS

THIN SKINS

A HASKELL BLEVINS MYSTERY

Taylor McCafferty

POCKET BOOKS

New York   London   Toronto   Sydney   Tokyo   Singapore

An *Original* Publication of POCKET BOOKS

POCKET BOOKS, a division of Simon & Schuster Inc.
1230 Avenue of the Americas, New York, NY 10020

ISBN: 0-671-79977-0

First Pocket Books printing April 1994

10 9 8 7 6 5 4 3 2 1

POCKET and colophon are registered trademarks of Simon & Schuster Inc.

Cover art by John Zielinski

Printed in the U.S.A.

Acknowledgments

I wish to thank Arbidella Dooley and the Shepherdsville Police Department in Shepherdsville, Kentucky, for taking the time to answer my questions. I'd also like to thank my agent, Richard Parks, for all his help, and my editor, Jane Chelius, for her wonderful guidance. And, as always, I'd like to thank my twin sister, Beverly Herald, for serving as my first reader.

CHAPTER

1

Private detectives are supposed to be suspicious. It's what we do. We suspect things, and then we go check those things out.

You'd think I'd have been instantly suspicious that hot Monday morning in August when Rigdon Bewley came running up to me in my brother Elmo's drugstore. After all, if you've been the only private detective in a small town for over a year—and lately folks have actually started giving you pitying looks on account of it having become pretty much common knowledge that there isn't enough detecting business around these parts to keep groceries on your table, let alone a roof over your head—it's probably a bad sign if anybody shows up *begging* you to help them.

Having such a thing happen is, no doubt, akin to staggering out of a desert somewhere, all covered in dust, your lips cracked and bleeding, and having some guy come up and start pleading with you to drink a little of his water.

A thing like that ought to make you suspicious.

In my case, I'm ashamed to say, it did not. Of course, when Rigdon Bewley first came running up to me, the ammonia fumes from my mop bucket might've clouded my judgment some.

"Haskell! Thank God you're here," Rigdon said. "You've got to help me! You've just *got* to!"

I'd just dipped my mop into my bucket and was right in the middle of taking another swipe at the floor in front of Elmo's tanning lotions display, but I stopped and stared at Rigdon.

Rigdon was actually shaking.

Which was, in itself, pretty amazing. I'd known Rigdon Bewley ever since we were in the same chemistry lab back in the ninth grade, and as best as I could recall, I'd never seen him rattled before. Matter of fact, if I remembered correctly, Rigdon had caught his lab coat on fire one afternoon in the chemistry lab, and he hadn't even quickened his step on his way to the water fountain to put it out.

Back then Rigdon had always been too cool to hurry— and far too cool to ever get upset. Moreover, I'd seen Rigdon around town several times in the last year or so, and he sure hadn't looked as if he'd changed much. Every time I'd seen him, Rigdon had always been sauntering along, thumbs hooked carelessly in his belt loops. I'd watched him and pretty much decided that Rigdon—even after all this time—was still doing a fair-to-middling imitation of James Dean, much like he'd been doing seventeen years earlier.

That's James Dean, mind you, the fifties movie actor who'd died too young, not *Jimmy* Dean, the one that sells the sausage. I mention this only because I know full well that there are quite a few male residents of Pigeon Fork who—if given the choice of imitating one of these Deans—would pick Jimmy, hands down. In fact, I do believe that these particular male residents would probably consider having a sausage named after you a thing to aspire to.

Rigdon, I have to hand it to. He was a tad more discriminating.

Rigdon had apparently once seen an old movie starring the non-sausage James Dean, and it had hit him hard. As far back as I could remember, Rigdon had always worn his wavy blond hair combed straight back from his forehead. Just like James Dean. Rigdon had always worn scuffed cowboy boots and faded skintight blue jeans rolled up at the ankles. Just like James Dean. And he'd always worn a plain white T-shirt, in the wintertime with a jacket, in the summertime, without. Just like—you guessed it—James Dean.

Rigdon's outfit today, in fact, looked to be exactly what James Dean had worn in *Rebel Without a Cause.*

I was pretty sure, however, that I'd never seen James Dean in any of his movies shaking in his shoes the way Rigdon was now doing. Or James's voice quavering that bad. Or his blue eyes showing the whites all around, the way Rigdon's now were.

"What's the problem, Rigdon?" I said.

"I'm in big trouble, *that's* the problem!" Rigdon said. "You—You've got to help me, Haskell!" In *Rebel Without a Cause,* James Dean had walked around with a cigarette dangling insolently out of the side of his mouth, but Rigdon, I don't believe, has ever smoked. Long ago Rigdon had solved this problem, though, by making a small substitution—a gnawed toothpick for the cigarette. Now, as Rigdon spoke, the toothpick sticking out of the left side of his mouth bobbled up and down with every word.

It didn't look insolent. It looked downright uncomfortable.

"What kind of trouble are you in?" I said.

Rigdon's answer was not nearly as specific as I'd hoped. "It's weird!" Rigdon said. *"Real* weird! And you're my only hope! You'll help out an old buddy, won't you, Haskell?"

From the way Rigdon sounded, you might've thought that Rigdon and I had been close friends or something. This was not exactly the truth. We'd been acquaintances, at best. Mainly, I believe, because back in high school, when a lot of the kids were comparing Rigdon to James Dean, they'd been comparing *me* to Howdy Doody.

To be honest, there are still those who do this today.

This unfortunate comparison might have something to do with the fact that I happen to have a head full of red hair and enough freckles to amply spatter the noses of every single citizen of a small Latin American country.

Today, at the age of thirty-four, I continue to hope, however, that the rumors of my being a Howdy Doody look-alike have never had any real basis in fact, and that the folks fueling these rumors are just doing it to be cruel.

I couldn't help but take into account, though, that the very same folks spreading unkind rumors about me were spreading nothing of the sort regarding Rigdon.

It also worried me some that, in my considered opinion, Rigdon *did* look quite a bit like James Dean.

At five ten, Rigdon was slender but muscular, and although he might not be as good-looking as James Dean, he was damn close. This last, I have no doubt, was a good part of the reason why, back in high school, Rigdon— again like the real James Dean—had pretty much had a new girl on his arm every other week.

Back then, believe me, I would've loved to have been a close friend of Rigdon's, being as how it might've put me in a good position to catch some of his discards.

There is, however, an unspoken rule that even in my teens I think I knew instinctively. This unspoken rule goes something like this: James Dean does not hang out with Howdy Doody.

At least, he didn't until now. "You'll help out an old buddy who's in big trouble, won't you?" Rigdon was saying. "I'll pay your fee, whatever you want!"

Now, this last part got my attention. Let me see now, this wasn't just a *favor* Rigdon was talking about. It actually sounded as if he wanted to *hire* me.

It was at this point, of course, that I started trying not to do what I always do when I'm first approached by somebody who might actually be a genuine, honest-to-God client.

I tried not to hyperventilate.

"What would you like me to do?" My voice was amazingly casual considering that I've had this long-standing agreement with my brother Elmo for the last year or so—in fact, ever since I opened up my private eye business. In exchange for Elmo letting me have office space rent-free over his drugstore, I actually agreed to mop Elmo's floors and run Elmo's soda fountain during my slow times.

My only excuse is that I made this agreement right after I moved back from Louisville. I'd been living in Louisville for over eight years before then, working homicide on the Louisville police force, and during that time, I reckon I must've completely forgotten the way Pigeon Fork is. When I made that agreement with Elmo, I don't believe I had any idea just how many slow times a private detective could have in a town with a population of only 1,511.

Now, of course, some thirteen months later, I realize that, in Pigeon Fork, Kentucky, if times got any slower, they'd be going backward. I and this mop have gotten to be real close. It's a relationship I don't exactly cherish. I tried to keep the eagerness out of my voice as I added,

"What exactly is the job you've got for me, Rigdon, old buddy?"

Rigdon swallowed once before he answered. "Well, uh, I know it sounds strange, but, uh, well—I, uh, need you to, uh—" Rigdon couldn't seem to find the right words. Finally, grabbing onto my sleeve, he managed to say, his voice getting ragged, "I'm a marked man, Haskell. A marked man, I tell you!"

The toothpick in the corner of Rigdon's mouth was bobbling up and down right smart now. You could get motion sick watching that thing. Not to mention, Rigdon's grabbing at my sleeve was pulling my shirt all sideways. I leaned away from him, hoping he'd let go. And, as I leaned, I remembered something else about old Rigdon.

He always did have a flair for the dramatic.

I reckon that's something you might reasonably expect from somebody who goes around imitating a movie star all the time.

Mind you, I wouldn't go so far as to call Rigdon an outright liar, but there was no denying that he'd always had the tendency to exaggerate a tad. Back in high school Rigdon had once told the entire chemistry lab—with a straight face—that he was a close, personal friend of the Rolling Stones. Come to find out, what Rigdon had apparently meant by that was that he'd just been to a Stones concert up in Cincinnati.

It was remembering Rigdon's tendency to exaggerate that made me ask, as I was still trying to shake off his hand, "Okay, what exactly do you mean by 'marked'?"

For all I knew, Rigdon had just gotten a little careless with a Bic.

"I mean just what I said!" Rigdon said. I'd succeeded in getting him to let go of my shirtsleeve, but you could tell he hated to give it up. For want of something to grab,

Rigdon plucked the toothpick out of his mouth and pointed it at me. "I'm a marked man, Haskell, and the police aren't doing a thing about it!"

I was trying to hold onto my mop and tuck my shirt back into my jeans at the same time. No easy task.

"The police just don't seem to care!" Rigdon was saying.

This last was a little harder to believe than Rigdon's Stones story. The police in Pigeon Fork pretty much boiled down to just one man—Sheriff Vergil Minrath—a guy I know fairly well, being as how Vergil had been my dad's best friend right up until the day Dad died. It has been my experience that if any Pigeon Forkians ever start considering themselves "marked," with a Bic or otherwise, Vergil is the first one to look into it. In fact, I do believe Vergil would take anything even approximating being "marked" in his jurisdiction as a personal affront.

Rigdon had reinserted his toothpick, and was now running a trembling hand through his blond hair. "There's a plot afoot, I tell you!"

I just looked at him. *Afoot?* Now there's a word you don't hear every day. It made you wonder if Rigdon had been recently reading a little too much Sherlock Holmes.

Rigdon's voice rose. "You got to believe me, Haskell, there's a plot to *kill* me!"

Rigdon was really getting agitated now, removing and reinserting his toothpick, fidgeting with his belt, and running his hand through his hair in a whirl of motion. When somebody starts acting this way around me, I always get ultracalm. To sort of defuse the situation.

I also wanted to get Rigdon to lower his voice some. A couple of Elmo's customers two aisles over had turned to give us curious looks.

I cleared my throat. "Okay, let me get this straight," I

said, turning my own voice down a notch in the hopes that Rigdon would follow suit, "you say you're a marked man . . ." I cocked my head in Rigdon's direction, and assumed what I hoped was an attitude of nonchalance, leaning on my mop. Like maybe I heard this sort of thing every day of my life. "What makes you think so?"

Rigdon did not follow my lead. If anything, his voice got even louder.

"It's my work, Haskell. My WORK!"

Beads of sweat were now popping out pretty good on Rigdon's forehead. It was, as I said, a hot day, but that was *outside.* Inside, Elmo's air-conditioning was going full-blast, giving the drugstore the kind of atmosphere you find in a lot of stores on hot summer days.

The kind of atmosphere in which you could possibly hang meat.

The way I looked at it, it took some doing to sweat in Elmo's these days, and yet Rigdon here was getting to be a regular fountain.

I can't say it was doing wonders for his personal hygiene. I leaned farther away from him.

"Somehow, they've found out what I'm doing, and they're trying to stop it!" Rigdon was going on.

I blinked at that one. From the way Rigdon was talking, you might've thought he was some kind of scientist or something. That maybe he was working on a new stealth bomber. Or that he'd just invented a motor that ran on water. *Or* at the very least, that Rigdon was working on something that could upset the apple cart of quite a few very important, very powerful folks.

Rigdon, however, was not a scientist.

He was a taxidermist.

The way I saw it, there probably weren't a whole lot of very important, very powerful folks for whom taxidermy figured prominently in their lives.

"They? Who do you mean, 'they'?" I tried to sound as if I were just asking a question, nothing more. There must've been, however, something in the way I said those words, because Rigdon stiffened and refused to say anything more.

"Look, Haskell, you don't have to take my word for it. I've got proof," he said. "Back at my place. Will you come with me so's I can show you? Please? Please, Haskell, *please?*"

This, of course, was precisely the point where my detective suspicions should've kicked into overdrive. Rigdon was actually clasping his hands together in front of my face as if he were praying to me. "Come on, Haskell," he pleaded, "do this for me. *Please?*"

In my defense, I should mention here that it had been over eight weeks since I'd done any detecting work whatsoever. My phone was not exactly ringing off the hook. In fact, Melba Hawley, the less-than-efficient secretary that I share with my brother Elmo, actually suggested last week that maybe I might ought to consider taking my extra phone line out. Melba was talking about the line that I've got strung up so she can answer it at her desk down in the drugstore, right along with Elmo's phone.

"You're just wasting your money, Haskell," Melba had told me cheerfully, patting her brown beehive hairdo with a plump hand. "You should just have your customers call up on Elmo's line." She'd leaned forward and given me a toothy smile. "I don't think your calls would tie up the drugstore phone one bit."

I'd just looked at her. Melba can be so supportive. I'd considered saying a few equally supportive things to her, but I decided against it. Melba takes offense real easy. And when she's offended, she sort of forgets to answer my phone. Of course, these days I probably couldn't tell the difference, but there was no reason to poke the tiger. Instead, I just took a deep breath and said, "Melba, we call them clients, not customers. Remember?"

To which Melba replied pretty much the way she always does.

"La dee da."

Patting her beehive some more.

Bearing all this in mind, I don't think I could be faulted exactly for doing what I did. I was plopping my mop back into my bucket and returning them both to the storeroom in the back of Elmo's before Rigdon had gotten to his last "Please."

"Okay, Rigdon," I said when I returned. "I'll follow you to your place, but I can't be gone real long, okay?" It was already ten-thirty by my watch. "I've got me another appointment at noon, okay?"

I wasn't just trying to cut our little visit short. I really was telling the truth. My appointment was a lunch date with my girlfriend Imogene, but I wasn't about to tell Rigdon that. There was every possibility that James Dean would never understand why Howdy Doody couldn't just have his girlfriend cool her heels for a while.

But then again, for James Dean, there was always another girl coming down the pike.

For Howdy Doody, what was coming down the pike was probably Clarabelle.

Rigdon was now nodding eagerly. "That's okay, Haskell. If you need to leave before noon, that's fine. Whatever you say."

I think I could've told him that we'd both needed to sit on razor blades on the way out to his place, and Rigdon would've said the same thing.

After that there was nothing else to do but tell Melba that I was going to be out on a case, get in my truck, and follow Rigdon's red Chevy pickup out to his place.

As usual, Melba was not at her desk, so I just left her a

note saying where I was going. I'd already told her about my date at Frank's, but in the note I reminded her again. The only thing reliable about Melba's memory is that you can pretty much count on it being real short.

It wasn't a long drive out to Rigdon's, only about fifteen miles outside of town. We headed down Main Street, passing Frank's Bar and Grill on the left some six miles later, and then we turned right onto Cedar Holler Road on the other side of Higgins's Stop 'n' Shop. A few miles after that we bumped over the railroad tracks, and then finally we made a real sharp right-hand turn onto a country road that was evidently so out of the way, it didn't even warrant a street sign.

On the way, the road Rigdon and I traveled went from blacktop to something folks around these parts call "chipped." It sounds as if maybe somebody took after the road with a pickax, or that maybe the road is crumbling like a cookie, but in actuality, chipping has nothing to do with chips.

Chipping is what the Crayton County Road Department does to a lot of the side roads around Pigeon Fork. I'm not exactly sure what the process entails, but I do know that it involves the Road Department guys laying down a lot of black, sticky oil, and then grinning at you real wide when all that oil splatters the underside of your truck as you go by. After the oil and the grinning comes a layer of fine gravel, spread real thin.

Chipping a road cuts down on dust, and it's supposed to be a whole lot cheaper than blacktop. It's this last that makes me believe—on account of there not being any actual chips involved—that long ago folks around these parts probably just misunderstood the term. Probably what it was really called originally was "cheaping."

Anyway, if the road Rigdon and I were traveling had not been cheaped, I surely wouldn't have been able to follow Rigdon as closely as I was doing. August in

Kentucky is usually a pretty dry month, and this one had been no exception. If this road had been your average dirt road, I probably wouldn't even have been able to *see* Rigdon by now. His truck would've just been this giant dust cloud up ahead of me.

The unmarked road Rigdon and I finally turned onto was also cheaped. It being unmarked is something you get used to around these parts. Sometimes I suspect that the Crayton County Road Department figures that if you don't already know where you're going, you shouldn't be out here in the middle of nowhere, driving around. And it's up to them to discourage you.

Even without a street sign, and even if I hadn't been following Rigdon so closely, I probably could've found Rigdon's house. Mainly because by now I'd started seeing small white signs on the side of the road about every thousand feet or so.

These signs reminded me of those little Burma-Shave signs you used to see lining the highways when I was little. Only instead of a rhyming slogan like the Burma-Shave signs, these small white signs all said the same thing. "Rigdon Bewley," in neat hand lettering. And under that, "Professional Taxidermist." With a red arrow pointing in the direction Rigdon and I were traveling.

I stared at the signs. Was there such a thing as an *un*professional taxidermist? So that it was necessary to make sure that folks understood that you were not one of these rank amateurs? Or could it be that old Rigdon was exaggerating again?

As we moved down the road, Rigdon's signs got bigger. And fancier. Now they had line drawings in each corner.

Unfortunately, what Rigdon had apparently not taken into account when he'd done these drawings was that folks viewing them would be traveling down a country road at forty-five miles an hour. The drawings were far too small and far too detailed for you to get a real good look before you were past them.

What Rigdon had also apparently not taken into account was that he was no artist. I actually had to slow down a little and really stare at several of the signs before I finally figured out what it was that Rigdon had been trying to draw.

The top left-hand corner was the easiest—a rabbit bearing a distinct resemblance to Bambi's Thumper. Rigdon must've traced this one out of a book because it was, without a doubt, his best. The other three were harder to decipher. By squinting, I finally decided that the strange smudge in the top right-hand corner was a fish jumping out of nonexistent water, and that thing in the bottom right corner with what looked to be tree branches growing out of its head was a deer.

It was the drawing in the lower left-hand corner of Rigdon's signs, however, that truly intrigued me. I couldn't figure out this one for the life of me. What it looked to be more than anything else was a large, furry thumb.

I believe, however, I could assume that this was not the sort of thing Rigdon stuffed and mounted.

By the time Rigdon and I had pulled into the long, gravel driveway of a small ranch-type house setting pretty far back from the road, I still hadn't made up my mind what that fourth drawing could be.

Rigdon's front yard looked to cover about an acre of ground, and there were two more signs in it, one real close to the road, and one real close to Rigdon's front door. This last sign Rigdon had apparently done up big. It hung around the neck of a large stone deer.

I got out of my truck, getting my best look yet at the rabbit, the deer, the fish, and the thumb.

It didn't help.

As best as I could tell, the thumb appeared to have a pointy thumbnail sticking out off the end.

I'd pretty much made up my mind to just come right out and ask Rigdon what in hell that thumb was, but straight away Rigdon came toward me, saying, "Did you notice my signs, Haskell? Pretty nice, huh? I drew them myself."

I didn't even blink. "No kidding," I said.

"I worked on them for weeks. *Weeks,* mind you." Rigdon started going on then about how many hours it had taken him to do the drawings, and how he'd worked on them over and over again to get them "just right."

I could tell Rigdon was pretty much talking just to put off going inside. All the time he was telling me about the hard work he'd done on his drawings, he kept glancing toward his house, his eyes growing more and more apprehensive.

I, of course, just stood there, listening to him, and yes, mentally shelving my come-right-out-and-ask-him plan. It didn't seem like good form to insult a client's art work right off the bat.

"I put up the signs," Rigdon was now saying, "because lately, my business has been dying off."

I wasn't about to touch that one with a stick. "No kidding," I said again.

"I thought maybe the signs would help," Rigdon added, "but they sure don't seem to have done the trick." He sounded a little bewildered.

I was feeling a little bewildered myself. Was it possible that Rigdon had actually been under the impression that putting up a few directional signs would cause a regular traffic jam heading his way? What did he think—that folks around town had a lot of recently expired dead animals lying around, waiting to be stuffed and mounted, and that his signs would serve as a quick reminder that they'd better get to it?

If such a thing *were* true, which was unlikely, wouldn't the animals themselves be reminder enough?

Staring at Rigdon, I remembered something else about him. Back in high school, he had not exactly been a member of the National Honor Society. Matter of fact, now that I thought about it, there had been more than a few bets wagered our senior year that Rigdon would not graduate with the rest of us.

He had, of course, fooled everybody. Mainly, as I recall, by coming up with an A in Art.

Looking over at the furry thumb on Rigdon's sign, I realized this was hard to believe.

Rigdon had apparently put off the inevitable for as long as he could. With a final uneasy glance toward the house, he squared his shoulders and started up the gravel path toward his front door.

With a final piercing stare at the thumb, I followed him.

CHAPTER
2

Rigdon's house looked like the kind of house you might draw in the first grade.

Come to think of it, it went right well with his sign in the front yard.

A small, rectangular box, Rigdon's house had a front door centered in the middle, two picture windows centered on either side of the door, and a single peaked roof sitting on top. The siding on the house was even a shade you might've colored it with your crayons back in the first grade—light blue with white shutters on either side of the windows.

In style, Rigdon's house pretty much matched the others on his street. The only thing that seemed to change was the color of his neighbors' siding. The house across the street was yellow with white shutters, the one next door to that, green with white shutters, and the one farther on down the street, gray with—you guessed it—white shutters once again.

Either every one of Rigdon's neighbors had identical

tastes in shutters, or the shutter department at one of the local hardware stores had had a white sale.

This kind of thing always amazes me. You'd think that folks would choose to live way out in a rural area somewhere so they could build themselves any kind of unique house they'd like. Likely as not, though, what you'll find on a remote country road like Rigdon's are houses that look every bit as much like each other as those you'll find in a subdivision in Louisville, or Nashville, or Atlanta.

Rigdon's house—like all the houses on his side of the street—did, however, have some things you didn't generally get in those big city subdivisions. Besides having an acre of yard in front and at least a half acre on either side, Rigdon's house backed up to dense woods. In fact, his tiny house looked even tinier, overshadowed the way it was by the huge maples, oaks, and evergreens towering over it in the back.

"Nice place you got here," I said. I was lying through my teeth, of course. Rigdon's house was one of the plainest, most unimaginative houses I'd ever seen. It didn't even have a porch, which might've added a little interest to the front. Instead it had a stoop. Which was mainly just a concrete block sitting out in front of Rigdon's door. A real small concrete block. There was barely enough room for both of us to stand on it while Rigdon fooled around with his key.

Rigdon nodded when I spoke, but he didn't answer. He was sure taking his sweet time, unlocking his front door.

This, believe it or not, was an odd thing to be doing around these parts. I don't mean, taking his sweet time. I mean, unlocking his door.

Folks around Pigeon Fork don't generally bother to lock their doors. Particularly out in the boonies like this. I reckon they figure that if a burglar has gone to all the trouble of finding the place, he deserves something for the effort.

Of course, I could understand why Rigdon might've made an exception on the door-locking issue. I reckon if you're under the impression that there's—how had he put it?—"a plot afoot," it might make you a tad cautious.

Come to think of it, Rigdon had probably only started locking his door just recently. That probably explained why it was taking him so long to get in his own front door. Having not unlocked it all that many times before, Rigdon was still getting the hang of it.

While I waited for Rigdon to finally get the door unlocked, I noticed yet another small sign taped on the picture window to the left of the door. "Walk-ins welcome. 24 hours a day."

I couldn't help staring. Once again Rigdon's thought processes totally escaped me. Did he think that his customers were the sort that just moseyed in off the street? Sort of like folks who needed a quick haircut? Did he expect them to show up at two or three in the morning with something they needed stuffed in a hurry?

Rigdon had finally finished with his key, and with his hand on the doorknob, glanced back at me before he went ahead and opened the door. Obviously he was making sure that I was still right behind him.

That's, of course, when Rigdon saw me staring at his window sign. "I just had that one made," he said. "I thought being open all hours might drum up a little extra business."

I stopped looking at the sign, and started looking at Rigdon. There was every chance that he was not a marketing genius.

Rigdon now stepped aside, letting me go in first. Just before he followed me inside, Rigdon peered into the house cautiously.

What Rigdon was looking for, I wasn't sure.

His apprehension, however, was catching. I found myself moving slowly into Rigdon's living room, my eyes darting this way and that, like maybe I expected something to jump out at me.

The things in that room, however, had done all the jumping they were ever going to do.

Rigdon had apparently transformed his living room into one large showroom of his work. On the two end tables on either side of his couch, on the coffee table in front of his couch, and clustered in groups of three here and there on the gray linoleum floor were innumerable motionless creatures. Squirrels, rabbits, raccoons, beavers, blackbirds, pheasants—you name it, and Rigdon had apparently stuffed it.

It was, however, the group of animals squatting on furry haunches on the brick hearth surrounding the small wood stove in the center of Rigdon's living room that pretty much caught my eye. Lord. It looked as if these poor rabbits, squirrels, and raccoons were huddling around that stove, hoping against hope for a little warmth.

They were out of luck, of course. Rigdon's little house must've had central air-conditioning, because it was as cool inside as a cave. It was just as well. You could tell, even from where I was standing across the room, that no amount of heat was ever going to do these particular creatures the least bit of good.

In back of me Rigdon suddenly let out with a bloodcurdling yell. "Shoo! Shoo! SHOOO-OOOO!"

The things in that room may have been beyond jumping, but I instantly proved I was still capable of it. I must've leaped a foot off the ground.

My heart in my mouth, I wheeled on Rigdon. "What in hell did you do that for?"

Rigdon didn't even look my way. Intent on searching

the room, his eyes moving quickly from one creature to another, he said, "I was just making sure that none of these animals were alive."

I stared at him. Wasn't that the sort of thing you generally checked for *before* you stuffed and mounted them?

Rigdon was not looking in my direction, so he pretty much missed the expression on my face. "You never can be too sure, you know," he added.

Oh yeah. Uh-huh. My goodness, yes. Stuffed animals coming back to life had to be a real problem for taxidermists. It had to happen *all* the time. What a nuisance.

I stared at Rigdon some more, getting a real sinking feeling for the first time. Like I said at the beginning, suspecting things is what we detectives do. Right now, for example, I'd started suspecting that Rigdon was not playing with a full deck.

Like I also said at the beginning, checking our suspicions out is another thing we detectives do.

"Uh, tell me, Rigdon," I said, trying to keep my voice real casual so as not to provoke another yell, "have any of these animals ever come back to life *after* you got through with them?"

Rigdon looked at me as if maybe *I* were the one with a few cards missing. "Of course not. The ones I stuff always stay dead." At this point it must've occurred to Rigdon what might've made me ask such a thing. He shrugged and then added, kind of sheepishly, "Oh. Yeah. Well, I guess my checking to see that all these animals are dead does sound a little strange."

I shrugged too, as if to say, "Reckon so." Actually, what I was thinking was that it didn't just sound strange, it *was* strange.

And not just a little.

Rigdon was hurrying on. "Actually, it wasn't the

stuffed animals that I was worried about. I was just making sure that no *other* animals had gotten in while we were gone." He gave me a significant look. "It would be real easy, you know, for an animal to hide in here, *pretending* he'd been stuffed."

Somehow, that little explanation did not make me feel all that much better. Oddly enough. I was now watching Rigdon every bit as intently as he himself had been searching the room.

Rigdon must have completed his search for stuffed-animal imposters, because he now seemed suddenly to relax a little. Glancing my way, he took in the entire room with a single sweeping motion of his hand. "Nice, huh?" he said.

Having been unable to bring myself to ask him about the furry thumb on his signs—and now beginning to wonder if Rigdon might not be more comfortable in a garment with very long sleeves that tied in the back—I wasn't about to tell Rigdon the truth: That what he had in his living room was not exactly the sort of home decor that I myself leaned toward. "It's nice, all right," I lied.

"They all look just like they were still alive, don't they?" Rigdon went on.

The answer to that was, of course: No, not at all. It was obvious that either all these creatures were very dead, or else we'd just stumbled into a game of animal "frozen catchers."

I didn't say a word, though. Instead I gave Rigdon an insincere smile and gave the room a quick look-see myself.

Hanging at eye level on the wall to my left was a large moose head. Mounted on a wooden plaque in the shape of a shield, the moose met my gaze with what could only be described as a long-suffering expression on its face.

Next, traveling clockwise around the room, there were three deer heads mounted on similar plaques. These three wore long-suffering expressions virtually identical to that of their moose neighbor.

It made you wonder. Was this the sort of expression Rigdon *meant* to put on these animals' faces? Or was it just there, and Rigdon couldn't do a thing about it?

I reckon it wasn't exactly possible to make them all smile.

After the moose and the deer came about a dozen small plaques holding bass, catfish, and bluegills—all apparently looking just as they'd looked the moment they'd been hooked (horrified)—and finally, positioned next to the wall directly in back of me, a large owl sat on a wooden perch.

The owl, unlike its neighbors, looked neither long-suffering nor horrified. It looked pissed.

Rigdon was following my gaze with obvious pride. "You notice," he said, "how all their eyes seem to follow you as you move?"

I took a couple of steps farther into the room and glanced around again. In my humble opinion, not a single glass eye now seemed directed my way.

Fortunately, Rigdon didn't seem to need me to agree. "It's the same sort of effect," he said, "that you get when you walk past the Mona Lisa."

I glanced over at the moose. Mona Lisa, it wasn't.

"Very nice," I lied again.

I reckon I might as well admit it. I'm not what you might call a taxidermy aficionado. In fact, I guess I'm pretty much of the mind-set that dead things need to be buried. The sooner, the better.

While I'm not one of those animal rights folks you see yelling on television every once in a while, I do tend to believe that taking the life of an animal just to make it into a wall decoration does seem a tad on the selfish side.

And, even if you didn't actually kill the animal yourself—say, it died of natural causes or, for example, from kissing the bumper of a semi—I still have reservations about the whole thing. When I'd heard years ago that Roy Rogers had had his horse Trigger stuffed and mounted, it had given me pause. Somehow, the thought of turning something as big as a horse into a room display seemed not quite in the best of taste. Not to mention, the thought of Roy and Dale walking past Trigger every day, maybe even hanging their cowboy hats on Trigger's velvety ears, was an image I sure didn't want to dwell on.

Rigdon was now directing my attention toward the far wall. "That there's my masterpiece," he said.

I stared. In the middle of the wall that Rigdon indicated was a raised wooden platform polished to a high gleam and illuminated by a single spotlight. In the middle of this platform, the light around the animal making a sort of halo, stood a large golden retriever. Carefully posed with one paw in the air, its nose lifted in an attitude of frozen expectation, the retriever carried a duck in its mouth.

I wasn't sure, but from where I stood, the retriever looked to be in a far better mood than the duck.

Rigdon cleared his throat, his toothpick wobbling precariously. "That's Shep," he said. "Best damn hunting dog you'd ever want to own." He blinked a couple of times, and added, "Shep lived to be almost fifteen, and, well, I just couldn't bring myself to part with him."

Once again I smiled insincerely. I've got a dog myself, one that I pretty much like—except, of course, during those times when he tries to steal a rib eye off my plate. When Rip finally goes to his reward, or meets his Maker, or whatever it is that dogs do, I will—without a doubt—miss him real bad.

Bearing all that in mind, I'd still say—without any hesitation whatsoever—that the idea of turning Rip's remains into something I had to dust every week does not appeal to me.

Not to mention, I'm pretty sure it wouldn't appeal to Rip either. Especially considering that Rip spends nearly every minute of his life these days curled up somewhere, sleeping. If Rip were forced to actually stand for, oh, say, an eternity, and moreover, to not only stand, but to keep one paw in the air much like Shep over there, I would bet money that Rip would be wearing the exact same expression as Rigdon's owl.

No doubt the first thing Rip would do when we met on the other side would be to bite me.

Apparently, Rigdon had stalled as much as he could. He now took still another deep breath, squared his shoulders, and led the way through the crowded living room and on into the small kitchen on the other side of the open door.

Rigdon stopped abruptly just inside the door. "In here is what I've got to show you," Rigdon said. His voice had started shaking some again.

Like Rigdon, I, too, stopped just inside the door.

Rigdon was now pointing dramatically at his kitchen table. "See?" he said. *"See?* What did I tell you?"

I don't know what I was expecting. From the way Rigdon's voice was shaking, though, I sure expected something more than what I saw: a glass of milk, a small blue bowl with a stainless steel spoon sticking out of it, and a jumbo box of Cap'n Crunch, all sitting innocuously on the white painted surface of Rigdon's kitchen table.

I must've taken too long to get the significance of all this, because in back of me Rigdon made an impatient noise. How he managed to do that and not lose his toothpick was beyond me. "Come on, Haskell, take a real close look!" he said. "Those aren't just Crunch berries, you know!"

Moving across the room so that I stood right next to the table, I followed Rigdon's directions.

Sure enough, mixed among the Crunch berries in the

blue bowl, a couple shiny black berries floated in the milk. These dark berries looked a lot like blueberries, but I recognized them instantly. Being as how my mother had carefully pointed these berries out to me when I'd been no bigger than a pup.

Small, shiny black globes, they were baneberries.

Baneberry plants grow wild around these parts, getting almost three feet tall in the real heavily wooded areas. You don't see them a lot, but because the berries are extremely poisonous and can actually kill you extremely dead, my mom used to point them out to me every time we ran across them.

You don't have to eat too many baneberries to do the trick either. Two just might do it.

I moved even closer to Rigdon's kitchen table and noticed something else. There were small animal footprints all over the tabletop, but particularly around the cereal bowl.

As if something with tiny, muddy paws had circled the bowl.

I was still, however, not at all sure what conclusion I was supposed to draw from all this. I glanced back over at Rigdon uncertainly.

"I told you," he said, his eyes now as wide as they'd been back at Elmo's. "It's proof! They really *are* trying to kill me!"

I just looked at him. Maybe I was being stupid here. *"Who?"* I said.

Rigdon gave me a look that said there was no maybe about it. I was stupid, all right. "Why, the animals, of course!" Rigdon said. "The *animals* in the woods have put out a hit on me!"

I blinked.

Evidently, when Rigdon said there was a plot *afoot,* he wasn't kidding.

Rigdon's voice was shaking so bad, you might've

thought we were in the middle of an earthquake. "This one was a squirrel that did this!" he said, pointing at the footprints on the table with a finger shaking every bit as bad as his voice. "I can tell, you know. I can recognize paw prints, and these were definitely left by a squirrel!"

Rigdon's tone appeared to imply that he was giving me quite a bit of help here. Real, solid clues to go on.

I just stared at him for a second. "You actually think a *squirrel* is trying to poison you?"

Rigdon shook his head. "Oh no," he said.

I felt an instant wave of real relief. Obviously, I'd misunderstood Rigdon badly.

My relief was short-lived, however. Rigdon hurried on. "It's not just squirrels, Haskell. Like I told you, there's a whole gang of animals after me!"

Rigdon was still hanging back over at the door to the kitchen, peering into the room this way and that. It took me a second to realize what he was doing.

Before he took it upon himself to move all the way into the room, Rigdon was actually checking to make absolutely sure that there were no homicidal bushy-tailed creatures lurking in the shadows. With, no doubt, large pawfuls of baneberries.

The sinking feeling I'd had in the living room had returned. "Rigdon, you can't be serious!"

Rigdon, however, was not listening. Having assured himself that the woodland equivalent of Pretty Boy Floyd was not at that moment scampering around the room, he walked straight past me to stand in front of the window over the kitchen sink. "I left this just exactly the way I found it. So's you could see. This," Rigdon said, "must've been the way the little devil got in, don't you think?"

I followed Rigdon over to the window. It was standing half open, so you could clearly see that in the lower left-hand corner the screen had been ripped away from the frame. In all likelihood, Rigdon was right. If a squirrel had gotten into this room, it probably had come in through the window.

I was even willing to concede that the "little devil" in question might even have left the baneberries in Rigdon's bowl. Maybe the thing really had been carrying a couple of berries around in its little paws and had dropped them into the cereal bowl.

Stranger things, no doubt, have happened. Hell, they're documented every week on *America's Funniest Home Videos.*

However, two berries do not a plot make. And malice aforethought in this instance, I believe, would be definitely hard to prove.

"Look, Rigdon," I said, "just because some animal might've tippy-toed in here and inadvertently dropped some berries in your bowl, and just because those berries happened to be poisonous, certainly doesn't mean there's some big plot—"

Rigdon interrupted. *"Happened* to be poisonous? Are you nuts?"

I stared at him. This guy believed that there were actually such things as squirrel hit men, and he was asking if *I* was nuts?

"There's no 'happened to be' about it! They're trying to poison me *on purpose,* I tell you!" Rigdon was saying. "How do you think those berries got in my bowl, huh, answer me that!"

Rigdon was really getting excited now. The toothpick in the corner of his mouth was going up and down like a trip-hammer.

That thing must be glued on.

Before I had a chance to answer his question, though, Rigdon went right on and answered for me. "I'll tell you how! They were put there. Not by accident neither!"

Rigdon was flailing his arms around so much that, in

order to keep from possibly being smacked, I took a step backward. And then, all of a sudden, it hit me. Wait a minute now, this was too bizarre. Rigdon *had* to be pulling my leg. Sure, that was it. Old Rigdon had heard around town about how my business had slacked off, and how I'd probably take any kind of case, and he'd decided to pull a fast one on me. He probably even had a bet going with somebody whether or not I'd fall for it. Hell, it was probably the same guys that had bet years ago on whether Rigdon himself was going to make it out of high school.

I was halfway tempted to start looking for a camera hidden in one of Rigdon's kitchen cabinets. Filming what was, no doubt, scheduled to be Saturday night entertainment at Frank's Bar and Grill up the road. "All right, Rigdon," I said, holding up my hands in a gesture of submission and already starting to grin. "You got me. You really had me going for a minute there, but I'm on to—"

Rigdon, however, did not grin back. Instead, he looked as if I'd slapped him. "Haskell, this is no joke! This is my *life* we're talking about! This morning if I hadn't noticed that a couple of them Crunch berries looked funny, why, I'd have been every bit as dead as all them animals out in my living room."

Rigdon's eyes were showing the whites all around again. I stared at him. The blood did appear to have drained out of his face.

James Dean might've been a good enough actor to pull this off, but I was pretty sure that Rigdon Bewley was not.

Rigdon, then, might actually be serious. Dead serious.

That sinking feeling was back.

I held up my hands. "Rigdon, listen to me, okay? Don't you think all this is a little farfetched? I mean, don't you think—"

28

Thinking, however, did not appear to be Rigdon's strong suit. He was too busy grabbing my sleeve again. "I even know *why* they've put out a hit on me, Haskell," he said. "I've figured out *exactly* why they want me dead."

"You have?" I believe I was showing real patience at this point.

Rigdon nodded. "The animals doing this must be *relatives* of the ones I've stuffed." Rigdon said this very slowly, as if he were explaining things to a kindergartner.

I blinked again.

Rigdon's nod this time was so vigorous, he finally managed to dislodge his toothpick. Retrieving it off the floor, he said, "That's it, all right, they're not happy about what I've done to their kin—" Rigdon was so excited now that when he tried to reinsert his toothpick, he missed the first time and nearly skewered his nose. Undaunted, he hurried on. "—and now they've heard all about my plans for this place, you know, all about my *big* plans, and—and they're *mad!*"

I was getting more and more convinced that it was not just the animals in the woods that could make such a claim.

I also now had a pretty good guess as to why the police had not been all that eager to help Rigdon out.

There was, however, no calming Rigdon down. He was pacing his small kitchen, flailing his arms around even more. "With my business dying off the way it's been, you see, I'd been looking for a way to add to my income. And I finally hit on it," he said.

According to Rigdon, he'd been planning for months to build an addition to his house, in order to have a kind of exhibit of his work in there. "It's going to be like a petting zoo," he said, "only without the petting."

Under other circumstances, this last might've sounded real funny. However, in view of what I'd been hearing up to then, this sounded like the first sensible thing Rigdon had come close to saying since we'd walked into his kitchen.

"A petting zoo without the petting, you say."

My tone must've been encouraging because Rigdon actually calmed down a little as he went on, telling me about his "big plans" to supplement his income by charging tourists and school kids to come all the way out here and see animals in their natural habitat. Or, at least, as natural as you could get, in big glass cases filled with sticks and rocks to simulate the great outdoors.

Because he didn't have the cash on hand to hire the work done, Rigdon had been making plans to build this addition himself. "My uncle, Ernal Bewley, you see, used to be a builder—fact is, he built all the houses on this road—"

This was not exactly a surprise. No wonder they all looked so much alike.

"—he's retired now, but I learned a lot from working for Ernal when I was younger. I installed my own central air, you know, about five years back. There ain't a doubt in my mind that I can do all the work myself."

Rigdon was now looking a *lot* more relaxed. I was even feeling slightly more relaxed myself, now that Rigdon was confining his discussion to the activities of actual humans for a change.

"For about a month now," Rigdon said, "I've been making drawings and getting together a list of materials." He paused and added, "Here, I'll show you." Striding out of the kitchen, down the hall, and through the door directly in front of him, once again he kept looking back at me to make sure I was following.

I was following, all right. Although I can't say I was real glad when we got where we were going. The room Rigdon and I entered was obviously his workroom. A long wooden worktable against the right wall was cluttered with the kind of things apparently no taxidermist can do without. Hammers, saws, scissors, tweezers, pliers, twine, modeling clay, needles and several spools of thread—to mention just some of the stuff—were spread from one end of the table to the other. There were also various small skulls and bones, several knives of one size and another, and a jar holding what looked to be dark brown glass eyes in varying sizes.

I swallowed uneasily. If this didn't look like Frankenstein's lab, nothing did.

At the end of the worktable closest to me, there was a large bucket filled with a dark red liquid.

I couldn't help staring at it. Good Lord.

Rigdon, however, was now staring at *me* and looking puzzled. "That there's tomato juice, you know. It's the best thing for getting the smell out of skunk skins. Works like a charm."

I cleared my throat and gave him a quick nod. "Oh yeah. Of course," I said. I tried to sound as if what he'd just told me was something I'd known ever since I was in diapers.

Rigdon now continued across the room and stopped at a small desk positioned against the far window. Opening the top drawer, he pulled out a sheaf of papers. "See?" he said. "This right here is more proof that what I'm telling you is the truth!"

It was already pretty light in the room, but Rigdon pulled the chain on the overhead light fixture. As if casting a little more light on the subject would banish any lingering doubts I might have.

He also apparently thought that it would help to wave his papers back and forth awful close to my face. To keep Rigdon from, say, poking out one of my eyes with those papers, I grabbed them the next time they went by and gave them a quick look. Sure enough, according to the sketches, Rigdon had been planning to knock out an

outside wall in his living room and add on a large room.
The new room apparently was going to be filled to
overflowing with glass showcases lining the walls.

"Just this week," Rigdon said, looking over my shoulder, "I started getting prices for the cost of materials.
And then"—he drew a long, shuddering breath—"the
animals found out about it!"

Rigdon was tensing up again. "In the last few days,
Haskell," he said, "they've really been after me!" According to Rigdon, raccoons had made their sneaky way
into his kitchen and left poison leaves in his salad.
Rabbits had hidden razor blades in the tomatoes in his
garden. And, of course, just this morning a squirrel had
come into his kitchen and put baneberries in his cereal
bowl. Rigdon had poured milk on his cereal and then,
remembering that he'd left a skin soaking in tomato
juice, he'd gone into his workroom for a few minutes.

"That damn squirrel must've been watching me, just
waiting for his chance!" Rigdon said.

I cleared my throat. "You think that squirrel could've
lifted the window over your sink all by itself?"

Rigdon didn't even blink. "Oh, I'm sure it had help
from the others."

I just stared at him. "Others?"

Rigdon was looking a tad impatient. "The raccoons
and the rabbits, Haskell. I'm telling you, it's a vendetta!
And I need help!" His eyes were pleading. "That's where
you come in."

I cleared my throat again. And then I believe I answered Rigdon pretty much the way any private detective
might have, under similar circumstances.

"Where do I come in?" I asked.

Rigdon gave me another impatient look. "Why, you've
got to find the animals that are doing this! You've got to
stop them before it's too late!"

For a second I couldn't speak. Even if there really were

such things as homicidal squirrels and raccoons and rabbits—which, I don't mind telling you, I had some serious reservations about—how in the world did Rigdon think I could stop them? Put them under arrest? I was pretty sure Vergil would not cotton to filling his jail cells with anything that needed its cage cleaned out on a regular basis.

If arrest was out of the question, then, did Rigdon actually expect me to pull a Rambo out in the woods, blasting away at any furry creature that made a move toward his house? If that was what he had in mind, Rigdon didn't need a detective—all he needed was somebody with a rifle who didn't much care that it wasn't yet hunting season.

Moreover, judging solely from the sounds that frequently came out of the woods surrounding my own house, I'd guess Rigdon wouldn't have a bit of trouble finding quite a few folks who met these particular qualifications.

"You *will* help me, won't you?" Rigdon added. "Please, Haskell?"

I swallowed uneasily. I know I should've only been thinking about what all Rigdon had just told me. And how real unlikely it was that Rigdon was anywhere near talking sense.

Instead, however, I was thinking about something else.

I was thinking about that damn mop waiting for me back at Elmo's.

You know, I don't believe Mannix or Peter Gunn or any of those private eyes I used to watch on TV when I was a kid ever faced this kind of a dilemma.

"Please?" Rigdon was saying again.

CHAPTER
3

Rigdon was running his hand through his hair again. "You will help me, won't you, Haskell? I know exactly what kind of animals we're dealing with here because of the footprints they left behind." He took a ragged breath. "So see? It's not as if you don't have anything to go on." Rigdon's eyes were now as wild as the creatures he thought were after him.

I was still trying to figure out what to say.

In the last year since I'd been back in Pigeon Fork, I'd worked some strange cases. I'd investigated a triple homicide—the murders, believe it or not, of a little old lady and her two pets. I'd investigated a kidnapping in which the ransom note had been received, but apparently the kidnapper had not yet seen fit to actually abduct the victim. I'd even investigated several break-ins around town in which absolutely nothing had been stolen.

Judging from all this, you might not think so, but I *do* have my standards.

I pretty much insist that my clients be sane.

Call me picky.

Logistics aside—how exactly would you go about questioning animal suspects?—it just didn't seem right to take money from Rigdon for a job like this.

Particularly since it was real clear that Rigdon needed all the money he could get his hands on to pay for psychiatric help.

I cleared my throat. "Rigdon," I said, "I don't think I'm your man."

Rigdon looked as if he were choking. "Wha-a-at?" The word was a wail.

I hated to say it again. "I don't think I can help you."

I could hardly believe my own ears. Me, turning down work? Was I as crazy as Rigdon?

In the Most-Crazy Contest, Rigdon, however, had clearly outdistanced me. He was now plucking at his toothpick with one hand, running his fingers through his hair with the other hand, *and* pacing his workroom, all in a whirl of motion. "Oh my God, oh my God, oh my God," he kept saying.

Rigdon probably wouldn't have been any too good at that walking-and-chewing-gum thing, because in the middle of doing what all he was now doing, he seemed to get confused. He ended up running the *toothpick* through his hair. Still pacing to beat the band. Like maybe he thought he was in some kind of imaginary cage.

When he finally stopped all this, I kind of wished he'd kept on. Because then he just stared at me, real pitiful-like, and said, "Haskell, come on, you're not really turning me down, are you?"

I nodded weakly. "I'm sorry, Rigdon," I said. I was telling the truth. I *was* sorry. For a lot of reasons, not the least of which, I might as well admit, was that I could still be listed among the unemployed.

It looked as if I might have to have that mop surgically removed.

Rigdon was sticking his toothpick back in his mouth. Not the most hygienic thing in the world to do. "Then you don't *care?*" he wailed. "You're just leaving me to *them?*"

I held up my hand in what I hoped was a calming gesture. "Rigdon, I'm not leaving you to anything." I took a deep breath, once again searching for the right words.

What I came up with was: "Look, Rigdon, I'm going to tell you something flat out, and I want you to listen." I paused, making sure that I had his full attention, and then I said, "Animals don't hunt people. It's the other way around."

I couldn't believe I was actually saying this to somebody. As if it were news.

Rigdon's answer was real quick, I'll give him that. "Nonsense! *That's* what they want us to think! They want us to think they're a lot dumber than they really are." He plucked out his toothpick again and pointed it at me. "Have you ever seen a wild animal eat a poisoned berry?"

He had me there. "Don't believe I have."

Rigdon looked triumphant. "Of *course* you haven't!" he said, flourishing his toothpick. "You know why? Because wild animals don't eat poison berries!"

"They don't?" I said.

Rigdon moved now so that his face was right next to mine. "Wild animals know, Haskell, they *know!*"

Up this close, I could see how bloodshot his eyes were. It looked as if he hadn't been getting much sleep.

I didn't have to guess why not.

Rigdon's voice was almost a shout. "Wild animals know *exactly* which berries are poison and which ones are not!"

I had had all the zoology lessons I cared to hear for one

day. "Rigdon—" I started to say, but he interrupted me. Reinserting his toothpick, running his fingers through his hair, and pacing his kitchen again. It looked to me as if Rigdon's imaginary cage was shrinking some. He was pacing in smaller and smaller circles.

"*Animals* are always careful, aren't they?" Rigdon was saying. "But are humans careful? No-o-o-o—"

For a second there, he sounded like the late John Belushi.

"—*humans* eat poisoned berries all the time!" Rigdon went on. He stopped suddenly and whirled to face me. "So *see?*"

Rigdon's logic was making me tired. "See what?"

"That *proves* that animals are smarter than us!"

I blinked. The way *I* saw it, Rigdon could very well be speaking the truth. About himself.

With regard to the rest of us, however, the jury was still out.

"The animals in the woods really are plotting against me, Haskell!" Rigdon went on. He hung his blond head and his tone got pitiful again. "There's nobody else to help me. I called the police, you know, right after I found the razor blades in my tomatoes, but when I told Vergil what was going on, the sheriff practically laughed in my face. Can you believe that?"

Actually, I could. I could believe it even though I knew full well that Vergil is not exactly what you'd ever describe as a Happy Camper. As a rule, the expression on the sheriff's face is always pretty much that of someone who'd just found he'd thrown away a winning lottery ticket.

Be that as it may, I'm pretty sure that if old Vergil ever *were* to break with tradition and actually crack a smile, no doubt the odds would've been best right after Vergil got through listening to Rigdon's little tale.

37

Rigdon was shaking again.

"Hey," I said, "calm down now—"

I'm not sure why I said this. It had about as much effect as saying "Cool off" to a fire.

"But Haskell, these animals *are* real smart!" Rigdon said, his voice threatening to go off into a solid scream. "They're going to get me unless you help me!"

I put my hand on his shoulder. "Rigdon, old buddy," I said, and I made my voice just as kind as I knew how, "you do need help. You really do. But not my kind of help. You need to talk to somebody."

Rigdon's answer was like a punch in the stomach. He lifted his chin, his eyes tortured. "Don't you think I already knew that?" he said. His toothpick bobbled piteously. "I knew I needed to talk to somebody. That's why I decided to talk to *you!*"

I just looked at him for a second. "No, Rigdon," I said, "I mean, you need to talk to a *doctor*. Somebody like that."

I didn't particularly want to blurt out right to his face that he needed to get himself to a shrink pronto, but I kind of hoped he'd get the message.

He didn't. "What do I need a doctor for?" Rigdon said. "I'm not sick! I'm not running a fever or nothing."

I swallowed uneasily, more at a loss for words than ever. How do you tell somebody that the kind of illness he had wasn't exactly measured with a thermometer? "Rigdon," I finally said, "take my word for it, you really do need to see a doctor."

As I said this, I was turning and heading out of his house toward my truck.

I didn't know what else to tell him. Crazy people, I have found, are not all that inclined to listen to reason.

Rigdon, of course, followed me. In fact, for a while there I wasn't sure if he was going to let me leave.

He trailed after me all the way out to the driveway, and

then stood, hanging onto the door handle of my truck. Even after I got in and started the engine.

"Haskell, come on now, buddy, I thought I could count on you." He actually sounded panicky.

I tried to answer him as best I could. "Rigdon, if you were thinking straight, you'd understand why I can't help you."

Thinking straight, however, was obviously not on Rigdon's list of Things to Do Today. "Haskell, for God's sake, they're going to kill me," he said. "And when they do, it's going to be all your fault!"

I had the truck in reverse by then, but if Rigdon didn't let go, I was either going to have to sit there idling until my truck ran out of gas, or else drag him down his own driveway.

It seemed like a real mean thing to do to the mentally ill.

"Rigdon," I said, "let go of my door."

Rigdon, if anything, tightened his grip. "You're my last hope, Haskell! Everybody else thinks I'm a nut!"

I didn't want to say so, but in my opinion, he could drop the "else" in that last sentence.

I decided maybe I should try a different tack. "Rigdon, remember how I told you I had an appointment? Remember?"

Unfortunately, at this point I couldn't help noticing that my voice had started sounding a lot like the soothing, placating tones that Nurse Ratched had used with Jack Nicholson in that movie, *One Flew Over the Cuckoo's Nest*. What bothered me most about this was that Nurse Ratched had turned out to be a real bad guy in that film.

I cleared my throat and hurried on. "Rigdon, it's getting late, and I really do have to go now." I started easing out on the clutch so that my truck began backing down the driveway real slow.

Rigdon ran alongside, his hand still on my door. "Haskell, without you, I'm a goner! Please, you've got to help me!"

"You'll be fine," I said. Nurse Ratched again. Even more soothing.

Rigdon may have been doing some major flying over his own personal cuckoo's nest, but evidently he wasn't quite crazy enough to let me drag him down the road. Abruptly, he let go of my door handle.

It was then, however, that Rigdon did something that made me feel even worse than my sounding like Nurse Ratched and all of his pleading put together.

He just stood there, staring at me.

Not saying a word.

Oh yeah, that did the trick, all right.

I pulled out of Rigdon's driveway, feeling like something a little lower on the evolutionary scale than a slug.

In fact, traveling down the road toward Frank's Bar and Grill, on my way to meet Imogene for lunch, I decided that a slug was probably something I'd look up to.

I couldn't get poor Rigdon's face out of my mind. I was riding along, bouncing around curves and going up and down hills, but if the truth be known, I was hardly seeing the road ahead at all. What I was seeing, instead, was Rigdon's tortured eyes.

I tried to tell myself that taking the money of a crazy man to do an even crazier job would've made me feel even *more* like something you'd scrape off the bottom of your shoe, but that didn't help a whole lot. Even if Rigdon were nuttier than a fruitcake—and, I do believe, if you did a personal survey, you'd find that most fruitcakes would be considered nut-free compared to Rigdon—he was obviously still sane enough to form an opinion. And that opinion appeared to be: Haskell

Blevins, his old high school buddy, was letting him down in a big way.

By the time I pulled into Frank's parking lot some ten minutes or so later, I was trying to get philosophical. I was telling myself: Hey, come on now, face it, some situations are just plain lose-lose. This, no doubt, was one of those situations. No matter what you did—whether you took Rigdon's job or you didn't—you were going to feel bad. Period. Besides, when it came right down to it, you did the only thing you could do.

I almost believed myself.

It was not quite noon, but Frank's gravel parking lot was already pretty crowded. At least, it was crowded by Pigeon Fork standards. There must've been twenty or more cars and trucks there. I immediately recognized my girlfriend Imogene's vintage sixties red Mustang over on the right side of the building. I parked beside it and hurried inside. Where, for the next few minutes, I pretty much just stood, right inside the entrance next to the cash register, in the only space in Frank's that doesn't have a table crowded into it.

I stood there, looking around the room. Trying, of course, to spot Imogene.

At just about any other time of the day, it would've been easy to find her. Frank's Bar and Grill, after all, is just one big room filled with tables.

In fact, Frank's used to be a feed store at one time. The feed store went bankrupt some years back, after which Frank Puckett bought the thing and turned it into a feed store for people instead of livestock.

Frank has kept a lot of the old feed store intact. The place is still real rustic inside, with exposed oak rafters overhead and wide plank flooring underfoot. Then, too, there's still all the old weathered metal signs from the feed store decorating the rough-hewn walls, advertising

Friskies dog food, Mail Pouch tobacco, Aubrey's Red Feed, and like that. These signs, according to Frank, give the place "amby-ants."

Ambiance, I believe, is what Frank means by this. Either that or Frank was trying to break it to us that his place needs a visit from the Orkin man.

Frank seems to be under the impression that it is his restaurant's "amby-ants" that keeps it so crowded during lunch. Of course, Frank also contends that his having the only neon sign around these parts—a real small red thing that hangs in his front window and says "Say Bull"—brings folks in from all over the county.

Nobody has ever had the heart to remind Frank that there are only two places to eat in Pigeon Fork—Frank's Bar and Grill and Lassiter's Restaurant. And for sure nobody will ever tell Frank the ultimate horrible truth— that quite a few Pigeon Forkians make their lunch decisions simply by flipping a coin.

Today must've been one of Frank's luckier days. It looked to me as if an awful lot of coins around town had come up Frank's.

Standing there just inside the entrance, scanning the room for Imogene, I spotted several familiar faces. Ruta Lippton, sole proprietor of the Curl Crazee beauty shop downtown, Pop Matheny of Pop's Barbershop, Zeke Arndell of Arndell's New and Hardly Used Furniture— it looked as if most of Pigeon Fork's downtown businesses were represented. Quite a few of these folks lifted their hand in a wave. Or nodded in my direction.

Most of the folks who waved and nodded at me I recognized, but a few of them I'd swear I'd never seen before. This is one of the things I really missed when I was back in Louisville. In Louisville, if a stranger starts waving at you, it's generally because he's trying to warn you about something.

I'm not sure why, but standing there waving and nodding at a few total strangers lifted my spirits a little.

My spirits escalated even more when—as I was still waving and nodding—something occurred to me.

Lord. If I thought I felt bad now, just think how bad I would've felt if I'd taken Rigdon's job and everybody here at Frank's—friends and strangers alike—had found out about it. Not to mention, not only everybody here at Frank's, but, say, every other person, big or small, within a twenty-five mile radius of Pigeon Fork?

There was, of course, not a doubt in my mind that, had I indeed gone to work for Rigdon, every single one of these aforementioned folks *would* have found out. The grapevine in Pigeon Fork is like the grapevine in every other small town in America. Nothing if not efficient.

Fact is, you could pretty much guarantee that news of my latest job would be all over Crayton County in a heartbeat. Moreover, my secretary Melba—who could easily qualify as Chief of Gossip Central around these parts—would, no doubt, help the grapevine along.

Standing there just inside the entrance to Frank's, I actually went cold, thinking about it. For crying out loud, if I'd taken on Rigdon's crazy case, no doubt by nightfall I'd have been known as "that slimeball private eye who bilks the mentally ill out of their hard-earned money." Hell, I might as well have had it printed on my business card.

Once all this went through my mind, I actually started to feel better. It also helped to finally locate Imogene.

She was sitting all the way in the back of the room, looking straight at me with one of her soft smiles.

That woman sure is a sight for sore eyes.

At least, she is for mine.

In fact, for the last three months or so, I reckon I've felt like the luckiest man in the world. Particularly since, the way Imogene and I met, you might've thought that Imogene and I would be the last two people to end up together.

Imogene and I met when I was investigating her sister's murder. It was a real dark time for us both, what with me feeling real bad about not being able to prevent what had happened, and Imogene feeling real bad about losing somebody she loved so much.

And yet, out of all that terribleness, something kind of wonderful happened.

Now, I found myself grinning like a total fool as I walked toward her.

There are those, I realize, who might say that Imogene Mayhew is not the most gorgeous woman in the world or anything. And, to be as totally objective as I can be— which is pretty hard to do these days when it comes to Imogene—even I would have to admit that Imogene is not exactly what most folks would call beautiful, technically speaking. She is real attractive, though, in a big-boned, farm-fresh sort of way.

Fact is, the only reason, in my opinion, that other folks don't seem to notice just how truly attractive Imogene happens to be is that Imogene herself does absolutely nothing to draw attention to her looks. Her brown wavy hair always looks as if it could stand a good brushing, and a whole lot of the time the only makeup she seems to remember to put on is a little lipstick.

Like right now, for example. Imogene looked as if she hadn't even bothered with the lipstick. A real estate agent, Imogene was wearing the kind of thing she usually wore to work—a gray pin-striped suit and a tailored white blouse with a burgundy bow at the collar—but her face looked freshly scrubbed.

I find this, I might as well admit, downright refreshing. My ex-wife, Claudine—I call her Claudzilla—would no more stick her nose out the door without makeup than she would go outside naked.

Come to think of it, I'm pretty sure Claudzilla considered being without makeup and being naked to be synonymous.

When Imogene isn't wearing makeup, it makes one thing real obvious—the one thing that she and I had in common, right from the start. Actually, to be precise, it's not just *one* thing. It's a whole lot of little things.

Freckles.

Imogene may very well be the only other person in Crayton County who could give me a run for my money in the freckle department. I've told her more than once that if there is ever a global freckle shortage, the world is going to beat a path to both our doors.

It's a credit to Imogene that as many times as I've said this to her, she always laughs. Right out loud, as if it were the first time she'd heard it.

This is another change from what I'd been used to. Claudzilla always used to roll her eyes whenever I told a joke she'd heard before. Claudzilla also pointed it out to everybody present. "Oh *God*," Claudzilla would say, in the tone of somebody about to go through the Inquisition, "not this again." Claudzilla always made this little remark as she was sticking her fingers in her ears.

Imogene was now waggling *her* fingers at me in a little wave.

I gave her an even bigger grin as I sat down opposite her.

"How's it going, Haskell?" Imogene said.

That's all Imogene said. Just that, just the kind of comment to which you pretty much answer "Fine," and let it go at that. I must've been more upset about the Rigdon situation than I thought, because before I knew it, my mouth had actually opened itself up and blurted,

"Well, things aren't going so good, Imogene. Can you believe I just had to turn down a job?"

I really hadn't meant to say anything to Imogene. By then I thought I'd pretty much made up my mind that I'd done the right thing, and that was that. I really didn't need a second opinion.

Or, at least, right up to the second Imogene spoke I didn't think I did.

I reckon I would've blurted out every detail of the entire Rigdon episode right then and there if Imogene and I hadn't been immediately interrupted by one of the teenage waitresses Frank always hires for the summer.

"Whaddyahave?" I believe this is what the girl said. It was hard to decipher what words she was trying to form around all the bubble gum in her mouth.

Imogene and I both went with Frank's Afternoon Special, a sign of true compatibility, if I do say so myself. Frank's Special is a quarter pounder, large fries, and a Coke, and it's the closest thing you're going to get to fast food within a hundred miles of Pigeon Fork. No doubt, Frank's would be called *Mc*Frank's except that he doesn't have a clown anywhere around.

Unless, of course, you count Frank himself.

Once the gum-smacking waitress flounced off to the kitchen with our orders, Imogene gave me another soft smile and said, "So, what's all this about having to turn down a job?"

All right, I'll admit it, it wasn't exactly as if she was twisting my arm. Maybe there *was* a pretty decent chance that I did need to hear someone else say, "Haskell, you did the right thing."

Unfortunately, just as I was starting in again, it suddenly got pretty hard to hear anything.

On account of Frank cranking up what he calls his "entertainment."

What *I* call it is something else again.

About a month ago somebody made the mistake of mentioning to Frank how Lassiter's Restaurant offers *its* customers musical entertainment. I have no doubt that whoever the fool was that told Frank about this did *not* also mention exactly what kind of musical entertainment Lassiter's offers. Or surely Frank wouldn't have thought he had to do something to keep up.

Cyrus Lassiter, you see, makes you listen to hymns. The whole time you're eating. Nothing but hymns, one after another, over and over. Cyrus has been playing hymns at his restaurant ever since his brother saw fit to die suddenly of a heart attack.

I don't think it's disrespectful to say that it's a tad disconcerting to be biting down on one of Cyrus's barbecue sandwiches just as "When the Saints Are Called Up Yonder" is pouring out over his loudspeakers. It makes you wonder if there might be something about his food that Cyrus is not telling if, while you're wolfing it down, Cyrus feels compelled to prepare you for the hereafter.

Whoever told Frank about Cyrus's music could not possibly have mentioned just how disconcerting listening to hymns while you eat can be. Or else, if Frank had been told, all he'd heard was that Lassiter's Restaurant was offering something that Frank's Bar and Grill wasn't.

So, late one afternoon, Frank suddenly jumped into his truck and drove all the way to Louisville to buy what has to be, bar none, the four largest speakers this side of Hollywood.

Hell, there have been rock groups that don't have speakers as big as Frank's.

Lined up against the back wall, these massive black things look a little like Stonehenge.

To make sure he's got something for all possible tastes, Frank doesn't confine the music he blasts out over these monsters to just one kind either. In fact, he runs the gamut—from elevator music to country, from pop to classic rock, from show tunes to rap.

The only thing that stays the same is the decibel level.

Oh yeah, no matter if it's Patsy Cline, or Michael Jackson, or M.C. Hammer, Frank's windows are rattling up a storm. No doubt, the windows of the cars out in Frank's parking lot are rattling too.

It is, to say the least, annoying as hell.

I believe, if he'd admit it, it also annoys the hell out of Frank. That's why he doesn't offer his "musical entertainment" all the time. Frank just cranks it up every so often, playing one or two songs, and then he gives everybody's eardrums a rest for a spell.

I personally think that Frank would give it up entirely, except that he's not about to admit that he hauled Stonehenge all the way back from Louisville for nothing. He's going to get full value out of those damn speakers, and if that means deafening a significant portion of the Pigeon Fork population, so be it.

Frank is a real humanitarian.

He proved it one more time just as I started to tell Imogene about Rigdon. That was, of course, when— thanks to Frank—Tammy Wynette started belting out "Stand By Your Man." It didn't help that Imogene and I were sitting with most of Stonehenge within a foot of us.

I leaned forward and tried to speak as slowly and as distinctly as I could. After a while, Imogene seemed to be following me pretty good, in spite of Tammy. I figured Imogene might be missing a few details, but she seemed to be getting the gist. She was nodding and smiling, and more or less encouraging me to go on.

I went over the whole thing, from beginning to end, even telling Imogene word for word exactly what I'd told Rigdon just before I pulled out of his driveway. "SO WHAT DO YOU THINK?" I finally finished. My voice at this point was a whisper compared to Tammy Wynette's.

Imogene didn't answer for a second. Then she reached for a pencil in her purse.

Tammy was winding up for a real big finish as Imogene carefully smoothed the paper napkin beside her plate, scribbled something on the thing, and handed it to me.

The napkin read: *"Why* did you turn down the job?"

Oh yeah. She'd missed a few details, all right.

I took a deep breath, cupped my hands around my mouth, and shouted, "I turned it down because Rigdon Bewley is crazy!"

Unfortunately, at that moment, Tammy Wynette wound things up in a hurry.

Into the sudden silence, then, the only thing that carried to what seemed like every single nook and cranny of the restaurant were my final four words.

If I need to spell them out for you, those particular words happened to be, "RIGDON BEWLEY IS CRAZY!"

To be exact.

I reckon every single head in the restaurant turned toward where Imogene and I were sitting.

This, in itself, would've been bad enough. But then I—along with a significant portion of the folks in Frank's—turned and saw that one of the heads that had turned in my direction was the head of what had to be just about the worst person in the world to hear me say what I did.

It was Rigdon Bewley.

To borrow a phrase from Rigdon himself: Oh my God.

Evidently, Rigdon had decided that it would no longer be prudent to eat any more meals at home—or, for all I knew, maybe he'd decided to follow me here to plead with me some more—whatever the reason, Rigdon had been strolling in the front door of Frank's at the exact moment Tammy's song ended.

Rigdon couldn't have timed it better.

Or, rather, worse.

My stomach wrenched.

Imogene followed my appalled gaze. "Oh dear," she said. "Do you think he heard you?"

The answer to that, of course, was: Unless Rigdon had very recently spent a significant portion of his life in Frank's Bar and Grill, sitting at the exact table Imogene and I now occupied, I believed so.

In fact, if there was any doubt about it, it was totally erased when, from all the way across the room, Rigdon's eyes met mine.

My stomach wrenched again.

Rigdon looked even more accusing now than he had earlier when I'd almost dragged him down his driveway.

In fact, that right there was what was so awful about it. Rigdon didn't look angry so much as he looked hurt.

Like maybe somebody he'd actually thought was a friend of his had just betrayed him.

Without a word, Rigdon turned abruptly on his heel and stomped out Frank's front door.

I started to jump up right then and follow him. I really did. I had every intention of getting up from the table, running lickety-split across Frank's Bar and Grill, dodging other diners like some kind of demented football player, and doing my darnedest to catch Rigdon out in the parking lot.

To try to explain.

And, even more important, to try somehow to apologize.

Unfortunately, as I shoved back my chair, ready to begin the Rigdon Marathon, I saw something so mindblowing that for a split second it drove every other thought right out of my mind.

So that I ended up sitting abruptly back down in my chair, like somebody who'd just found out his legs had turned to jelly.

Actually, to be precise, what stopped me in my tracks was not a *something* at all. It was a *someone*—a someone I hadn't seen in almost eighteen months.

Nonchalantly strolling into Frank's, as if she did it every day of her life—in fact, *passing* Rigdon, who was on his way out just as she was on her way in—was, of all people, Claudine.

The woman I'd been proud to make my ex-wife not quite two years before.

The woman, need I remind you, that ever since our divorce I'd been fondly referring to as "Claudzilla."

Good Lord. What was *she* doing here?

CHAPTER
4

For a long moment Claudine stood in the entrance to Frank's Bar and Grill, much as I'd done minutes earlier, her eyes traveling around the room.

Unlike yours truly, however, who—when *I* had been standing exactly where Claudine was standing now—had only rated a few nods and waves, Claudine seemed to be causing a sort of ripple effect all over Frank's. It looked to me as if everybody's eyes—men's and women's alike—were rapidly traveling in Claudine's direction.

Lord. It was like watching the pull of the North Pole on a room full of compasses.

Even as this thought occurred to me, mind you, it did not escape my notice that the thing I'd immediately come up with to compare to my ex-wife was a thing that was extremely cold and very distant.

I believe that says it all.

I also noticed something else. There appeared to be a slight difference in the reaction of all those eyes around me. I may have been wrong, but it looked to me as if this difference depended solely on whether a given set of eyes happened to belong to a man or a woman. If the eyes focusing on Claudzilla were a man's, they appeared to increase in size, oh, maybe four or five times. If the eyes, however, were a woman's, the reaction was just the opposite. The eyes began to shrink, becoming smaller and smaller until, in some cases, they ended up being little more than slits.

Claudzilla *was* a sight to see, I reckon. Wearing a crimson-red, halter-top dress that probably couldn't have been any tighter without cutting off significant blood circulation and, no doubt, rendering her unconscious, Claudzilla stood at the front of the restaurant, scanning the room as she slowly wound a platinum curl around a crimson fingertip.

I was pretty sure Claudzilla's hair had *not* been platinum the last time I'd seen her. Of course, I couldn't be positive, being as how toward the last her hair had been in curlers a good deal of the time. I didn't think, however, that her hair had ever been quite this white. Evidently, at her last beauty shop appointment, Claudzilla had decided to throw caution to the wind.

Or else she'd had a bad scare recently.

She'd probably gotten a good look at her last Visa statement.

Claudzilla's hair had changed in other ways too. It had to be at least three inches longer than I remembered, and unlike the windswept Farrah Fawcett look she used to wear, it was now parted in the middle and hanging in smooth, sleek waves just past her bare shoulders.

Glancing around, I decided I was probably the only person in Frank's looking at Claudzilla's *hair*. Most folk's eyes appeared to be focused on a place inches below her platinum waves. It was at this place that a good deal of Claudzilla herself seemed to be overflowing the low-cut neckline of that tight red dress.

Claudzilla's dress must've been even tighter than I thought. Apparently, just pulling it on had worked all excess flesh upward.

Sort of like the effect you might get from squeezing a toothpaste tube up from the bottom.

The way it looked to me, if Claudzilla wasn't careful, her toothpaste was going to pop out right in front of everybody.

Imogene had been looking at the door toward Rigdon, but even her attention was diverted by Claudzilla. "My goodness," she said. Sure enough, my theory was holding up. Imogene's eyes *did* seem to be shrinking some. "Who in the world is *that?*"

I would've answered her. I really would've, but I didn't get the chance. At that moment Claudzilla spotted me and began making her way through the crowd. Waving animatedly, so that her entire body reverberated with the motion, she also began yelling so loud I could hear her faintly even over the new song now booming out over Frank's speakers—Garth Brooks's "I've Got Friends in Low Places."

Tell me about it, Garth.

"Haskell! HASK-ell!" Claudzilla yelled. "Why, *there* you are!"

Everybody in Frank's may have been staring at Claudzilla, but the second she yelled my name, all that changed. Now the eyes of every single person that she passed—all of whom, I suppose, could hear her all too clearly as she went by their tables—suddenly began to swivel in my direction.

In some instances this eye-swiveling appeared to be accompanied by jawdropping.

You could actually get the idea that of all the men in Frank's who might possibly appear on a list entitled

"Most Likely to Know a Platinum Blond in a Tight Red Dress," I would appear real close to the end.

If, indeed, I appeared on the list at all.

A thing like this could really hurt a guy's feelings.

Imogene's eyes swiveled just like everybody else's. I did take some comfort in the fact that Imogene's jaw, unlike some of the others, did not go slack. "Haskell," she said, "I think that woman over there might be yelling at you."

I may have been taking comfort a tad prematurely. Although Imogene's tone was not hostile or anything, she did, however, sound real concerned.

For a second I just stared back at her. Blankly.

I reckon I ought to establish something right now. When it comes to women, I'm pretty much just like the next guy. A damn coward.

The idea of running into my ex-wife while my new girlfriend looked on was enough to make my knees wobble a little.

Even sitting down.

"Haskell," Imogene was now saying, "that woman *is* yelling at you." Imogene was leaning away from our table and screwing up her face some, as if that might help her hear what all Claudzilla was saying.

Claudzilla was still at least ten tables away. She might've gotten to us a lot faster if she hadn't been wearing red high heels at least four inches high. It also didn't help any that the skirt of her knee-length dress was so tight. It was like watching somebody try to run with her legs bound in a crimson-red tourniquet.

Fact is, there was a real good chance—in that particular crimson-red dress—Claudzilla could qualify for handicapped parking.

"Can't you hear her? She's yelling *your* name," Imogene said. Was I imagining it, or had Imogene's eyes gotten a LOT smaller?

I took a deep breath before I answered.

"My name? Really? *Mine?* Well, uh, yes, uh, I, uh—"
That, I'm ashamed to say, is pretty much an exact quote.
I believe I need not demonstrate any further what a truly
silver-tongued devil *I* happen to be.

While my mouth was uttering mostly monosyllables,
my mind was racing through possible courses of action.

I could hide under the table, but obviously Claudzilla
had already spotted me. While she was, admittedly, not
exactly a rocket scientist, I was pretty sure she'd know to
look for me there.

I could also run for the men's rest room, but from what
I knew of Claudzilla, she wouldn't have the slightest
hesitation about following me inside. In fact, she might
even enjoy it.

Then again, I could act as if I were having some kind of
seizure, fall down on the ground, shake all over, begin
swallowing my tongue, and upon regaining conscious-
ness, pretend as if whatever fit I'd just gone through had
resulted in amnesia and I didn't know Claudzilla from
Adam.

Believe it or not, I actually considered this last one. I
know, I know. I realize it sounds a tad extreme, but at
that moment Claudzilla was getting real close, tottering
even more quickly around tables filled with goggle-eyed
diners. I was feeling more than a little desperate. I might
even have given the fit thing a whirl, except that I was
afraid Claudzilla would never buy it.

Just to prove her suspicions wrong, I probably
would've had to let myself get put into a home.

Claudzilla was yelling again. "Haskell! Haskell!
HASK-ell!" She was now waving even more excitedly, as
if maybe I were a rapidly departing cab she was trying to
flag down.

I'd like to think that I was still a little stunned about
what I'd just shouted to the world at large, right in front

of Rigdon. And that was why, more than anything else, I ended up just sitting there as if I were paralyzed, watching Claudzilla head my way.

To be honest, though, the Rigdon fiasco probably did not completely account for the expression on my face. Which, no doubt, mirrored that of the captain of the ship in that movie, *The Poseidon Adventure,* when he first spotted the tidal wave coming toward him.

"Haskell, do you know this woman?" Oh yeah. Imogene's eyes had gotten smaller, all right. She was obviously trying to sound real casual, but her voice had an unmistakable edge to it.

I cleared my throat. "Well, uh, Imogene, as a matter of fact, yes, she's, uh, well, she's, uh, my—"

My tongue was once again demonstrating how silver it was.

I might actually have finished the sentence—I was making real headway, I thought—except by then Claudzilla had reached our table.

"Hass-KULL!" she squealed.

I took a deep breath. My mama taught me that a gentleman always stands when a lady approaches. Even though I wasn't altogether sure that Claudzilla met the necessary qualifications, I knew that Mama, God rest her soul, would not think that got me off the hook. I got to my feet.

"Claudzi—" I stopped myself just in time. "Clau-*dine!"* I put a little extra emphasis on that last syllable. "Well, well, this sure is a surprise."

Claudine didn't seem to notice the total lack of enthusiasm in my voice. She let loose a giggle. "I *meant* to surprise you, you big lug," she said.

I blinked. Claudzilla's hair wasn't the only thing that had changed. Her tone had undergone a metamorphosis too. My goodness. She actually sounded *nice.*

Of course, the last thing, as I recall, that Claudzilla had

said to me was something on the order of: "Get out of my life, you scumbag." A statement which, I do believe, might've easily dictated her tone.

Claudine was giggling some more. "Your secretary told me where you were, so I hurried right over here!"

Wouldn't you know it? The first time ever that Melba remembered what I'd told her and then actually passed the news along to somebody, it would turn out to be my ex-wife.

It figured.

"Oh, Haskell, I am so-o-o glad to see you!" Claudine had stopped giggling, and was now leaning toward me, arms extended, fingers spread wide.

The last time Claudine had come toward me with her arms in this position, she'd been going for my throat. As I recall, it had been right after she'd found out that the court had only awarded her alimony for a year.

Remembering that particular little scene, I couldn't help it. It was practically a reflex action to take a quick step backward.

Claudine, however, immediately closed the gap, crushing her body to me in a huge, shirt-wrinkling hug.

"Haskell, Haskell, Haskell." That's what Claudine said while she was hugging me.

I didn't know what to say back. If I was supposed to repeat *her* name three times too, she was out of luck. I decided to go with saying nothing.

It was during the second or two while I was saying nothing and Claudine had me in a body lock that I realized that Garth Brooks had stopped singing, and that Frank's restaurant had gotten awful quiet. This was real odd too. Usually, in the brief moment between songs, the place is about as quiet as a train wreck as everybody hurries to say what he has to say before Frank cranks up more "entertainment."

A quick glance around the room, however, immediately told me why Frank's was suddenly so quiet. You can't talk with your mouth hanging open.

The mouths of just about every one of the folks in that room could've been rented out as birdhouses.

Not only were their mouths wide open, but every one of their eyes appeared to be riveted to me and Claudzilla. Every tiny slitlike female eye and every huge, saucerlike male eye.

I couldn't help noticing that my theory was still holding up right nice.

I also noticed something else. Lord. A whole lot of the saucer eyes aimed in my direction looked downright envious.

I swallowed and actually felt a wave of pity for those guys. As a responsible member of the male sex, I felt like maybe I should warn them. Because, let me tell you, if there was ever a woman who needed a surgeon general's warning, oh, say, maybe *tattooed* on her forehead—or perhaps somewhere near her toothpaste tube overflow— Claudzilla was it. The warning, in fact, ought to be pretty direct. Something on the order of: *Contact with this person could be hazardous to your health.*

Or maybe it should be something even stronger. Something that would strike terror into a man's heart the second he read it. Something like, *Contact with this person could be hazardous to your credit rating.*

That ought to do it.

Claudzilla had pulled away and was now beaming at me. "Guess what, Haskell? I've got two weeks of vacation coming to me, and I've decided to spend them both right here in Pigeon Fork, seeing the sights!"

My stomach wrenched.

Uh-oh. This didn't sound good.

For one thing, there are no sights in Pigeon Fork. Believe me, I know. Other than the eight years I'd spent in Louisville, I've lived here all my life. If there was a single sight to see anywhere around these parts, I'd have spotted it by now.

So what exactly was Claudine up to?

"Isn't it going to be great?" Claudine said. Her big blue eyes were dancing merrily.

It was, of course, at this point that I became acutely aware of another set of eyes.

Imogene's.

I gave Imogene a quick sideways glance, and realized that she was now leaning forward a little. As if she might be real interested in how I answered Claudzilla's question.

I think, under the circumstances, that I did real good just to remember what Claudzilla had asked. How'd that go again? Isn't it going to be *great* to have my ex-wife in town for the next two long, interminable weeks?

"Uh, well," I said, "uh, well, uh, uh, well, uh—"

I might've gone on that way for maybe the next hour or so except that Imogene interrupted me. "Haskell," she said, "aren't you going to introduce us?"

The second Imogene spoke, Claudzilla turned in her direction, her face registering surprise. As if perhaps Claudzilla was noticing for the first time that there was somebody else besides me sitting at the table. I couldn't speak for Imogene, but personally I didn't buy it. I myself had spotted Imogene clear across the room. Somehow, I tended to believe that Claudzilla had done the same.

"Why, yes, Haskell," Claudine said, turning back toward me, her smile now a shade too bright, *"aren't* you going to introduce us?"

Now, mind you, this was the very first time since our divorce that I'd ever run into Claudine when I was in the company of a woman with whom I was having an intimate relationship.

The very first time.

Come to think of it, this was the very first time in my entire *life* that I'd ever run into Claudine when I was out with another woman—period.

Being as how I'd never been unfaithful to Claudzilla while we were married.

A thing, I might add, that Claudzilla herself cannot say.

This, I believe, is why I started feeling so rattled. I believe it's also why I immediately started acting as if my *wife* had just caught me running around on her.

"Uh, well, Claudine—" I was actually stammering. "—uh, well, this is, uh, my *friend,* Imogene."

As soon as the words were out of my mouth, I realized that I'd made a tiny, insignificant, barely noticeable omission.

The word "girl." As in, for example, the word *"girl-friend."*

In my opinion, anybody—in a similar situation—could've made a mistake like this. *Anybody.* Particularly if he was as rattled as I was. How something like this could happen is a real easy thing to understand.

Glancing in Imogene's direction, I realized that it might not be quite as easy to understand as I thought. In fact, judging solely from the look on Imogene's face, I'd say that I had about as much chance of Imogene understanding this as my dog, Rip, understanding the Gettysburg Address.

Claudine smiled real big, stuck out a crimson-tipped hand, and said, "So-o-o glad to meet you, Emma Jane!"

That surgeon general's hazardous-to-your-health warning would, no doubt, be a real good idea, because Imogene was definitely looking a little sick. "It's Imogene," she said through her teeth, as she took Claudine's hand. *"Not* Emma Jane."

Claudine gave Imogene's hand a quick shake, and came out with another one of her shrill giggles. "Dear me," she said. "Well, one country name sounds just like another country name, doesn't it?" She smiled even wider and added, "Like I said, I am so-o-o glad to meet you. I'm *Mrs.* Blevins."

Was it my imagination, or had Claudzilla raised her voice some? It seemed as if her voice echoed all over Frank's as she said that last sentence.

Of course, as quiet as it was, it might've just been my imagination.

Wouldn't you know that Frank had apparently picked this moment to give his "entertainment" a rest? I mean, where were Garth Brooks and Bette Midler and Lawrence Welk when you really needed them?

Of course, come to think of it, it probably wasn't a coincidence at all that Frank's entertainment had dried up when it did. Hell, Frank himself was probably lurking around somewhere, eavesdropping on the three of us, just like apparently all the rest of his lunch crowd.

Imogene was now, if anything, looking even sicker.

I wasn't feeling so great myself. I hurried to correct Claudine. "Uh, Imogene, what Claudine meant by that is that she's the *ex*-Mrs. Blevins," I said. I tried to say this loud enough so that my voice carried all the way to Frank's front door. "What I mean is, Claudine is my *ex*-wife. We're *not* married anymore. That's why Claudine probably should have called herself the *ex*-Mrs. Blevins instead of *Mrs.* Blevins. Because we're *not* married. Not, uh, anymore . . ."

My voice sort of trailed off at this point, being as how I really couldn't think of anything else to say.

I've never been good at public speaking.

I did think, however, that I'd clarified things nicely.

I might've overdone it a tad, however. Imogene was now looking at me as if questioning whether she'd been overestimating my intelligence these last few months.

Claudine didn't seem to appreciate my attempt at

clarification either. She actually looked a little hurt. She blinked a time or two, and then with a little shrug, said, "Oh, Haskell, I don't think you have to spell out every little thing to Imogene here. I think Imogene knows *exactly* who I am."

At this point something happened that completely baffled me. The two women just looked at each other. Without speaking. Or anything. They just stared into each other's eyes. I looked from Imogene to Claudine and back to Imogene, and I'm here to tell you that whatever was exchanged between them was completely lost on me.

Imogene finally broke off the staring contest and looked over in my direction. There were now two bright spots of color on each of her cheeks. "You know, Haskell, your *ex* is absolutely right," she said. "I do know *exactly* who she is."

Claudine, inexplicably, giggled again. "Listen," she said, "you two don't mind if I join you for lunch, do you?"

Before either Imogene or I could answer, Claudine had tottered over on those high-heeled stilts of hers to the table on our right. There, two elderly men were sitting with two empty chairs on either side of them. "Mind if I borrow a chair?" Claudine said.

I didn't know either of these men. Both looked to be in their sixties, both were wearing faded overalls, and both had the dark red sunburn characteristic of men who make their living riding a tractor.

The mouths of these two old guys had already been hanging open even before Claudine spoke to them. That was probably why neither one of them seemed able to answer her. Instead they just stared, saucer-eyed, and nodded. Very slowly. As if they were in some kind of trance.

I do believe if Claudine had asked for all the money

those two had in their pockets, they would've handed it right over.

Claudine seemed unaware of the effect she was having on these two old guys. She gave them both an even bigger smile and said, "Thanks, lammykins, you two are so-o-o sweet."

It's hard to tell if a red-faced man is blushing, but I'd say both of them were. One of them, I'd swear, was drooling a little.

That surgeon general's warning had better be in even bigger print than I thought.

Claudine scooted the chair back over to our table and sat down on my left. "Now, you don't have to order anything for me, Haskell," she said. "I don't want to be a bother. In fact, I'll just have something to drink." She paused and added, "Even though, as yet, I haven't had a thing to eat all day, but, well, I sure wouldn't want to tie you two up, waiting on an order for little ol' me."

That, of course, was pretty much how I ended up sitting myself down, calling over a waitress, and buying Claudine the Complete Fried Chicken Extravaganza Platter.

The Extravaganza Platter, by the way, is the most expensive thing on Frank's menu.

Oddly enough.

That was also pretty much how Imogene and I both ended up spending the next hour or so watching Claudine wolf down fried chicken and listening to her go on and on about the different things that had happened to her and me while we were married. Claudine talked about the vacation we took in Hawaii, the vacation we took in Jamaica, and the vacation we took in Florida. She talked about the apartment we had back in Louisville, the old VW bug we used to drive, and the great furniture buys we found at the Salvation Army Thrift Store in Louisville's South End.

It was amazing how that woman could talk and eat at the same time. Without losing any speed doing either thing. And without choking. Of course, maybe that right there is why Claudine had chosen to wear that particular red dress into the restaurant. If she did happen to start choking, a dress that tight could probably perform the Heimlich maneuver all by itself.

I can't say it was all that much fun to listen to Claudine go on and on about our relationship right in front of the woman I was having a relationship with now. This was just like Claudzilla, though, to talk first and think of folk's feelings later. I did all I could to shut her up, but it was like trying to turn off the TV when you don't have the remote control. By the time Claudine had polished off most of her fried chicken, I was starting to think that if she began another sentence with the words, "Remember when you and I . . ." I might actually throw up.

Claudine's chattering didn't seem to be doing much for Imogene's digestion either. Imogene barely touched her Frank's Afternoon Special.

When Claudine started describing the hot tub she and I had bought one year with our income tax refund, Imogene abruptly got to her feet. "Well," she said, "this has been real nice, but I've got to get back to work."

I didn't believe the part about this lunch being real nice, and I sure didn't believe the part where she had to return to work. As a real estate agent, Imogene can pretty much dictate her own schedule. I, however, knew a cue when I heard it. I scrambled to my feet. "Me too," I said.

Claudine's face fell. "Oh, Haskell, do you have to?"

A quick glance at Imogene told me the answer. Oh yeah. I had to.

I might've liked to have stayed and gotten Claudzilla to tell me exactly what she was doing here in Pigeon Fork, but that suddenly didn't seem like all that good an idea. Besides, I was pretty sure I'd find out sooner or later.

"I'm real busy, Claudine," I lied.

I gave Claudine enough money to pay for her Extravaganza Platter, and I followed Imogene toward the door as fast as I could, pretty much ignoring all the eyes that were now swiveling in our direction.

If, however, I'd known what Imogene was going to say to me once we were out in the parking lot, I might've slowed up some.

No sooner had we cleared Frank's front door and our feet had touched gravel than Imogene stopped abruptly and wheeled in my direction. "How could you?"

I was caught off guard. "How could I what?"

Imogene rolled her eyes. "What? What do you mean, *what?*"

I was losing the thread of this conversation fast, so I came up with the sort of snappy comeback I think I'm known for.

"Huh?"

What I meant by this, of course, was that I needed a little more clarification. From Imogene's reaction, though, you might've thought I'd slapped her.

Imogene's mouth went white and her eyes glittered. "How in the world could you tell your ex-wife right in front of me that I was just your *friend?*"

It was at this point, of course, that I realized the reason Imogene's eyes were glittering was that they actually had *tears* in them.

Oh God.

I'd really hurt her.

Imogene's voice was shaking now. "Up to now I was under the impression that you and I were more than just friends."

I took a step toward her. "We are, Imogene. We're a *lot* more than just friends. We ARE." Actually, I couldn't believe she was even questioning such a thing. Particularly since two nights ago I'd finally gotten up enough courage to tell her that I loved her.

I don't know, maybe in California men say "Love ya, babe" to just about every female they run into, and it doesn't mean a thing, but around these parts I was under the impression that mentioning the word "love" was pretty significant. It was certainly significant to *me*.

Two nights ago when Imogene had answered me with an "I love you" of her own, I'd actually thought for a second I might burst, I was that happy. And now Imogene was wondering if we were more than *friends*? Lord. What was wrong with this picture?

"Imogene, you've got to understand," I said, "I was just real rattled in there, that's all—"

Imogene was clearly not listening. "Did you know your ex-wife was coming to Pigeon Fork? Have you known for a while that she was coming to town and you didn't even tell me?"

I just looked at her. Wasn't this just like a woman? You do something incredibly callous and stupid, and right away they start thinking you could do something really mean. My God, did Imogene actually think I'd *planned* on Claudine showing up today so that I'd have this golden opportunity to act like a total jerk?

"Of course I didn't know she was coming!" I said. "I didn't have the slightest—"

Imogene was at that moment standing not five inches in front of me, so she probably did hear every word I said. You wouldn't have thought so, though, judging from what she did next. Right in the middle of what I was saying, she started waving her arms around. "And *then*," she said, "you just *sat* there while that woman went on and *on* and ON about your life together, for God's sake—"

I held up my hand. "Now, Imogene, Claudine was just

making conversation, that's all. She didn't mean anything by it."

Imogene actually staggered backward. "Are you NUTS?"

It was the second time today I'd been asked this. It could actually make you start feeling a tad uneasy.

I decided to ignore the question. "Imogene," I said, "Claudine talks a *lot* before she thinks." I didn't think it polite to mention, but to the best of my recollection, there had been entire days in our marriage when Claudine had appeared not to think at all. "Believe me," I went on, "Claudine did not mean anything by what she said."

Imogene blinked. "Haskell, of *course* Claudine meant something by it! Of course she did!"

I just looked at Imogene again. "What do you think she meant?"

I wasn't being deliberately thick-headed. I really did want to know what Imogene's line of thinking was here.

Imogene, however, gave me the kind of look I give my dog Rip when he won't fetch. "Oh brother," she said. Then, unbelievably, Imogene threw up her hands and stalked off to her car.

Just like that.

I decided it would probably not be a good idea to hurry after her and try to get a kiss good-bye.

Instead I just stood there, in Frank's parking lot, watching Imogene get into her red Mustang, start it up, and roar away in a cloud of gravel dust.

For a long moment I didn't move. I was that perplexed.

Now why in the world would Imogene be acting so sensitive all of a sudden? If I didn't know better, I'd have actually said that it was because she was afraid I might still care about Claudine. And yet, that would be ridiculous. Hadn't I told *her* I loved her? And hadn't I made it abundantly clear just exactly how I felt about Claudine these days?

I don't know, but it's my general impression that you don't refer to a woman you're still in love with as "Claudzilla."

At least, *I* don't.

So what exactly was Imogene's problem?

I turned to head toward my pickup. When we were married, Claudzilla had told me more than once that I didn't know the first thing about women. More and more I was starting to believe she might be right.

I started up my truck and drove over to where Frank's parking lot emptied onto the state road. Sitting there, waiting for a car to pass so I could pull out, I don't mind telling you I was feeling more than a little depressed. In the space of only an hour or so, I'd insulted an old high school buddy and hurt the feelings of the one woman in the world I cared most about.

I was two for two, and the day wasn't even over yet.

I took a deep breath. Well, maybe I didn't know what to say to Imogene, but I sure knew what to say to Rigdon.

I pulled onto the state road and headed back the way I'd come.

It didn't seem to take any time to get back to Rigdon's little ranch house. His truck was in his driveway and his front door was standing a little ajar when I pulled up.

I took still another deep breath before I got out of my truck. Apologizing to Rigdon was definitely going to be difficult.

I reckon that's why I wanted to get it over with as quick as I could. I hurried up the gravel path to Rigdon's front door, pushed it all the way open and stuck my head in. "Rigdon?" I called.

There was no answer.

I stepped through the door, walked around all those

motionless animals in Rigdon's living room, and moved quickly into the hall.

"Rigdon? Hey, Rigdon?" I called again.

He wasn't in the kitchen, so I turned to head into his workroom.

That's when I saw him.

A rope twisted around his neck, Rigdon was hanging from the light fixture in the middle of the room.

Oh God.

Apologizing was going to be even more difficult than I thought.

CHAPTER
5

Hanging from the overhead light fixture, his feet almost a yard off the floor, poor Rigdon looked like a rag doll. On the linoleum floor a wooden chair lay on its side.

I tried to move as fast as I could, but it seemed suddenly as if I was traveling not through air, but through water, dragging at my legs and arms, slowing me down. Lord. It seemed to take forever to get to Rigdon's side—and to grab his hand.

"Rigdon!" I said. "Rigdon!"

I don't know why I called his name. As soon as I touched his hand, I knew that Rigdon was not ever going to answer me.

The poor guy had spent his entire life trying to be cool, and he'd finally made it.

Matter of fact, Rigdon wasn't just cool. He was cold.

I didn't want to look up into Rigdon's face, but my eyes seemed irresistibly drawn in that direction. The way sometimes you're drawn to look at an awful car accident.

You don't want to look, you know you're going to hate yourself after, but you just can't help it.

Oh God. I hated myself, all right. Rigdon's tongue was protruding, his eyes bulging, his face swollen and distorted. His lips—and the skin all along his jawline—were an ugly, mottled purple.

I dropped Rigdon's hand and took a couple of stumbling steps away from him, nearly falling over the wooden chair beneath his feet. My breath was now coming in short, ragged gasps, and my heart pounding so loud, it seemed to fill the entire room.

There are those who'll tell you that people like me, who've worked homicide investigations for years, eventually get used to seeing folks in the condition poor Rigdon was in. I'm here to tell you we don't. Not ever.

For a long moment I couldn't even think. I just stood there, my mind emptied of everything except the terrible shock of seeing poor Rigdon Bewley, my old friend from high school, hanging there like a piece of meat.

Not looking a bit like James Dean anymore.

It was when my mind had cleared some—when I'd finally started actually *seeing* once again whatever it was I happened to be looking at—that I spotted the note.

Handwritten in ballpoint pen on a sheet of notebook paper, the note was lying faceup on top of Rigdon's worktable. I stepped around the overturned chair beneath Rigdon's feet, being careful not to look back up at Rigdon again. Lord knows, one look was all I needed. If anything, I was going to need help *forgetting* what I'd just seen. I certainly didn't need any quick refresher courses.

My back to Rigdon, I moved close enough to the worktable so that I could read the note without touching it.

I guess it's pretty clear by now how bad I feel about what happened. It's no use going on. I'm ending it once and for all. Good-bye forever. Rigdon.

I must've read that thing ten times.

It seemed pretty cut and dried. Of course, I couldn't tell for sure if the note really was in Rigdon's handwriting, but from the dramatic tone, it sure sounded like Rigdon, all right.

The note—and, of course, Rigdon himself suspended from the ceiling in back of me—pretty much added up to one inescapable conclusion.

Rigdon Bewley had committed suicide.

Don't worry. I wasn't exactly congratulating myself on my amazing deductive powers at this point. I knew very well that you didn't exactly need to be a crackerjack private detective to deduce *this* from the clues on hand.

And yet, standing there at Rigdon's worktable, reading that note again and again, I just couldn't believe this particular deduction was correct. I just couldn't believe Rigdon had really taken his own life.

Why on earth would he do such a thing? Why would a man who'd only hours before been pleading with me to protect him from homicidal squirrels and raccoons suddenly turn around and do to himself exactly what he'd wanted me to keep the squirrels and raccoons from doing to him?

Of course, it probably could be argued that anybody who was afraid of animal hit men might not be capable of real logical thinking.

Moreover, Rigdon's note did seem to offer something of an explanation. In fact, if the truth be known, it was this part of his note that I found myself reading over and over. The part that said "how bad I feel about *what happened.*"

I swallowed uneasily. Surely Rigdon hadn't been referring to today's little episode at Frank's Bar and Grill? Surely Rigdon could not have been so thin-skinned that what I'd said about him in front of everybody at Frank's could have actually driven the poor guy to this?

Just *considering* such a thing made my mouth go dry.

No, the idea was preposterous. Surely nobody could be that thin-skinned.

I resolutely put the thought right out of my mind, moved away from Rigdon's worktable and hurried out of the room to look for a phone. I found it on the wall in the kitchen right next to the door. Dialing up the sheriff, I started talking as soon as I recognized the voice on the other end. "Vergil? It's Haskell. You better get out here to Rigdon Bewley's place right away."

I never call the sheriff just to chat. Even if Vergil was my dad's best friend at one time—and, no doubt, they would still be real close today if my dad were still alive—Vergil and I don't exactly have that kind of relationship. The few phone calls, in fact, that I've made to Vergil in the last year or so have always been under pretty urgent circumstances. I reckon this is why it didn't take any more than just those few words for Vergil to get the message.

I'd say the sheriff took the news with his customary stoic attitude. "OH MY GOD!" Vergil screamed. "You don't mean to tell me Rigdon Bewley is DEAD?"

"I'm afraid so—"

I started to tell him the rest of it, but Vergil drowned me out. "NO-O-O-O! Oh my Lordy, Lordy, Lordy! I can't believe it! Oh God, oh God, oh God! OH, this is awful, this is really awful, this is TERRIBLE—"

Vergil was carrying on so much, I started thinking that he must've been a lot closer to Rigdon than I'd thought. I hadn't been aware, of course, that Rigdon and Vergil were real close buddies or anything, but for all I knew, they'd gotten to be friends in the years I'd been away.

Which meant, of course, that I'd been an insensitive jerk to just blurt out the news like that. When Vergil finally toned down enough so that I could be heard, I said, "Verg, I'm *real* sorry. I had no idea you knew Rigdon that well—"

Vergil was right in the middle of an "Oh my God," but he broke off to say, "Rigdon? Naw, I didn't know him. He was a hunter or something, wasn't he?"

"No, Vergil, he was a taxiderm—"

Vergil interrupted me. Not surprisingly, he was revving up again. "I tell you, Haskell, everywhere you go, somebody up and gets killed! I just can't believe you've found yourself another *murder!* My GAWD in heaven! Lordy, Lordy, LORDY . . ."

I understood then. It wasn't so much that Rigdon himself was dead. It was that Vergil thought Rigdon had been *murdered.* Vergil pretty much takes any crime committed in Crayton County as a personal affront. He actually appears to believe that folks around these parts are just committing crimes to spite him.

In Kentucky, however, suicide is not considered a crime. I reckon it's pretty easy to understand the thinking here. If suicide were a crime, there would, no doubt, be a real problem arresting the folks who'd been successful committing it. There'd also be a definite problem with sentencing. What I mean is, you might actually be able to charge somebody posthumously and even convict him, but how in the world were you going to punish him? Spit on his headstone?

All these problems must've occurred to Kentucky's lawmakers. Their solution, evidently, had been just to let folks kill themselves all they want.

Vergil was still carrying on, so I hurried to straighten him out. It took some doing because for a while there I couldn't get a word in edgewise. Vergil kept on chanting "my GAWD in heaven" until finally I had to scream to get myself heard.

"Vergil. Vergil! VERgil! VERGIL, this doesn't look like a murder!"

Vergil's chanting abruptly stopped. "What do you mean, it doesn't look like a murder? What's it look like?" Vergil always sounds as if he just got out of a funeral, but now he managed to sound both mournful and irritable at the same time.

"It looks like Rigdon hung himself." Just saying the words was a shock all over again. "There's a suicide note."

There was a moment's silence while Vergil apparently digested this last bit of news. "No kidding," he finally said. "Why, that's a shame. A crying shame."

Vergil didn't sound like it was a shame. He must've been very well aware that suicide would not appear on any list of possible things you could do to break the law in Kentucky, because Vergil sounded as if all this were suddenly a load off his mind.

Vergil evidently realized that he'd let a little too much relief seep into his voice, because he quickly cleared his throat and added, "Was Rigdon already dead when you got there, Haskell? I mean, do you think there was any way I could've gotten there and stopped him *before* he'd done what he did?"

I knew, of course, what Vergil was getting at. Believe it or not, even though suicide itself is not against the law in this state, it's perfectly okay to use force to stop a suicide in progress. In other words, law enforcement folks can actually shoot somebody who's shooting himself.

I don't mind telling you, the thinking here totally escapes me. I knew, however, that this was what was bothering Vergil now. Vergil, like I said, takes his law enforcing real serious. Old Vergil wanted to make damn sure he'd done everything he was supposed to.

"Vergil," I said, "Rigdon had been dead quite a while."

I thought Vergil would've been feeling a little kindlier toward me, being as how I'd just reassured him and all.

His next question, however, was—in my opinion—less than kind. "Was Rigdon a client of yours, Haskell? Have your clients stopped being killed off by other folks and now started killing off *themselves?*"

There was no other way to look at this. *This* was a cheap shot.

It was pretty typical, though, of Vergil lately. Not only has Vergil actually suggested that my arrival in town has started some kind of crime wave, he has also been real vocal in his belief that a significant portion of my clients meet with untimely ends.

All of this, of course, is blatantly untrue. Folks were cheerfully breaking the law long before I got there, and they would, no doubt, keep right on if I left.

And most of my clients have survived hiring me. In fact, only two of my clients have ever been murdered, and in both those cases Vergil knew very well that their demises had nothing whatsoever to do with the person they'd happened to hire to do their detecting work.

It was on the tip of my tongue to ask Vergil if he'd ever heard of the word "coincidence," but I thought better of it.

The last time Vergil made this little accusation, I'd totally embarrassed myself by naming off every client I'd had who was still walking around. I hadn't had all that many clients, so I'd ended up even mentioning the names of two librarians for whom I'd located some lost books.

Oh yeah. My last response to Vergil's accusation had already pretty much guaranteed me a nomination for Total Idiot of the Year. I really didn't have to do anything more. So all I said, after I gritted my teeth a little, was, "No, Vergil, Rigdon was *not* a client of mine." I thought I'd just skip the part where Rigdon had indeed tried to hire me only this morning. No use confusing the issue. "Rigdon was just a friend."

I don't know why, but for some reason my voice

cracked a little when I said this last sentence. It was kind of embarrassing.

It must've been embarrassing for Vergil too, because right after that he seemed real anxious to get off the phone. Of course, it might've been because he was suddenly in an all-fired hurry to get his entourage together and come on out to Rigdon's. I suspected, however, it was something else.

Vergil, for all his walking around looking like a thunderstorm himself, doesn't particularly cotton to dealing with anybody who's not in his best mood. In fact, Vergil actually told me once that he can't stand being around anybody who's "whining."

This, from the man who, if he can't say something nice, will talk your ear off.

After I hung up the phone, and while I waited for the sheriff and the coroner and anybody else Vergil brought with him to arrive, I decided to give Rigdon's workroom another look-see.

For one thing, in spite of what I'd just told Vergil, I was still having trouble actually believing that Rigdon really had taken his own life. I reckon maybe I was hoping I'd run into something that would convince me once and for all.

For another thing, I knew very well that this was going to be my last chance to look around in there. Being as how Vergil has gotten so persnickety ever since I moved back to Pigeon Fork, I knew what was going to happen.

I don't know why really, but somehow—in addition to suggesting that I'm a crime wave starter and the equivalent of the Kiss of Death for my clients—Vergil has latched onto the dumb idea that I'm some hot shot detective from the big city who's trying to tell him how to do his job. I've tried to convince him otherwise, but once the sheriff gets something into his head, it's hard to shake it loose.

Working on cases here in town, I've had folks try to kill me a few times, I've had my tires slashed, my dog nearly murdered, and I've even ended up in the hospital. Every time something awful has happened to me, Vergil's been so mad, he can't see straight.

He's been sure I was hogging all the glory.

For a while there I thought I might actually have to make a few attempts on Vergil's life just to even things up.

Even the times I've helped him catch a culprit, Vergil has only been grudgingly grateful.

Now, there wasn't a doubt in my mind that once Vergil got here, I wouldn't be allowed to so much as stick my toe into Rigdon's workroom. Nope, Vergil was going to waltz in here and fence me out about as fast as you could say "Official Police Business."

That meant I didn't have much time. Hurrying back into Rigdon's workroom, I wasn't even sure what I was looking for.

I was sure of one thing, though. I was not going to do any more looking at Rigdon. I purposely avoided even glancing in his direction.

In my opinion, if you've seen one purple, swollen face, you've pretty much seen your quota for a lifetime.

Instead I concentrated on looking around the room. I moved real slow, checking all around, trying to find out if maybe there was something I'd overlooked before, in the first awful moments after discovering Rigdon's body.

I would've liked to have said I was confining my search to tiny, insignificant details that might've managed to escape my notice earlier, but let's face it, after one look at Rigdon, I probably could've overlooked the *Titanic,* had it been sitting next to Rigdon's worktable.

I went over and looked at the note again. Nothing new there.

I also looked at Rigdon's worktable. Just as I remembered it from my visit earlier, the surface was cluttered with bones, wire, tools, and various knives. The bucket holding the tomato juice was gone, but other than that, the table looked pretty much the same.

I particularly stared at Rigdon's assortment of knives. There were a couple of carbon steel medium-sized knives, a small paring knife, a broad-bladed butcher's knife, and an open pocketknife. All lying right out in plain view on the table.

Those knives did make you wonder. Why would Rigdon choose to hang himself when he'd had another method so readily available?

Of course, hanging *was* a whole lot neater, I suppose. Maybe Rigdon hadn't wanted to leave a mess for anybody to clean up.

Although if Rigdon were the neat type, his cluttered worktable sure didn't prove it.

You'd also think if Rigdon were really trying to be considerate of those he left behind, he might've given a little more thought to what he was going to be looking like once the awful deed was done.

This last, now that I thought about it, was not a bit consistent with the Rigdon I had known. Surely a man who'd spent a good portion of his life trying to look like a movie star would've been far too vain to leave such an unattractive corpse. Wouldn't he?

On the other hand, if you were about to kill yourself, you might not be terribly inclined to think too far into the future. Then, too, there was probably also a good chance you might not be terribly concerned about your appearance anymore.

Although this sure didn't sound like Rigdon either. Rigdon, I'd have sworn, would've been one of the few men in the world who would insist on having a mirror installed on the inside lid of his coffin.

It was at this point, of course, that I realized I was thinking in circles. So I decided to stop thinking for a while and just concentrate on looking around. I stepped away from the worktable and started moving around the room.

It was while I was doing a methodical search of the floor, particularly in the area of the overturned chair, that I saw it.

Rigdon's toothpick.

It was lying less than an inch to the left of the overturned chair, one end of the toothpick characteristically chewed into pulp.

Staring at that thing, I found myself blinking again, real fast this time. Somehow, that solitary little toothpick lying there on the linoleum floor made everything seem even more awful.

Judging from where it was lying, the toothpick looked as if it might've actually fallen from Rigdon's mouth as he breathed his last.

It was so sad.

And so *odd*.

I squatted and peered at the toothpick real close. If you were hanging yourself, would you do it with a toothpick in your mouth? Would you climb up on a chair, put a noose over your head, carefully work the rope *around* the toothpick sticking out of the corner of your mouth, and then tighten the rope around your neck?

Having never killed myself before, I couldn't exactly speak with authority, but wasn't it a lot more likely that you'd put your toothpick in the garbage, or leave it on your worktable, or even stick it in your pocket *before* you climbed up on the chair?

I stood up and took a long breath. There was also something else bothering me. During the eight years I'd spent as a cop in Louisville, I'd had the misfortune of running into quite a few suicides. Nearly every one of these had involved the use of a gun. In all those years, in fact, I'd seen only two suicides by hanging.

I'm not sure why folks don't usually hang themselves these days. Maybe word had gotten out just how bad you were going to look once you'd done such a thing to yourself, or maybe folks just didn't know how to tie a good knot anymore. Whatever the reason, hanging yourself was definitely not the "in" way to go. If, indeed, it had ever been.

What's more, in both the hanging suicides I'd seen, the feet of the dead person had been *touching* the floor. At the time, I'd been kind of surprised that this was the case, so I'd asked around. What I'd found out was that this was actually *common* in suicidal hangings.

According to what one of the other detectives had told me, folks who commit suicide by hanging themselves almost always do it the same way. This particular detective had gone into considerable detail describing what he referred to as "the most popular hanging method." At the time, I'd just gotten myself married to Claudine, and I remember feeling downright uneasy the way this guy went on and on and on, letting me know exactly how you went about hanging yourself properly. As if it were information I might find personally useful.

What the guy had told me was that you tie one end of a rope around a firm support, like a rafter or a shower curtain rod. Then you tie the other end around your neck, and apply pressure against the rope by crouching down, if you're standing, or by leaning forward, if you're sitting. This standing/leaning action pretty much cuts off all the blood flow to your brain, which causes you to black out.

Once you've blacked out, the full weight of your body gets applied to the noose. This, of course, cuts off every bit of your oxygen and finishes the job.

The reason folks almost always do it this way, so this guy told me, was that this particular method was the most comfortable way to do it.

Back then I'd thought the guy had been looking at me with a little too much sympathy, and I'd been real anxious to end our little conversation. Now, however, I have to admit, that guy had been right.

If I *were* interested in committing suicide, comfort would, no doubt, be a real important factor in deciding how I went about it.

In fact, it might very well be the *most* important factor.

Like I said before, call me picky.

I took another deep breath and gave the room a long, long look. All the stuff I'd noticed during my search was, when you came right down to it, not exactly earth-shattering. And yet, added together, all these non-earth-shattering things were enough to make me wonder.

Was it possible that Rigdon's death had not been a suicide after all? Could he have been murdered, and all this *staged* to look as if he'd taken his own life?

I was starting to feel almost as cold as Rigdon himself. Which was going some.

I was also starting to feel as if I had quite a few questions to put to Vergil the minute he showed up.

Questions, no doubt, that Vergil was going to be tickled pink to hear.

The last time Vergil arrived at a crime scene, he'd acted so embarrassed that a crime had happened in his jurisdiction, he hadn't even run his sirens when he pulled up. It had been as if he were *sneaking* in to do his job, hoping no one would notice that yet another person had had the audacity to break the law during his watch.

Like I said earlier, though, that had been three months ago. The humiliation must've worn off. Or else being under the impression that the scene he was about to arrive at wasn't technically a *crime* scene at all had done wonders for Vergil's confidence. Vergil's siren and the siren of the deputy car following him were going full-blast when they pulled into Rigdon's driveway.

I've never been real sure why Vergil and his deputies even bother to run their sirens on their way to things like this. It's not as if there's a whole lot of traffic they've got to weave through on their way out of town. And, in this case, it was certainly not as if they had to worry about Rigdon getting away before they got here.

The only explanation I've been able to come up with is that the sirens must be a public relations ploy. It's Vergil's way of letting folks know that he's on the job, protecting and serving, catching the bad guys, doing whatever good sheriffs do.

I was still in Rigdon's workroom when I first heard Vergil's public relations message wailing in the distance. I took one last look around, noticed nothing more than I'd noticed before, and immediately headed out to the living room, making my way around the motionless menagerie out there, toward Rigdon's front door.

Vergil and his two deputies, the Gunterman twins, were just pulling their cars into Rigdon's long driveway when I walked out of the house.

Horace Merryman, the assistant coroner, was also pulling into the driveway right behind the two police cars. Horace drives a big, black Ford limousine that's real easy to spot around town. I reckon it's the only limo within a hundred-mile radius. If that alone wasn't enough to make it stand out, the way it says CRAYTON COUNTY CORONER in large, metallic-gold, capital letters on one side, and MERRYMAN'S FUNERAL HOME in even larger capital letters on the other side, makes it just about the eye-catchingest vehicle around these parts. Both sides of Horace's limo also display the same Pigeon Fork telephone number. The numbers aren't quite as big as the letters just above them, but they're close.

It's always bothered me some that the coroner here in Crayton County also happens to be the owner of Pigeon Fork's only funeral home. It appears to me to be a clear-cut conflict of interest if the guy who's about to pronounce you dead is the exact same guy who is also about to immediately profit from his pronouncement.

Nobody but me, however, has ever seemed to see any problem with this.

Vergil, Horace Merryman, and the Gunterman brothers got out of their cars, slamming their doors right and left, and came hurrying up the gravel path toward Rigdon's house in what had to be record time. The four of them were moving so fast, it almost looked as if they were racing each other to where I stood in front of Rigdon's stoop.

Vergil had the early lead. In his tan, crisply pressed sheriff's uniform, he traveled up the gravel path so quickly, I thought any minute he was going to break into an outright run.

Running, though, is a thing, I believe, that Vergil considers unseemly for a person of his elevated social stature. I hated to tell Vergil, but walking real fast like he was now doing probably wasn't seemly either. On account of the way the rapid motion made his beer belly bobble up and down.

Vergil's stomach looked like a tan beach ball bouncing in my direction.

If, however, Vergil's stomach looked like a beach ball, the stomachs of the two Gunterman twins in back of him looked like identical medicine balls bouncing toward me.

You might've expected that the twins' size would've slowed them down some, but at six feet three and at least 240 pounds apiece, the twins appeared to be gaining fast on Vergil.

Watching the Guntermans head my way, I halfway expected the ground to start shaking.

Bringing up the rear, clearly out of the money, his short legs moving twice as fast as the Guntermans' but not covering anywhere near as much ground, came Horace Merryman.

Merryman is pretty much a misnomer for Horace. A merry man he has never been. The kind of man he has always been, in fact, is nervous. Even now, as Horace scampered after the others, he was fidgeting with the lapels of his black undertaker's suit, fidgeting with the latch of his medical bag, and fidgeting with the ends of his pencil-thin mustache, all in a whirl of motion.

As thin as a reed, and not an inch over five feet five, if Horace had any kind of a ball for a stomach, it had apparently never been inflated.

With all these folks running straight at me, it took some doing to hold my ground. Particularly when self-preservation pretty much dictated that I just step aside when they got within a few feet of me.

I was determined, however, to talk to Vergil before he got a look at Rigdon. I had hoped to talk to him alone, but Vergil and the Guntermans arrived at the finish line at almost the same time.

I've always thought the best way to tell somebody something they might not want to hear was just to spit it right out. I took a deep breath and moved so that I blocked Vergil's path. "Vergil?" I said.

He put on the brakes the second I spoke.

The Gunterman twins must not have expected Vergil to stop that quick, because the two of them had to veer off to one side to keep from mowing him down.

Vergil gave the twins a long, infinitely sad stare as the Guntermans hurried to rejoin him on the gravel path, before he answered me. "Yeah, Haskell?"

"Vergil, I think I might've been wrong over the phone."

I was standing right in front of Vergil, but I still didn't

have his full attention. Horace Merryman had just arrived at the bottom of the stoop too, and both his and Vergil's eyes had apparently been caught by the sign hanging around the neck of the stone deer in Rigdon's front yard.

Judging from the direction they were looking, I'd say Vergil and Horace were particularly taken with Rigdon's drawing of the furry thumb.

No doubt they were both marveling at the craftsmanship of the thing.

Vergil cleared his throat before he answered me. For a split second I was afraid he was going to ask me what in hell that thumb drawing was, and I would've had to admit that I didn't have the slightest idea. Fortunately, though, it must've occurred to Vergil that this would've entailed admitting that he himself didn't know either.

"What do you mean," Vergil asked, "you were wrong over the phone?" Running his hand through his thinning salt-and-pepper hair, he was—oddly enough—*still* staring at Rigdon's thumb.

I took another deep breath. "Vergil," I said, "this might not be a suicide after all."

Oh yeah. Vergil was every bit as tickled pink to hear what I had to say as I'd expected him to be.

"WH-A-A-AT?" Vergil screamed. "What in hell are you talking about?"

With his eyes bugging out like that, Vergil even scared the Guntermans. They took several quick steps away from him.

CHAPTER
6

I'd accomplished one thing anyway. Vergil and Horace were no longer staring at Rigdon's sign. Their eyes, in fact, seemed pretty much riveted to my face.

"What do you mean, this isn't a suicide?" Vergil said. "I thought you said there was a suicide note." Vergil's got a whole lot of fine tiny lines like spiderwebs crisscrossing his face. These lines deepen quite a bit when Vergil gets upset. Right now, as he spoke, the lines around his mouth looked like ravines.

"Well, yes, Vergil, I did say there was a suicide note, but now I'm not so sure it really is—"

I would've continued to explain, but at that moment Horace jumped in, looking affronted. "Wait a minute," he said. He was now fidgeting with his hair, brushing it out of his face, and fiddling with the cuffs of his sleeves. "Aren't I the coroner around here? I believe it's *my* job to determine whether a death is a suicide or not."

If anybody else had said this, it probably would've sounded like a reprimand. Horace, however—his voice a hushed monotone—sounded as if he were merely point-ing out a fact that I might've overlooked. In much the same calm, low-key way as he would've directed me into the correct parlor for a final viewing.

I just stared at him for a second. There are those around town who think that Horace has been an under-taker so long, he's forgotten how to talk normal, but I know for a fact that Horace has always sounded like this.

According to my dad, who went to high school with him, even back then if you ran into Horace Merryman at a ball game or a pep rally, Horace would be cheering the team on in this same hushed monotone. The way my dad told it, Horace never did have much choice as to what occupation he was going into. With a voice like that, he was either going to be a funeral director or he was going to do the play-by-play for golf tournaments.

Right now, I sort of wished he'd chosen to do the golf thing.

"Horace," I said, "I certainly am *not* trying to tell you how to do your job."

I thought I sounded downright sincere. It did not help my case any, however, to have Vergil make a real skeptical sound in the back of his throat.

And roll his eyes.

I ignored Vergil and hurried on. "Horace, I just want you to keep an open mind when you go in there, because this whole thing just doesn't feel right to me." Turning back to the sheriff, I added, "Vergil, I really think—"

That was all I managed to say before Vergil held up his hand. Much like he would've held it up to stop oncoming traffic. "Maybe in the Big City," he said, "law enforce-ment folks go around taking a poll of what everybody thinks, but around these parts we generally just let the professionals do their job."

Uh-oh. There was no doubt this time. That one *was* a reprimand.

I could've kicked myself. In my hurry to tell Vergil about Rigdon, I'd forgotten how touchy he can be in situations like this. Lord. I should never have started giving Vergil an unsolicited opinion in front of witnesses.

Mainly because Vergil, for some reason, actually seems to entertain the notion that I'm after his job. He apparently truly believes that I left law enforcement in Louisville just so I could go into law enforcement in my hometown. As if it had been so much fun arresting total strangers and sending them away to prison that I was real anxious to do that kind of thing with folks I knew.

Vergil had to be kidding.

And yet, no doubt about it, I'd just stepped on Vergil's toes in a big way.

He was now looking straight at me and frowning, but he was clearly directing his comments to the Guntermans. "Jeb? Fred? Keep the *civilians* out here in the yard."

While a quick glance around told me that Vergil's previous public relations message had apparently been heard all up and down Rigdon's road—and, as a result, there were indeed quite a few folks sticking their heads out of their doors and looking this way—at that moment there were no "civilians" standing around in Rigdon's yard except Horace and me. And since I was pretty sure *Horace* was going to be allowed inside Rigdon's house, I believe I could assume, then, that the "civilians" Vergil was referring to pretty much dwindled down to just one—me.

This didn't look good. Vergil, obviously, had kicked into Official Police Business mode in a big way.

Which meant I'd be lucky if he gave me any more information other than what I could read off his sheriff's badge.

It also meant I'd be lucky if he bothered to listen at all

to any new theories I might have regarding Rigdon's death being something other than a suicide.

"Vergil?" I said.

Vergil was now ignoring me. He turned to the Guntermans. "Nobody gets in or out. Got it?" Vergil's voice was a bark. "We professionals are going inside to do *our jobs.*"

I may have been being a little thin-skinned here myself, but it seemed to me that Vergil took particular relish in saying this last sentence. And emphasizing those last two words.

"I'll take statements from the *civilians* when we come back out," Vergil was now saying to the Gunterman twin on his left. It was either Jeb or Fred, I couldn't tell which.

It really didn't matter which twin was which. With beefy jaws, short pug noses, and burr haircuts, the Guntermans are pretty much identically ugly. They're also pretty much identically threatening. And pretty much identically dimmer than a burnt-out light bulb.

When Vergil finished telling them what to do, both twins nodded in unison.

And saluted.

Vergil had been turning to move past me, up the stoop, but when the twins saluted him, he stopped mid-stride to give them both another long, sad look.

He must've decided after the salute that the twins needed additional instruction. *"Stay here by the stoop,"* he said, enunciating every word very carefully.

It was at this point that Jeb and Fred, oddly enough, both looked in *my* direction and smirked.

It took me a second to realize why it was that the twins were looking at me in this way. Then, unfortunately, it hit me.

The Guntermans thought that Vergil was referring to *me.*

As "the stupe."

I took still another deep breath. It's misunderstandings like this that have led folks around town to speculate that the sum of the twins' shoe sizes would far exceed the sum of their IQs.

Vergil looked now as if he was more than ready to cast his vote in favor of the shoe sizes. "Jeb, Fred, on second thought, maybe you better stand *up there,*" he said, pointing at the stoop and putting a little extra emphasis on his last two words. "On the little porch. In front of the door. So you can stop anybody who might be wanting to go inside."

That seemed to me about as clear as you could make it without putting down those paper footprints they use in dance classes, so that the twins could follow them.

Apparently, dance footprints would not be necessary. "Oh. Uh, *sure,*" the twin nearest to me said. "Come on, Fred."

Fred was still smirking at me as he and his brother followed Vergil and Horace up onto the stoop as far as the front door. Vergil, with Horace at his heels, disappeared inside, and then, of course, the twins turned around, their backs to the door, and just stood there. Twin Incredible Hulks, taking up just about every inch of space on that small stoop, now smirking in unison in my direction.

I considered explaining the whole thing to them. More or less telling the twins that they really had misunderstood Vergil, maybe even pointing out the stoop they were now standing on. Perhaps even *spelling* it for them.

There was always the chance, though, that this whole stoop thing could be a concept too complex for the twins to follow. These were, mind you, the very same guys who'd once told me with straight faces that the reason their mama named them Jeb and Fred was on account of her wanting names that rhymed.

It would also be just my luck that the twins would think I was not pointing at the stoop at all, but at one of them. They then might possibly conclude that I was calling whichever-it-was a stupe, and by the time Vergil came back out, the stupe in question would've beaten me to a bloody pulp.

Or maybe they would've taken turns.

For some reason, I decided it wasn't an issue worth discussing.

It was, however, a real disconcerting thing to have the *Gunterman twins,* of all people, looking at you as if you were dumb.

It was even more disconcerting to notice that, while I'd been momentarily distracted by the smirking stupes on the stoop, all those folks who'd been poking their heads out their doors had now apparently decided to head this way.

All up and down Rigdon's road people were coming out of houses the way bugs come out of woodwork.

Unlike bugs, however, some of these folks were getting into trucks and driving this way. After a while it looked like a convoy snaking down the road.

All this, of course, was not exactly a surprise. For the most part, when you live way out in the country, it's understood that you'll mind your business and everybody else'll mind theirs. However, you let a few police cars and a coroner's limo show up in your driveway, and that kind of understanding goes out the window. I can guarantee you're going to have company. Real quick.

In fact, it's occasions like this that let country folk know just how many neighbors they've got. You'll see faces you're sure you've never seen before in your life, not to mention, faces you'd not seen in years.

Two faces I personally had not seen in years belonged to a man and a woman in their late fifties who came hurrying out of the house with the yellow siding directly across the street.

I took one look and my stomach wrenched.

It was Agnes and Ernal Bewley, Rigdon's aunt and uncle. I hadn't realized they lived this close to Rigdon.

Agnes and Ernal may have been Rigdon's aunt and uncle, but they might as well have been his parents. I'd never known Rigdon to have any other folks. From what I'd heard around town, Rigdon's real mom and dad had died or disappeared or some such when he was still in kindergarten, and after that Agnes and Ernal had taken Rigdon and his younger sister in, and raised them ever since.

Even though I hadn't seen either one since Rigdon and I were in high school, they were pretty easy to recognize. Agnes's round, pink face was creased with a few more lines maybe, and wiry Ernal now had himself a little bit of a gut hanging over his belt buckle. Other than that, though, they looked pretty much the way I remembered them.

Agnes's hair had already been gray all those years ago, and she was still wearing it the same way she'd worn it back then. Pulled back from her face into a topknot, sort of like the way Gibson girls wore their hair.

Only if Agnes was a Gibson girl, she was a Gibson girl with muscular forearms that looked as if they could've belonged to Popeye, and a soft, plump body that looked as if it could've been constructed out of pillows. *King-sized* pillows, in fact. Agnes had to be at least five ten.

Today Agnes's king-sized pillow-body was stuffed into a pink, sleeveless housedress, covered by an old-fashioned bib apron in a pink floral pattern. Her pillow legs were stuffed into hose rolled down at the knee, and her pillow feet were stuffed into the shoes that at one time had been the source of quite a bit of teasing directed at Rigdon. You know that old cliché of an insult, "Your mom wears army boots?" In Agnes's case, it wasn't an insult. It was a statement of fact. She was clumping toward Rigdon's front yard in big, black, orthopedic clodhoppers.

Next to Agnes, Ernal looked downright dapper in his tan slacks, plaid short-sleeved shirt, and discolored tennis shoes. With bony legs and arms that seemed far too long for the rest of his body, Ernal was only about two inches taller than Agnes, but where she was soft and plump, he was all lean, hard muscle. He had thinning, black wavy hair, high cheekbones, deep-set eyes, a protruding lower lip, and frankly, if anybody had ever asked me who Ernal Bewley looked the most like, I'd have said without even hesitating—Abraham Lincoln. No kidding. I'm pretty sure they could've run Ernal's face on the five dollar bill and nobody would've known the difference.

Except, of course, that Ernal doesn't have the Lincoln whiskers. What he does have is real long sideburns reaching almost to his chin. So Ernal pretty much looks just like Lincoln after a shave.

I watched Agnes and Ernal heading my way, and I couldn't help it, I started blinking real bad. I could still see the two of them all those years ago—the king-sized Gibson girl and Lincoln in a plaid shirt—sitting there in the front row of the auditorium during the Pigeon Fork High senior play. Rigdon had only had two lines in the last act, but Agnes and Ernal had come to every performance.

I would've paid good money not to be anywhere around when the two of them found out what had happened to their boy.

I blinked some more and looked away. Directly at somebody else I recognized almost as quickly as I had

Rigdon's aunt and uncle. Across the street, hurrying out of the house with the green siding, was Curtis Strait. Rigdon's best friend ever since elementary school.

My stomach wrenched again.

Curtis had practically been Rigdon's shadow. He'd even tried to dress like Rigdon, wearing faded jeans, scuffed boots, and his hair combed straight back.

However, where Rigdon had succeeded real good at looking like James Dean, Curtis hadn't even come close. Of course, Curtis hadn't had much of a chance to start out with. At least six inches taller than Rigdon, with black, curly hair, and a five o'clock shadow so heavy that he never quite looked clean-shaven, Curtis was almost Rigdon's exact opposite.

You had to hand it to Curtis, though. Even though our classmates started calling him "Rebel Without a Clue," Curtis never did give up. Why, he'd even started running around with a toothpick sticking out of the side of his mouth right after Rigdon thought it up.

Now, I could see that Curtis, even after all these years, was apparently still giving it the old college try. Or, more appropriately, the old high school try. As Curtis hurried this way, dressed in—you guessed it—faded jeans and a white T-shirt, I could plainly see that Curtis had a toothpick dangling out of the corner of his mouth.

Evidently, Curtis's mama had never told him not to run with something in his mouth.

Running alongside Curtis was his wife, Bertie Lee. Like Agnes, Bertie Lee had a cliché of a saying that seemed to follow her around town too. It was, I believe: "Built like a brick outhouse." Bertie Lee's face was none too pretty, but a lot of the menfolk around these parts never made it up to her face.

Even if they did, they wouldn't have been able to see much anyway. Bertie Lee's got this real straight, chin-length black hair that she parts on the right side and lets fall over her left eye. I reckon she's trying to look alluring or something, but I don't mind telling you, talking to Bertie Lee is a lot like talking to the Phantom of the Opera. You never get a good look at half her face.

The Phantom, however, never wore the kind of outfit Bertie Lee had on today—a body-hugging pair of denim cutoffs and a red gingham halter top.

Bertie Lee must've been getting her wardrobe ideas from reruns of *Hee Haw*.

I can't say I objected. In my humble opinion, Bertie Lee's outfit showed off every brick in her outhouse to perfection.

The Bewleys and the Straits met up with each other right after they set foot on Rigdon's front yard. Even from where I was standing in front of the stoop, with nearly an acre of ground between us, I could hear what they were saying to each other. "What's going on?" "What's the police doing here?" "And Merryman's Funeral Home?"

I think everybody probably had already guessed what the answer was to all those questions, but nobody wanted to say it out loud.

I knew one thing for sure. *I* didn't want to be the one who told them.

Fortunately, by this time Rigdon's yard was starting to look as if he were having a garage sale. The folks in my immediate vicinity were men and women I didn't know at all, and I was real glad of that. They were just nameless women in sleeveless summer dresses or shorts outfits, and equally nameless men in jeans or overalls.

I quickly turned my back to the Bewleys and the Straits and sort of melted into the crowd. I realize this makes me sound like a damn coward, but I was sure hoping that the Bewleys and the Straits wouldn't recognize me anywhere near as quickly as I had them.

Right after I melted into the crowd, however, I spotted

the tall woman in her early thirties, running out of the pink house next door to Rigdon's house on this side of the street.

Seeing her made my stomach wrench more than seeing anybody else.

It was Louise Dossey, Rigdon's sister.

Lord. What was this, a club? Did every one of Rigdon's relatives and friends all live on the same road? Of course, I reckon I shouldn't have been surprised. As I recalled, the Bewleys had always been a real close-knit family. And Curtis probably would've followed Rigdon to the North Pole, providing there was a vacant igloo somewhere nearby.

If I didn't want to tell the Bewleys and the Straits what had happened to Rigdon, I sure didn't want to tell his sister Louise. There was such a thing, I believe, as "killing the messenger," and from what I remembered about Louise, she might be all too glad to demonstrate just how messenger-killing worked.

Even if I hadn't already known who she was, I probably would've guessed. Louise always has looked a whole lot like her brother. Which means, unfortunately, that, unlike Curtis, Louise looks a *lot* like James Dean. Without even trying.

In fact, what Louise mainly looked like, as she headed in my direction, was James Dean wearing a curly, brown, shoulder-length wig, a purple flowered T-shirt, green plaid shorts, and red plastic flip-flops.

Either Louise was making a bold fashion statement or else she'd been taking a bath when she'd heard the sirens—and had just grabbed whatever was handy so she could hurry right over here.

I sort of leaned toward this last theory, being as how Louise's brown hair looked a little damp around the ends.

I stared at her as she went by me. Looking like James

Dean, as you might imagine, is not nearly so attractive on a woman as a man.

Matter of fact, Louise's resemblance to James Dean probably explained why back in high school she hadn't dated all that much. She was three years younger than Rigdon and me, so I didn't know her anywhere near as well as I knew him. Generally, as I recall, she'd confined her considerable energies to winning prizes for her beef cattle at the Crayton County Fair.

Some of our more cruel classmates back then—oddly enough, the same ones who'd called me Howdy Doody and Curtis "Rebel Without a Clue"—had frequently pointed out the strong resemblance between Louise's figure and that of her heifers, but they never did say it to her face. Being as how, if she'd ever heard them, Louise would've, no doubt, made sure that these particular classmates of mine would've immediately started bearing a strong resemblance to somebody who'd been hit by a truck.

Louise's main claim to fame during the four years she spent at Pigeon Fork High, as I recall, was that she'd been the first girl to be elected President of the Future Farmers of America. Rumor had it, however, that she'd gotten herself elected by threatening every other member with major hurt if the votes didn't go her way.

Louise could do some damage, believe you me, if she set her mind to it. Like her aunt Agnes, Louise was not small. She was at least two inches taller than Rigdon, and she had to outweigh him by at least thirty pounds.

I'd heard that Louise had married a guy named Floyd Dossey, who'd moved into town shortly after I left. I'd never met him personally, but I assumed that the muscle-bound guy with the shaggy, shoulder-length brown hair who'd followed Louise out of the pink house had to be Floyd.

Floyd was a good five inches shorter than Louise, but

he looked like the sort of guy you wouldn't want to tease about it. Barefoot and wearing just a pair of faded Levi's jeans, he had a large, multicolored drawing of a snake tattooed on his chest.

Its fangs dripping blood, the snake seemed to move in and out of Floyd's chest hairs.

It was quite an effect.

As if the snake wasn't impressive enough, Floyd's left forearm displayed a snarling bear, and his right forearm showed off a growling tiger.

If Floyd was even half as tough as his tattoos, I'd say Louise had met her match.

Louise must not have seen me, because she brushed right past me, climbed up the steps, and headed straight toward the Gunterman twins. There wasn't room for her on the stoop, so she stopped at the top step.

"What's happened here?" she demanded.

Louise probably ought to stand next to the Guntermans more often. Next to them, she looked downright petite.

Louise was obviously directing her question to Fred, the twin standing directly in front of her, but her eyes kept traveling over to Merryman's car in the driveway. And to the words stenciled on the side. CRAYTON COUNTY CORONER.

Fred's answer may not have been all that informative, but it *was* real quick. "Uh," he said, "well, uh, well . . ."

Louise leaned forward. "Look, I—I want to know what's happened here," she said, her lower lip trembling.

Fred just looked at her, obviously hesitating. The size he was, I knew Fred wasn't afraid on account of the "kill-the-messenger" thing. Hell, he'd probably never even heard of it.

Nope, what had to be bothering Fred was, no doubt, something that had happened at the last crime scene he and I had visited. The one I mentioned earlier. Fred had taken it upon himself to notify the next of kin. As a result, he'd had to stand around and listen to the guy carry on, weeping and wailing, for the next several hours.

This must've made a definite impression on him. Now, in response to Louise, Fred scratched his medicine ball stomach, grunted a couple times, and then abruptly turned to his brother. "Jeb, you tell her."

Jeb's answer was real quick too. "O-h-h-h no you don't, not me, I ain't a-gonna tell her. Uh-uh, no-sirree—"

Louise took all this with the kind of patience she'd often displayed back in high school. Grabbing the front of Jeb's shirt, she yanked him toward her and screamed, "Tell me NOW!"

It was apparently the kind of argument Jeb couldn't resist.

He shrugged and said, "Some guy hung hisself."

That pretty much did the trick. Louise let go of his shirt.

She also stumbled backward down the steps.

And let loose a scream of anguish that echoed off the hills in the distance.

With the kind of tattoos he had, I might've thought that Floyd was not exactly the empathic sort, but as soon as Louise started screaming, he stepped right in and gathered her into his arms. In fact, the way he more or less caught her as she was falling, and the way he staggered only a little under the load, gave a whole new meaning to the word "supportive."

Louise being so much taller than Floyd made the two of them look a little funny, particularly since she was all hunkered over, leaning on him like maybe he was a human cane. I was willing to bet, though, that not a person there would ever mention it to either of them.

Evidently, several of the others standing in Rigdon's yard had heard what Jeb had just told Louise. And those that didn't hear were told by those that did. In about a minute everybody in the yard was sobbing and screaming and wiping their eyes. Some louder than others. The Straits, Curtis and Bertie Lee, for example, looked almost hysterical as they cried in each other's arms.

The one person, though, that I might've expected to have made the most fuss was just standing there. Rigdon's aunt, Agnes Bewley, looked positively shell-shocked as she pressed her already thin lips into an even thinner line and stared straight ahead, unblinking. On the other hand, standing right next to her, her husband Ernal was blinking up a storm.

The blinking evidently wasn't helping. Tears began to slowly streak down Ernal's face.

I looked away. Lord. I'd seen a lot of photographs of Lincoln looking real sad, but this was like watching him cry.

Having started all this commotion was evidently too much for Jeb. The huge twin took one harried look around the yard, his eyes darting from one anguished face to another, and then without a word he turned, opened Rigdon's front door, and ran inside.

Almost immediately, however, Jeb reappeared, running out of Rigdon's house even faster than he'd gone in.

His tiny eyes looked to be about ten times their regular size, so for a second there I thought maybe Jeb had gotten a look at Rigdon. It didn't seem, though, as if he'd been inside long enough to have made it all the way back to the workroom.

Jeb himself straightened me out. Running directly to his brother, he grabbed Fred's arm. "The place is crawling with animals, Fred! They's all over the place—and they's all standing real, real still!"

I thought Fred took the news well. "You're lying!"

Jeb shook his massive head. "Naw, it's true! See for yourself!"

Fred actually turned to go inside, but all the commotion outside had evidently brought Vergil to the front door in back of the twins. The sheriff must've overheard the entire conversation between the Gunterman brothers, because when he opened the door, he stared at Jeb and Fred for yet another long, sad moment.

Finally, heaving a huge sigh, Vergil said, "Boys, the guy was a taxidermist."

Jeb and Fred just looked at him.

I believe I've seen broken televisions with screens that didn't look any blanker than the Gunterman twins' faces.

Vergil heaved another sigh. He took a real quick glance around the yard, apparently decided that everybody was still too preoccupied with the grieving process to be listening to him, and then said, leaning toward the twins, his voice very low, *"A taxidermist stuffs animals. That's why they're not moving. The animals are dead."*

Jeb's answer was even lower than Vergil's, but I wasn't standing very far away. I heard every word. "Really?" Jeb said. "I thought, uh, a *taxi* dermist was just a fancy name for a guy who drives a cab."

After that one, Vergil must've stared at Jeb for a full thirty seconds.

I don't reckon I've ever seen Vergil look sadder.

What Jeb had said might not have sounded quite so bad except that in Pigeon Fork there's no such thing as a taxi. In fact, if you really wanted to call a cab around these parts, the closest one you could call is all the way in Louisville, and it would probably cost you a fortune to get it here.

Louise's sobs had died down a little by now, and for some reason Vergil now seemed downright anxious to take his leave of the twins and go have a talk with Rigdon's sister.

Oddly enough.

Vergil squeezed by the twins on the stoop and headed directly toward Louise. When he passed by me, I noticed that Vergil was taking out of his pocket one of the clear plastic evidence bags he always seems to have with him.

I could see through the plastic that the bag contained a sheet of notebook paper.

Apparently, Vergil's little chat with the twins had not left him in all that good a mood. As he went by me, he gave me a look almost as long and almost as sad as the one he'd given Jeb. *"Good-bye forever?* And you think maybe this isn't a suicide note?"

Oh yeah. I'd say the tone in which Vergil said that was pretty much contemptuous.

When Vergil got to Louise's side, his tone softened considerably. "Is this your brother's handwriting?"

Louise read the note and immediately started nodding her head. "Yes, that's Rigdon's, all right." That was all she got out before she started crying again.

Louise must've sobbed for a full minute.

Vergil either wanted to make sure I had not missed what Louise had just said or else he was just using this as an excuse to step away from somebody who was that upset. The second Louise started crying again, Vergil came back toward me and said, with a pointed look, "She says it's Rigdon's handwriting."

I kind of wished Vergil had not done that. Not just because it was obvious that he was rubbing it in a little, but also because if it hadn't been for Vergil, Louise might not have realized it was me standing there.

As soon as he spoke to me, Louise seemed to notice me for the first time. "See?" she said, pulling away from

Floyd and coming toward me. "See?" she said again, tears streaking down her face.

I just looked at her, not quite getting her drift. Was she wanting me to take a look at Rigdon's note?

Louise, however, didn't keep me in the dark for long. *"See what you did?"* she yelled.

And then, of course, she lunged for my throat.

CHAPTER
7

To give Vergil the benefit of the doubt, maybe Louise's sudden movement was so unexpected, it left him paralyzed with shock.

That could, no doubt, easily explain why the sheriff just stood there and let Louise try to kill me right in front of him.

Without him so much as moving a muscle.

Or, say, indicating in even the slightest way to the Guntermans, who were still standing up there on the stoop, that they might ought to step in and help me out a little.

You could tell Vergil's inaction was a real disappointment to the Guntermans too. The two of them were practically quivering as they kept glancing first at me and Louise, over at Vergil, and then back over at me and Louise again. Like huge, identical retrievers eagerly waiting for the signal to fetch.

On the other hand, it might not have been shock at all that momentarily paralyzed Vergil. There was a distinct possibility, I believe, that old Verg could be actually enjoying himself, watching me get attacked by a very large woman with very sharp fingernails.

If, at the time, I'd gotten a good look at the expression on Vergil's face, I probably could've made up my mind which one of these possible explanations was the correct one. I was, however, a tad too busy to give the sheriff much more than a startled glance once Louise pounced on me.

I hated to disappoint Vergil and all, but back in Louisville I'd had extensive training in dealing with just this sort of situation. Years ago I might've been at a real disadvantage, but not anymore. The training I got back in Louisville was not, of course, training I received in my official capacity as a homicide cop. No, it was even better. It was training I received in my official capacity as Claudzilla's husband.

Now I was relieved to find out that, even after all these months without practice, my reflexes were still right on the money.

Before Louise's fingernails had even grazed my throat, I'd grabbed her wrists. And locked them in place.

For a moment there, while Louise and I swayed back and forth, you might've thought we were dancing.

Except, of course, for the way Louise kept trying to break my grip.

And the way she kept screaming, "Murderer! *You* killed Rigdon! Just as sure as if you'd put a gun to his head! MURDERER!"

When Louise first started yelling, I was so appalled, I couldn't even speak. My God, could Louise actually believe that what I'd said earlier at Frank's had really driven Rigdon to take his own life? My stomach wrenched again just thinking about it.

In fact, for a second there I was so stunned, all I could

do was stare at Louise. And, of course, continue to try to keep her fingers away from my throat.

Vergil, however, seemed to have no trouble at all finding *his* voice. His salt-and-pepper head went up and he immediately moved closer to Louise. "What do you mean, Haskell killed Rigdon?"

I don't think Louise even heard Vergil. She was concentrating too hard on breaking away from me and, of course, strangling me as soon as she broke away. There was also the distinct possibility that her own screams might've drowned Vergil out. "MURDERER! You damn MURDERER!"

I couldn't help being painfully aware that Louise was calling me this in front of an entire yard full of people. I found my voice. "Louise, come on now, people can hear you. They might actually get the impression that I was some kind of—"

"MURDERER!" Louise thoughtfully finished for me. At the top of her lungs, I might add. "You killed Rigdon! You DID!"

I'd say, people getting the impression that I and, say, Ted Bundy had a lot in common was pretty much what Louise was aiming for.

Vergil had now moved around Louise so that he was standing pretty close to my right ear. Leaning even closer, Vergil asked, "What does she mean, *you* killed Rigdon?"

I would've liked to have turned and looked him straight in the eye, but I didn't dare give Louise that kind of an advantage. "Vergil," I said, "I didn't kill anybody."

Louise apparently had a sharply differing viewpoint. "YOU DID TOO! YOU KILLED RIGDON, AND YOU KNOW IT!" she screamed, grabbing for my throat again with renewed energy.

My hands tightened on her wrists.

Vergil sighed. It was one of those long-winded, extremely put-upon sighs that Vergil is pretty much famous for. Vergil's sigh could easily make you think that he'd rescued me from stranglers six or seven times already today. And now, wouldn't you know it, he was having to rescue me *again*.

Nodding toward the Guntermans, Vergil said, his voice infinitely weary, "Okay, boys."

He apparently couldn't have said anything to the twins that they would've liked to hear more. Their beefy faces looked as if they'd just been plugged in. With identical gleeful grins, the Guntermans moved toward Louise and me like twin tanks.

The twins' progress, however, was slowed somewhat by all the other folks who'd suddenly decided to move our way too. Louise's screams had apparently grabbed the attention of every single person in Rigdon's front yard. All these folks were now trying to get closer to us, each vying with the other for a better view. Even the Bewleys and the Straits, who'd been standing some distance away, seemingly lost in their own grief, were now elbowing their way toward the front of the crowd.

Louise and I were rapidly turning out to be the afternoon's Main Event.

We were even getting cheered. Sort of. Curtis Strait, his eyes red and teary, was now yelling as he headed toward us, "Get him, Louise! Get him!" Curtis managed to yell all this without dislodging the toothpick in the corner of his mouth. I might've been impressed except I really couldn't get past what Curtis was yelling. "After what Haskell done, he deserves it!"

I believe I could assume from this that Curtis, like Louise evidently, had also heard about the earlier scene at Frank's. I believe I could also assume that I probably shouldn't be putting Curtis down as a character reference anytime soon.

At Curtis's side, his wife, Bertie Lee, was shaking her fist in my direction, punctuating Curtis's cheers.

In back of Curtis, Agnes Bewley was also cheering. Only her cheer was a tad different from Curtis's. Hurrying toward us with her husband Ernal at her side, Agnes was waving her pillow arms in the air in an apparent attempt to distract Louise. "Louise, honey," Agnes shouted, "now you stop that right now! You know you don't want to kill nobody!"

Louise obviously disagreed. To prove the point, she made an even wilder grab for my throat. "MURDERER!" she was still yelling. "MURDERER!"

I can't say it was one of my better moments. Out in the crowd I could hear folks begin muttering to each other. I couldn't quite make out what they were saying, being as how I could only hear bits and pieces between Louise's yells. The words "murder," "Rigdon," and "Haskell" did seem to be cropping up pretty often, though.

Before the crowd in Rigdon's yard turned itself into a mob, I decided I'd better start trying to outshout my accuser. "LOUISE," I yelled. "LISTEN! RIGDON DIDN'T KILL HIMSELF! SOMEBODY MURDERED HIM!"

Even as I was shouting at Louise, I realized that I was suddenly sounding an awful lot more convinced than even *I* had thought I was. It was as if the more Louise accused me of causing Rigdon's suicide, the more determined I got that Rigdon had not taken his life at all.

Strange how that worked.

My shouts sure seemed to take the wind out of Louise's sails. Her hands suddenly went limp, dropping to her side, and she just stood there in front of me, eyes getting real round.

The Guntermans had reached us by then. Seeing Louise drop her hands and more or less call off her attack made the two of them stop dead in their tracks. It also made them look as if somebody had just broken their favorite toy.

"Wh-a-a-at?" Louise said, running her hand distractedly through her still-damp hair. "Rigdon was *murdered?*"

You might've thought, having spent the last few moments calling *me* a murderer, that the concept of Rigdon having been killed by somebody would not be one that was entirely foreign to Louise. Apparently, however, it was. Louise's face had gone chalky white.

It wasn't only Louise who looked stunned either. Several heads out in the crowd surrounding us had also sort of jerked to attention. The Bewleys' and the Straits', among others.

In fact, as best as I could tell, the only person near us who didn't look stunned was Vergil. What Vergil looked was annoyed. I reckon I'd just stepped on his toes again. Evidently, announcing in front of a crowd of witnesses what my personal conclusions were regarding one of *his* cases was downright uppity of me.

To tell you the truth, I was beginning not to care all that much about Vergil's confounded toes. If not stepping on them meant I had to stand idly by and let myself get accused of being the cause of Rigdon's suicide, then Vergil had better get ready to have both his feet trampled.

I fully intended to go ahead right then and explain to Louise—and anybody else who was listening—all the reasons that made me think Rigdon had not killed himself. As I was actually opening my mouth to do it, however, something occurred to me. All the things about Rigdon's death that bothered me—Rigdon hanging himself with his toothpick still in his mouth, the way his feet weren't touching the floor like most folks who hang themselves, and how Rigdon could've easily have cut his wrists instead of using a rope—all these things were things you might discuss with Vergil, but they sure weren't the most tactful subjects to go over with Rigdon's next of kin.

In front of the neighbors.

It didn't exactly make sense to try to convince all these folks that I had not been an insensitive jerk earlier today by being an insensitive jerk right this minute.

So all I ended up saying was, "Yes, Louise, Rigdon was murdered. I think so. I really do."

Which, even I will admit, could've rung with a tad more conviction.

It didn't help any, as I made this unbelievably persuasive statement, that Rigdon's front door was opening. I reckon everybody in Rigdon's yard turned to watch Horace Merryman make his way down the steps.

Horace, at first, didn't even seem to notice that anybody was looking at him other than Vergil. Fidgeting with that pencil-thin mustache of his, Horace walked straight over to the sheriff. "Did you get somebody to identify the handwriting on the suicide note?" he asked.

Vergil gave him a quick nod, his eyes still on me. Still real irritated. Which wasn't exactly a surprise.

Horace cleared his throat. "Well, then, that's that. It's a suicide, all right. No doubt about it."

Louise took in a breath that sounded a lot like the intake of a jet engine. Her voice, however, was real calm as she turned toward Horace. "Mr. Merryman, did you say my brother committed suicide?"

Horace turned and apparently noticed for the first time that Rigdon's front yard was pretty much filled with people. He all but gulped before he answered Louise. "Yes, ma'am," Horace said, fidgeting with his lapels now. He turned to look straight at me. "It was an *obvious* suicide. Plain as day. Open and shut."

I returned Horace's look. Was I imagining it, or was

Horace overdoing a little how obvious everything seemed to him?

I believe I could assume from this that Horace didn't cotton to my horning in on *his* investigations any more than Vergil did.

Speaking of Vergil, he was no longer looking irritated. What he was looking was victorious. "Then, Horace, what you're saying," Vergil said, his voice now unnaturally loud, "was that this was NOT a murder—in your EXPERT opinion."

I blinked at that one. Vergil was making Horace sound as if his one and only profession was that of Chief Medical Examiner for all of Kentucky. Come on now. The man was an *undertaker,* for God's sake. Horace just did a little coroner work on the side. More or less in between funerals. I don't think that exactly qualified old Horace as an expert.

I'd swear, though, that the second Vergil finished speaking, Horace's thin chest puffed itself out a little. "Yes sir," Horace said, fidgeting with his cuffs. "In my *expert opinion"*—here Horace seemed to linger almost lovingly over the words—"it's a suicide. DEFINITELY."

There was a moment of total silence, and then Louise reacted. "Murderer! You lousy murderer!" she suddenly screamed at me.

Horace and Vergil both jumped, and their mouths simultaneously dropped open. I think for a split second there Horace might've even thought Louise was talking to *him.*

Right away, though, Louise, no doubt, took a load off Horace's mind by turning and throwing herself bodily in *my* direction, going for my throat all over again.

My reflexes might've been a little rusty after all. This time Louise managed to gouge my neck some before I could grab her wrists.

Once Louise had made it clear exactly who it was she wanted to kill, a look of relief flooded Horace's face. For about a half second. Then he started fidgeting something awful again. "Uh, ma'am?" he called to Louise, fooling with his cuffs *and* his tie *and* the buttons on his coat. That hushed monotone didn't carry too well over Louise's shouts, but eventually Louise did glance Horace's way. "Uh, you must've misunderstood me. Haskell didn't murder your brother," Horace said. He was holding up one finger real timidlike, as if pointing out a mistake to a superior. "Your brother committed *suicide.*"

I grimaced. Thanks so much, Horace. The next time you want to help me out, why don't you just pour a little kerosene over a match I'm holding?

Louise's response to Horace's latest bulletin was to try to kick me with her red flip-flops.

I had to try to keep Louise's hands off my throat and dodge her kicks all at the same time.

I was also a tad concerned about something else. Floyd, Louise's husband, was just standing there, watching Louise and me start our dance again, but his tattoos looked as if they might be getting real mad.

It was also getting real hot out there. Perspiration was running down Louise's face, mingling with her tears, and my shirt was clinging to my back and underneath my arms. In a few minutes Louise and I were going to be, to use the words of Jimmy Connors in that deodorant commercial, "not easy to be around."

I myself would've preferred to just let go of Louise's wrists and walk away from the whole scene—it *was* kind of embarrassing to be fighting with a woman, particularly in front of so many witnesses—but I was pretty sure Louise wasn't going to let me get away that easy.

I didn't particularly want to let Louise strangle me,

and yet, I didn't really want to hurt her either. It seemed like bad form to rough up the recently bereaved.

Moreover, it seemed like particularly bad form to rough up the recently bereaved in front of a crowd.

This was assuming, of course, that it really was possible to rough Louise up. The rumors back in high school about Louise being awful strong had apparently not been rumors. It was all I could do to hold onto her wrists while I tried to calm her down. "Louise," I yelled, "LISTEN! Listen to me!"

"I'm through listening." Louise answered. "You killed him. You're a damn murderer! A cold-blooded *killer!* A no-good CRIMINAL—"

Okay. Okay. I was getting her drift. I interrupted. "Louise, LISTEN—"

Louise doing any listening, however, was obviously out of the question.

Nearby the Guntermans were exchanging a delighted look. Evidently, it had taken them this long to realize that Vergil's last order was still standing. Looking pleased as punch that Louise was once again attacking me, Jeb and Fred eagerly resumed lumbering toward us.

Unlike yours truly, the Guntermans apparently had no reservations whatsoever about roughing up the bereaved. I was still holding Louise by the wrists when Jeb and Fred got to us, but they plucked her right out of my grasp without even hesitating, swung her around, and then held her in place by her upper arms. One twin to an arm.

Having the Guntermans touch her did nothing for Louise's mood. "Let me go, you DAMN goons!" she yelled.

"Goons," I have found, is a word the twins really don't like to hear. Both their faces darkened.

Vergil must've noticed the thunderclouds gathering because he quickly stepped in. "That'll do, boys," he said. It was obvious to me that the sheriff meant for Jeb and Fred to release Louise, but neither twin seemed to get the message. If anything, they tightened their grip.

Vergil sighed, and raised his voice. "Jeb? Fred? LET HER GO."

That certainly didn't seem to leave anything to interpretation.

The faces of both twins fell. "But, uh, Sheriff, she's dangerous," Jeb said.

Fred nodded. "Uh, she might *kill* Haskell," he put in.

Vergil glared at them, and the Guntermans finally released their quarry.

A casual onlooker might've actually gotten the idea that the twins really liked me, but I knew better. Jeb and Fred don't like me so much as they like manhandling folks. They're pretty much equal-opportunity manhandlers too, not really drawing much distinction between men and women.

Louise, oddly enough, didn't seem to appreciate the twins' truly liberal attitudes. As soon as they let her go, she muttered, "Damn assholes."

Fortunately, with her muttering and all, the twins didn't quite catch what Louise said. "Whud she say?" Fred was asking Jeb as Louise moved to stand behind her husband.

Floyd didn't look at all delighted to be the only thing between Louise and the Guntermans while she was calling the twins names. Floyd's eyes went about three sizes bigger and his face lost some of its color.

I just looked at him. Was it possible old Floyd's tattoos were false advertising?

"Whud she say?" Fred was now asking Vergil.

Vergil wisely decided not to answer. Instead he moved closer to Louise. "I'm real sorry about Rigdon, I really am," he said, staring at Louise over Floyd's shoulder. For once Vergil's infinitely mournful voice was perfectly appropriate. "But ma'am, you need to understand, *nobody* murdered him. He really did commit suicide."

Even though Louise seemed a tad preoccupied with rubbing her arms where the Guntermans had been holding her, her answer was real quick. "You're the one that doesn't understand, Sheriff. Haskell is the 'what happened' in Rigdon's note."

Vergil blinked once, and then slowly turned to give me a long look.

I did a quick shrug, trying my best to look completely innocent. I've always been real bad, though, when folks suspected me of something. Even back when I was a kid, I always managed to look guilty whether I was or not. Right now, in the looking-innocent department, Charles Manson probably could've outdone me.

"What do you mean, Haskell is the 'what happened' mentioned in the note?" Vergil asked.

"I mean," Louise said, her tone irritated, "you gotta arrest him, Sheriff. If you won't let me kill him, you gotta arrest him right now!"

Vergil asked what I thought was an astute question. "What exactly would I be arresting him for?"

Louise lifted her chin, glaring at me. "Why, isn't there a law against driving somebody to suicide?" Louise's voice sounded loud enough to be heard in Indiana. "Haskell killed my brother just as if he'd put a gun to Rigdon's head!"

I sort of wished she'd stop saying that.

"Haskell humiliated Rigdon something awful!" Louise went on. "He called Rigdon a lunatic in front of the whole town!"

I couldn't let this pass. "I did NOT call Rigdon a lunatic!"

Louise's eyes looked as if you could light a cigarette off them. "Didn't you say he was crazy?"

She had me there. "Well, yeah, I did say that." The

moment I answered, I could hear mutterings again out in the crowd. They didn't sound friendly. I hurried to add, "But I didn't say it in front of the *entire town—*"

Louise rolled her eyes. "Didn't you say it in front of *every single person at Frank's Bar and Grill?*"

She had me again. "Well, yeah, I did do that—" The mutterings gained a little strength. They sounded even less friendly. "—but I had no idea that my voice was going to carry all over—"

Louise was no longer interested in hearing what I had to say. I decided this when she said, "Haskell, I don't want to hear your excuses—" That sort of tipped me off.

Louise had stepped out from behind Floyd and was now waving her arms and looking around at the folks standing near us, as if making a summation to the jury.

"—because there *aren't* any excuses. You ridiculed a poor, mentally unbalanced man in public." Wheeling around and pointing her finger with a flourish in my direction, she said, "Haskell Blevins, YOU KILLED MY BROTHER!"

I swallowed. The woman should've gone to law school.

A quick glance of my own around Rigdon's front yard told me that, if the folks presently milling around there could be taken as a random sampling, a significant portion of the town was ready to pronounce me guilty as charged.

In fact, I could see quite a few heads actually *nodding* in agreement.

One of these heads belonged to Curtis Strait. Once he started nodding, Bertie Lee, who was standing right next to her husband, started nodding too.

My stomach was no longer just wrenching. It felt as if I'd just tossed down a few burning rocks.

Vergil was now directing a mournful look my way. "Well, Haskell," he drawled, "I can see now why you might be leaning toward thinking Rigdon was murdered."

That made me mad. "Vergil," I blurted, "I would be convinced that Rigdon hadn't hung himself even if I hadn't caused him to do it!"

I probably should've given that last statement a little more thought. As soon as the words were out of my mouth, I could've cheerfully torn out my tongue.

Vergil's look was now not only mournful, but pitying.

Louise, though, flew into a frenzy. "See, see?" she screamed. "He's admitted he caused Rigdon to do it!" She turned to her husband. "Get him, Floyd! Get him! He killed Rigdon, and now you've got to make him pay!"

There didn't seem anything else to do but turn and face Floyd. He was quite a bit shorter than me, but he looked as if he'd recently spent a lot more time in a gym. Maybe, oh, say, bench-pressing three or four men my size. That was, no doubt, how Floyd's upper arms had gotten to be so close to the size of my own thighs.

I took a deep breath.

By this time, of course, I'd already pretty much decided I was not having a good day. Matter of fact, I was fairly certain that the only person I knew who was having a worse day than me was inside hanging from a rope.

Now, as I looked at the snake on Floyd's chest—a creature that now appeared to be glaring ominously at me through Floyd's chest hairs—another thought occurred to me.

My day wasn't over yet.

The way things were going, there was a good chance I could still beat Rigdon out.

CHAPTER
8

I braced myself, fully expecting Floyd to make some kind of real quick move in my direction. A karate chop maybe. A judo kick. Or perhaps just a good old American knee to my groin.

Floyd, however, didn't move a muscle. Which, for him, was saying a *lot*. Instead, he said, his voice dangerously close to a whine, "Now, Louise, honey—" He ran his hand through his shoulder-length hair. "—you cain't go around trying to kill people."

I blinked. Well, what do you know, Floyd's tattoos really were false advertising.

Maybe that snake wasn't glaring at me ominously through Floyd's chest hairs. Maybe it was *hiding* behind them.

For a second there I thought Louise might prove Floyd's statement wrong by trying to kill *him*. I think Vergil thought so too, because he took a quick step toward Louise and said real fast, "You know, Louise, just

120

calling somebody a name doesn't usually make that somebody take his own life."

I stared at Vergil. Lord, it actually sounded as if he was coming to my defense.

In front of all these people.

I was starting to feel downright touched, and then I realized that this was just Vergil's way of pumping Louise for more information.

And distracting her from strangling her own husband.

"Oh yeah?" Louise said. "Well, you didn't see how upset Rigdon was right after he got home from Frank's." She swiped at her eyes with the palm of her hands "I was out in my yard when Rigdon drove up in his pickup, and he told me what happened." According to Louise, Rigdon had told her *exactly* what I'd said in front of everybody at Frank's, and then he'd added, "I'm so embarrassed I could just die."

My stomach wrenched again when I heard that.

What Louise had just said still didn't make me believe that Rigdon had killed himself because of me, but it made me feel damn guilty all the same. I may not have driven poor Rigdon to suicide, but I certainly hadn't made the last few minutes of his life any too pleasant either.

I swallowed past the lump in my throat. Exactly how does a person go about apologizing to a dead man? Tell me that.

I think Louise knew that what she'd just said had really gotten to me too, because she repeated it. Slower. And louder. *"'I'm so embarrassed I could just die.'* THAT'S what Rigdon said." She turned and looked at the crowd standing around us, as if to make sure nobody had missed what she'd just said. Then she drew a ragged breath. "I tried to talk to him some more, but Rigdon wouldn't let me. He said he wanted to be alone, and then he just went straight into his house and shut the door."

I remembered that when I'd arrived, I found Rigdon's front door standing ajar. "Did Rigdon lock the door when he shut it?"

Louise looked at me as if I were talking nonsense. "How the HELL do I know? What I'm saying here is that Rigdon was UPSET! Now *you* might not care anything about that, but Sheriff, you do, don't you?" Louise's eyes were filling up again. "Sheriff, you got to show me you care about what Haskell did to Rigdon by putting Haskell's butt in jail! I mean, can't you arrest Haskell as an accessory to suicide? Like that there Kevorkian guy? Haskell killed Rigdon just the same as if he'd put a gun to his head!"

Have I mentioned that I wished she'd stop saying that?

"It's pretty obvious that if it weren't for Haskell, Rigdon would still be alive!" Louise said, and then suddenly it was as if the awful news hit her all over again. She stood stock-still for a moment, her eyes filling, and then she began to sob. Loud racking cries that were almost painful to hear.

By now Agnes had moved so that she was standing right next to Louise.

When Louise began sobbing anew, Floyd made a motion as if to take his wife into his arms again, but evidently, his reluctance to kill me earlier had not endeared him to her.

Louise broke off mid-sob to give Floyd a look that could've been classified a lethal weapon.

"Now, hon—" This time there was no doubt. Floyd was definitely whining.

Louise turned her back to him, and Agnes wrapped up Louise in her big pillow arms, just as if Louise were still a little girl.

Agnes was now wagging her gray Gibson-girl head, and blinking real bad. So far, from what I could tell, Agnes had not yet shed a single tear, but it seemed to be costing her a monumental effort to maintain her composure. She was actually trembling some as she patted Louise's back and said, "There, there, sweetie, there, there."

Ernal had followed Agnes over to Louise, and now, his own eyes moist, he was awkwardly patting Louise's shoulder. Looking more like Lincoln-in-a-plaid-shirt than ever, Ernal stood there, solemnly repeating, "There, there, Louise, there, there."

This is what everybody seems to say in situations like this. I've never figured out what it means. It must've helped some, though, because Louise's sobs died down a little.

That must've been all Ernal was hoping to achieve, because he stopped with his patting. Agnes, however, kept right on. "Come on now, Louise," Agnes said, "after all, it's not as if we weren't expecting something like this to happen."

That one got my attention.

It also got Vergil's. Before I could speak, he'd jumped in with, "What? You were *expecting* it?"

Agnes wagged her gray head at him, still sheltering Louise in her arms. "Sheriff, our entire family was afraid one day Rigdon would take his life. Just exactly like—"

"Agnes!" Ernal's deep-set Lincoln eyes no longer looked moist. They looked as if they were shooting fire in Agnes's direction. "What have I told you about airing family laundry in public?"

I stared at Ernal. Evidently, he didn't know his wife very well. Around these parts, Agnes had a reputation not unlike my secretary, Melba. What this meant, in essence, was that Ernal didn't have to worry about Agnes just *airing* their family laundry. Agnes not only aired it—she folded it, pressed it, and wore it out, in every sense of the word.

In fact, there were those in Pigeon Fork who insisted that the reason Agnes Bewley's lips were so thin was that they got exercised so often.

Even now you could tell that Agnes clearly was not cowed a bit by Ernal. She shrugged her big shoulders as if she were shaking off a bothersome gnat. "Ernal," she said, giving him a level look, "I have kept my mouth shut all this time so's folks wouldn't know we had ourselves a suicide in the family, just like you told me—"

At this point, those mutterings out in the crowd started up all over again. With a vengeance. I knew, of course, what was being said. Folks weren't talking about there being a Bewley suicide in the past so much as they were marveling that Agnes Bewley had apparently known a scandalous secret for *years* that she'd actually kept to herself.

Up to that moment I'm pretty sure nobody in Pigeon Fork would've thought this possible.

Agnes was hurrying on, "—but glory be, Ernal, look around you. *Everybody knows* we got ourselves a suicide in the family now." Agnes blinked a couple more times and added, her voice cracking a little, "Ain't no use keeping quiet no more."

I thought her point was well taken.

Ernal must've thought so too. Or else he wasn't about to argue about it with Agnes in front of all their neighbors. He took a ragged breath, and then just stood there with his eyes staring straight ahead, his shoulders slightly stooped, and his bony hands clasped in front of him as if he were silently praying for strength.

I stared at Ernal some more. I'd bet Lincoln himself looked exactly like that when they told him about Fort Sumter.

It was just as well Ernal had decided not to make a fuss. Short of gagging her, Agnes probably couldn't have been stopped at this point. She'd even quit patting Louise and pulled away so that she could devote all her attention to telling what she had to tell. Turning toward Vergil, Agnes said, "As I was saying, we was all afraid one day Rigdon would take his life *just like his own mother.*"

Agnes put a little extra emphasis on those last five words, and was immediately rewarded by another wave of mutterings from the crowd.

Agnes was also rewarded by Vergil's eyes widening. "Rigdon's *mother* committed suicide too?" Vergil still sounded mournful as usual, but his grief now appeared to be mixed with a heavy dose of curiosity.

Agnes nodded. "Nobody knew," she said. "It was hushed up right away. Back then it wasn't all built up out here the way it is now, so it was pretty easy to just tell folks in town that Margaret got herself a bad case of pneumonia real suddenlike. That wasn't what really happened, though." Agnes took a deep breath here and leaned toward Vergil, saying in a whisper loud enough to be heard across the street, "That poor woman hung herself from a tree! In the front yard of this very house!"

At this point Vergil, Horace, I, and a significant number of the folks standing near us all turned and looked toward Rigdon's front yard. It was real clear that there was not a single tree out there. In fact, there was only the stone deer with Rigdon's sign around its neck.

Agnes looked toward the front yard too, and shrugged again. "Well, *of course,* that tree got cut down right after."

Of course. If you left something like that standing in the yard, it could prove to be too much of a temptation.

Agnes apparently agreed with that line of thinking. "We sure didn't want nothing to happen to—to anybody else!"

I decided I probably shouldn't point out that even if

you did cut down a tree in the front yard, there was still a whole forest of them to contend with right behind the house. I also decided not to mention that Rigdon's own untimely end had not required the use of so much as a shrub.

"Fact is," Agnes was now saying, "we've all been afraid ever since Margaret died that suicide might run in the family!"

I just looked at her. Agnes made the tendency to kill yourself sound like the same thing as color blindness. Or being left-handed. I was pretty sure it didn't work that way.

Louise, however, evidently believed it did. After Agnes had pulled away from her, she'd been just standing there, wiping at her eyes with both hands and nodding as Agnes talked. Now Louise jumped in with, "There's statistics, you know." She pronounced the word as if it were spelled *stay-tis-ticks.* "I looked it up once, and it's a proven fact that folks who have parents that killed themselves are a lot more likely to do it too!" Louise punctuated this last by wiping her hands down the front of her flowered T-shirt.

Vergil was either getting real antsy being around somebody who continued to be as upset as Louise or else he didn't want to be that close to somebody who used her T-shirt as a handkerchief. He now took a couple of steps away from Louise.

Agnes jumped in again. "So naturally, after what their mama done and all, we was all real worried about the kids." You could tell that the story Agnes was now relating was making her feel sad and all, and yet, at the same time, she'd waited an awful long time to tell it. What's more, she was actually getting to tell it to a whole lot of folks. All of whom seemed to be hanging on her every word.

Sadness and excitement seemed to be warring in Agnes's eyes.

I may have been wrong, but it looked to me as if excitement was winning.

Agnes was now talking real slow, almost as if she were savoring the words. "We was worried particular about Rigdon, being as how he was at a real impressionable age when all this happened. He was only eleven." She sighed, a real long, drawn-out thing. She was almost as good at it as Vergil. "Lordy, Lordy, I reckon that had to be nigh on to twenty-two years ago."

Vergil cleared his throat. "Did anybody ever find out why Rigdon's mom did such a thing?"

Agnes gave Ernal a quick look before she answered.

Ernal did not look back. Mainly because he'd closed his eyes, as if by shutting out the sight of Agnes telling all the family secrets, he could shut out the sound.

Agnes must've taken this as blanket permission to tell the rest of it. Her voice was almost eager as she hurried on. "Oh, we all knowed the reason right away. Poor Margaret hung herself right after her husband, George—that's Ernal's brother—up and ran off."

"Ran off?" Vergil asked.

Both Agnes and Louise nodded their heads in unison.

"Nobody in the family ever saw him again," Louise put in. "I myself don't hardly even remember my daddy. Of course, I was only eight at the time, so I—"

Apparently, Agnes wasn't about to let Louise tell a story she'd been waiting this long to tell. She stepped closer to Vergil and, interrupting Louise, said in another loud whisper, "There'd been rumors, though. Lots of rumors. George, you see, apparently had himself a lady friend. All the way up in *Elizabethtown.*"

Elizabethtown is only about sixty miles up the interstate from Pigeon Fork. Agnes made it sound as if it were someplace just outside of Chicago.

"We all knew he'd run off with her. It just broke Margaret's heart all to pieces." Agnes's eyes were actually sparkling, but she shook her head real pitiful-like. "You know, before this happened, I'd have sworn George was plumb crazy about his family, and that he'd never do such a thing." Agnes was still shaking her head. "But it just goes to show you. When a trashy woman gets her hooks into a man, why, he can turn into a—a—" For a second I thought Agnes might actually curse, but she must've gotten control of herself. "—a *no-account* over night!"

"No-account" was evidently the worst word Agnes could think of.

Agnes was now staring out into the crowd as she made this little pronouncement. She seemed to be looking straight at Curtis, but it was hard to tell, being as how there were so many folks in her line of vision.

Curtis must've thought Agnes was staring at him, though, because he started nodding, as if he were hearing the gospel being preached.

Agnes was still preaching. "That's right," she said, giving one of her Army boots a little stomp for emphasis. "Some floozy without so much as a shred of decency got ahold of George and turned him into an idjit!"

It took me a second to realize that what Agnes meant by "idjit" was "idiot." I could see quite a few folks in the crowd were a tad confused too. They were leaning toward each other and whispering, "Idjit? *What's an idjit?*"

I took a quick glance at Ernal. This was, after all, his own brother that Agnes was bad-mouthing. In front of an awful lot of people.

Ernal seemed to be taking it surprisingly well. His eyes were still shut, of course, but just glancing at him, you might've thought he'd fallen asleep standing up.

On the other hand, maybe he hadn't figured out what

an idjit was either. It could be Ernal didn't realize Agnes was bad-mouthing his brother.

"If you'd seen Margaret, you'd have thought George was an idjit too," Agnes was now saying. "She was a real pretty thing. *Real* pretty. Fact is, Margaret was a fine wife, even if she was high-strung."

I didn't even blink, but to tell you the truth, that particular phrase is probably the last thing I'd use to describe a woman who'd hung herself.

I believe Vergil agreed with me. He was staring at Agnes without blinking, just like me, but the sheriff's mouth was doing this little twitching thing.

"Margaret got even more high-strung after George left," Agnes went on.

The sheriff's mouth twitched a little bit more.

"It was like she was cracking up inside, you know?" Agnes tried to sigh again, but on some level, she must've been enjoying herself too much. It sounded more like a hiccup. "Yep, Margaret's heart just broke all to pieces. And she was a real pretty thing too. But high-strung."

Agnes had evidently run out of story. She'd started repeating herself. Her voice sort of trailed off as she wagged her Gibson-girl head from side to side. "It was sad," she said. "Real sad." Agnes sounded sad too.

Of course, I couldn't be sure if Agnes was feeling sad because of what had happened so long ago, or because she'd come to the end of her story.

Louise took up the slack. "Rigdon never got over Mama's suicide. He just adored Mama, he did," Louise said. "I, of course, don't hardly remember her any more than I remember my daddy, but Rigdon, well, he was always talking about her. Rigdon was really very fragile—a real sensitive type."

Okay, I admit it, I may be a little on the cynical side, but I found this a tad hard to believe. I could not possibly feel any worse about what had happened to him, but let us not forget, Rigdon had been a man who'd made his living skinning dead animals and stretching that skin on wire frames. I wasn't sure, but to my way of thinking, that didn't exactly sound like the overly sensitive type to me.

"Rigdon was an artist, you know," Louise was now saying. As if to back up her statement, she took in Rigdon's sign in the front yard with a sweep of her hand.

As if by signal, once again Horace, Vergil, and I—and quite a few of the other folks standing around—all looked toward Rigdon's sign.

Vergil cleared his throat. "That Rigdon was, uh, a real artist, all right," he drawled. From the expression on Vergil's face, you could tell that he was already feeling bad about what he was about to do, but he'd seen an opening and he wasn't about to pass it up. "Why, I do believe those are the best dang drawings of, uh, a rabbit, and a deer, and, a, uh, fish, I think I've ever seen."

Horace's eyes darted to Vergil's face. Clearly, he'd figured out where Vergil was heading with this. Horace jumped in too, his whispered monotone sounding, for once, perfectly appropriate. He actually sounded a little awed. "It sure is," Horace said. "Why, those drawings take real talent."

Louise nodded, her eyes glistening again with tears.

Vergil cleared his throat again. "You know, uh, Louise, it's that, uh, *last* drawing that's the best."

Horace thoughtfully helped Vergil out by pointing directly at the furry thumb.

Louise wiped her eyes with her hands again, wiped her hands once more on her T-shirt, and nodded sadly. "Would you believe it? That's what everybody says."

Matter of fact, I did find that hard to believe, but I didn't say a word. I was pretty sure one word from me would shut Louise's mouth for good. No doubt, if that happened, I'd not only have Louise going for my throat, I'd have to contend with Vergil and Horace too.

Agnes was also looking at the sign now and nodding her head. "That there's the drawing that's the most original," she said.

"Yep, you don't see many of them drawn that way," Ernal actually put in. He sounded downright relieved to have folks talking about something other than his family's scandals. His eyes were even open. "That one took real talent."

Vergil and Horace both looked at each other and nodded. "Now, that's the truth," Vergil said.

"What's so amazing is that when Rigdon first started drawing it, I had no idea what it was going to be," Louise said, shaking her head. "Can you believe that?"

I certainly believed it, and I had no doubt whatsoever that both Vergil and Horace believed it too.

"It's real original, all right," Horace said. Apparently, the possibility of finding out what that furry thumb could be was getting to be too much for Horace. He was fidgeting something awful now, pulling at both cuffs, twisting his mustache, and fiddling with his collar.

Ernal was still nodding. "Oh, yeah, it's the best dang drawing I've ever seen of—" Here Horace and Vergil clearly leaned a little forward. "—one of them, that's for sure," Ernal finished.

Horace and Vergil's faces both fell.

They fell even more when Louise started sobbing again. "I only wish Rigdon could be alive to hear what you all just said!" Gulping back sobs, she turned to glare at me. "Of course, he would be alive if it weren't for *you!*"

I reckon I'd been feeling a lot like Ernal. Relieved that the subject of the discussion had moved in another direction. Now, having it return so suddenly made my stomach wrench even worse than before.

It didn't help that every single person in Rigdon's yard seemed to be looking in my direction. I hoped I was wrong, but it also seemed as if every one of these folks looked accusing. Agnes and Ernal, Curtis and Bertie Lee, and Louise and Floyd. Not to mention all the folks I didn't even know.

Even Vergil and Horace seemed to be glaring at me.

Of course, they were probably blaming me more for Louise's switching the topic of conversation off of Rigdon's sign as anything else.

In fact, the only two people that didn't seem to be looking at me accusingly were the Guntermans, but I don't think they even counted. They were both, at that moment, picking their respective noses, and that activity seemed to be taking every bit of their concentration.

Standing there, glancing around, I reckon I felt just about as popular as Dr. Frankenstein right after his monster got loose in the village. "Look," I said, as much to the crowd as to Louise, "I did NOT drive Rigdon to commit suicide. NOBODY drove him to commit suicide! Because he did NOT commit suicide!" I was now, I believe, pretty much babbling. "Somebody murdered him!"

Once again I hoped I was wrong, but none of those accusing eyes seemed to be looking any less accusing. If I needed proof of that, I got it when Curtis Strait shouldered his way to the front of the crowd. "Hell," he said, "you're just saying Rigdon was murdered to soothe your own conscience, that's all."

Curtis may have been talking solo, but he was being backed up by a chorus line. When Curtis said this, Bertie Lee and five or six others nodded in back of him.

Curtis took his toothpick out of his mouth and pointed it at me. It was a gesture so like Rigdon himself that for a split second I could hardly breathe. *"You know* what you did, Haskell. The whole town knows what you did."

I didn't have a toothpick to point at him, so I just pointed my finger. "I don't care what you say, Curtis," I said, "I think Rigdon was murdered, and I'm going to look into this until I get some answers." I was trying to sound real determined and all, but to tell you the truth, I believe my not having a toothpick to point hurt my credibility some.

Floyd, Louise's husband, now evidently decided to make up for his reluctance to kill me earlier. He moved to stand shoulder to shoulder with Curtis. Giving his blue jeans a hitch, Floyd said, "Well, nobody ain't paying you a red cent."

I guess he told me.

After that, the discussion seemed pretty much closed. Where I was concerned anyway. Folks standing out in Rigdon's yard appeared suddenly to have a lot to say to each other, but pretty much nobody seemed to have anything to say to me.

I would've liked to have just left at this point, but I couldn't. Being as how Vergil announced right then and there that he wanted to take statements from everybody. And nobody should even *think* about going anywhere.

I just looked at him. And actually had several very long thoughts about going somewhere.

A lot of good it did me.

Vergil went inside Rigdon's house, got himself a kitchen chair, sat it out on Rigdon's stoop, and had folks come up one by one to talk to him. It was sort of like watching folks go up to tell Santa what they wanted for Christmas.

Only Santa's identical elves were, of course, a little bigger than the ones you were accustomed to. And they were still picking their noses.

It seemed to take forever for Vergil to get around to talking to me. Matter of fact, I believe he talked to just about every single person in Rigdon's yard before he called my name.

No doubt old Vergil was punishing me for acting uppity.

It was a real punishment too. Still feeling a whole lot like Dr. Frankenstein, I now couldn't help but remember that scene in the movie when the villagers gather sticks and light them on fire and then rush up the hill to more or less show Frankenstein just how much they think of his handiwork.

By the time Vergil finally called my name, I was beginning to wonder if the folks standing around weren't about to go out and start collecting sticks. By then it seemed like everybody there had looked my way several times, and whatever they were muttering to each other didn't sound at all complimentary.

I was feeling every bit as fidgety as Horace.

In fact, the only person who gave me any sympathy at all was one of the ones I would've expected it from the least. When Vergil started taking a statement from Ernal, and I was standing pretty much by my lonesome off to one side, Agnes suddenly appeared at my side. "Haskell," she whispered. This time Agnes's whisper was real. *I* could barely hear her. "Don't blame yourself," she said. "It wasn't all your fault. Rigdon's not been himself ever since, well, ever since . . ."

I turned to look at Agnes. "Ever since what?"

All Agnes would do, though, was fold her huge forearms across her pillow chest and shrug.

"Ever since what?" I repeated.

Ernal must not have had all that much to say to Vergil. He was already coming down the steps. I could see his head turning as he scanned the crowd for his wife. It didn't take him any time at all to find her either. Of course, there weren't all that many giant gray-haired Gibson girls wearing army boots standing in Rigdon's yard.

You could tell when Ernal spotted Agnes, because he immediately stepped off the stoop and began heading our way. "All I'll say is that Rigdon had a *lot* to be depressed about lately," Agnes whispered. "That's all I'll say."

With that, she moved away from me and hurried toward Ernal.

I didn't even have time to think about what Agnes had told me, because right then Vergil sent one of his twin elves to get me.

After I'd told Vergil everything I could remember—which wasn't much—I decided to give it one last try. "Vergil," I said, "don't you think it's odd that a man who'd wanted to hire me this morning to protect him from homicidal woodland creatures would turn around and take his own life?"

Vergil clearly missed my point. "I thought you said Rigdon was *not* a client of yours?"

"Well, yes, I did." I stared right back at him, the way you used to back in high school when somebody challenged your word. "Technically speaking, Rigdon wasn't a client of mine. On account of my deciding not to take his case."

Vergil held up his hand. "Wait a minute, *you* turned down a job?" He made it sound as if Ed McMahon had tried to contact me and I'd refused all his calls. "Why on earth would *you* turn down a job?"

I sort of hated the way Vergil kept emphasizing the word "you." As if he could understand why anybody else in America might turn down work, but not me. Oh no. Everybody knew *I* was desperate.

Now I was not only somebody who drove the mentally ill to kill themselves, I was also an indigent.

I lifted my chin. "Well, Vergil, now that you ask, I turned down Rigdon's job because Rigdon seemed to be—well, he was—uh, that is, he seemed—"

I was trying to think of a polite way to describe Rigdon's mental state, but apparently Vergil didn't want to wait. He thoughtfully helped me out. "Is 'nuttier than a fruitcake' the words you were looking for?"

I stared at Vergil. Unyielding. "Okay, so Rigdon might've been a tad unbalanced, still, he——"

Vergil sighed. Have I mentioned how good he is at sighing? Fact is, if there's ever an Olympic event in Sighing, Uphill or Downhill, Vergil's got himself a real shot at the gold. "And, in your opinion," he said, "folks who are 'a tad unbalanced' don't commit suicide?"

I can't say I liked the way this conversation was going. "Well, now, maybe sometimes they do, but——"

Vergil didn't let me finish. "You know, Haskell, Rigdon came to me first with that crazy tale about the animals in the woods having some kind of a vendetta against him. Anybody who listened to it *had* to know Rigdon wasn't right in the head." Vergil was lecturing me. He does this a lot. One of these days I fully expect him to try to teach me to tie my shoelaces. "Haskell, you should never have said what you did right in front of him." Vergil scratched at his bald spot before he went on, his tone even more mournful than usual. "I hate to say this, but it probably was the straw that broke the camel's back."

I don't think he hated to say it.

I took a deep breath. "Vergil," I said, "I've got good reason to believe that Rigdon did not kill himself. In fact, I've got quite a few of them." I laid it all out for him then. Every single thing I hadn't wanted to discuss in front of Rigdon's family and neighbors. I told Vergil about the toothpick, about Rigdon's easy access to knives, and finally about how most suicides who hang themselves do it with their feet touching the floor.

Vergil did hear me out, I'll give him that. He sat there

in that kitchen chair, staring up at me, and when I was done, he leaned back, tilting back his chair precariously, and stared at me some more.

"Well, Haskell," he finally said, "I reckon Rigdon had never committed suicide before, and he just didn't know how to do it right."

I believe you could say that I had not exactly won Vergil over.

Vergil did mention that Horace still had to do the autopsy as required by law. Before I could get my hopes up, however, the sheriff added, "But I don't think Horace is going to find anything that isn't consistent with suicide, do you?"

I just looked at him. For once we agreed on something. "Nope," I admitted.

Horace was not going to find a thing, all right. Mainly, I'd say, because old Horace wasn't going to be looking terribly hard after he'd already announced his findings to everybody standing in Rigdon's yard *before* he'd done the autopsy.

After I finished talking with Vergil, I would've headed straight home to, no doubt, lick my wounds, except that I thought I probably ought to check in with Melba before I called it a day. When I got to Higgins's Stop 'n' Shop up the road, I did as Higgins's sign out front said. I stopped. I also parked, got out of my truck, and headed inside.

I may have been wrong, but it seemed to me that the entire store went quiet the second I walked in. I hoped, of course, that I was just being paranoid, being as how I had just spent quite some time having accusing looks directed my way.

Still, there was no getting around it. The place did seem awful silent as I headed directly toward the pay phone on the back wall, dialed up my office, and waited for Melba to answer.

As soon as I heard her on the end of the line, I wished I hadn't even bothered to phone.

Melba had let it ring five times, and then when she finally did pick up, she said, "Is this another call about that nut who killed hisself on account of what Haskell said to him?"

My breath caught in my throat.

CHAPTER
9

For a brief moment I actually considered driving straight to my office and demonstrating for Melba exactly how Louise had gone for my throat.

"Melba, what in the world do you think you're doing?"

There was a clicking sound over the phone. I thought for a split second that Melba had hung up on me, and then I realized she was chewing gum. "Why, I'm answering your phone, silly," she said, clicking her gum again. "I was, um, just trying to save time, that's all. By, um, you know, finding out right away what the call was about."

I took a deep, deep breath before I could trust myself to speak. "Melba? Don't try to save time, okay? In fact, DON'T EVER ANSWER MY PHONE THIS WAY AGAIN."

"Well, my goodness," she said, smacking her gum for emphasis, "aren't you the touchy one! I mean, just because the whole town thinks you made that guy kill hisself, that's no reason to jump down *my* throat."

Melba's tone, believe it or not, sounded injured. "I'll have you know that because of what *you* did to that poor man, I've had a god-awful day. Why, this phone's been ringing off the hook with folks wanting to know all about it. Lord knows, I've tried to explain, but—"

Melba's words actually caused a chill to go down my back. Oh my God. If *Melba* was fielding questions, I could forget about the villagers and the burning sticks. I was probably due to be tarred and feathered within the hour.

"—believe you me," Melba was saying, "it's been a real pain in the—"

I interrupted. "Melba, from now on, if anybody calls with questions, just refer them to me. Okay?"

"Well, sure, Haskell," Melba said, "but you ought to know, a lot of folks don't want to talk to you direct. They're kind of upset. On account of you driving that poor guy to—"

"Melba, I didn't drive anybody to do anything—"

"Uh-huh," Melba said. "Of course, folks who are guilty always say that."

It was right then I decided I'd better end this conversation before Melba drove *me* to suicide. "Melba," I said, interrupting again, "do I have any messages?"

Melba punctuated her answer with yet another gum smack. "Nope. Not a one. Unless, of course, you count the death threats."

"Death threats?" I asked. "Did you say I've gotten death *threats?* With an *s?* As in, more than one?"

"Oh, my goodness, yes," Melba answered cheerily. "There certainly have been more than one." She made it sound as if it were something I should be proud of.

At this point, I do believe any other secretary in America would've gone right ahead and filled me in on all the details. Without being prompted. Not Melba, though. Oh no. All I heard on the other end of the phone line was more gum smacking.

It's taken me almost the entire year since I've been back, but I think I've finally figured Melba out. Melba, I've decided, lives in abject fear that one day she might actually do more than her job strictly requires.

She needn't worry. Believe me.

I mentally counted to ten before I spoke. "Melba, do you suppose you could tell me exactly how many death threats I've gotten? And who called?" I tried to sound real casual, like maybe I was just asking the question out of curiosity, nothing more. But to tell you the truth, Melba's answer *was* kind of important to me.

"Well now, let me see," Melba said. "I did write them down and put them on my desk somewhere, but now— my goodness, where on earth did I put them, where could I have—"

Melba went on like this for the next several minutes, giving her gum an extra loud smack about every thirty seconds or so.

While I waited, leaning against the back wall of the Stop 'n' Shop, holding that receiver to my ear, I passed the time by thinking up a few death threats of my own.

It's times like these that Melba should thank her lucky stars she's got job security. It's heavy-duty job security, as a matter of fact, in the form of five kids, ranging in age from four to fourteen.

Of course, I can see how Melba might not readily see her good fortune, being as how she's a widow lady and all. And being as how there's been some speculation around town that her kids are not kids at all, but five manifestations of the anti-Christ. Still, Melba ought to give every one of her children a big kiss every day.

They certainly were doing their part to keep their mom employed.

It seemed like an hour had passed before Melba smacked her gum one final time and said, "HA!"

"Ha?"

"There they are, I knew I'd find them, I wrote those messages down and put them under this here bag of potato chips so's they wouldn't get lost, but wouldn't you know it—"

I actually had to interrupt her again. "Melba, how many threats were there?"

Melba was already counting. "One, two, three. That's all there was. Just three."

Just three? Maybe I was being a little oversensitive, but in a town of only 1,511, three death threats sounded like a lot.

One, in fact, would've been plenty.

"You don't have anything to worry about, though, Haskell," Melba added. "I don't think any of them threateners were really serious. None of them left their names."

I blinked at that one. Did Melba actually think that folks who intended to kill you generally identified themselves over the phone? I decided to let that one pass, though. Getting into an extended conversation with Melba is something I generally try to avoid.

"Melba, did you recognize any of the voices?" As unofficial head of Gossip Central in Crayton County, Melba has probably talked to every single person within a five-mile radius of Pigeon Fork. Hell, she'd probably talked to every one of them since *breakfast.* If anybody could recognize a voice around these parts, it had to be Melba.

"Nope," she said. Her voice was still, it seemed to me, inordinately cheery. "I didn't recognize a one. They were all men, though. Or else they were women disguising their voices to sound like men."

I didn't say anything, but I was not thinking kind

thoughts. In fact, what I was thinking was: Okay, let me get this straight. The callers were positively either men or women. Thanks so much, Melba. That certainly narrows it down.

She was still talking. "Anyways, I wrote down what every one of them said."

"You did?" I tried not to sound as surprised as I felt. But, my God, for Melba this practically amounted to service above and beyond the call of duty. The woman deserved a medal.

"The first one went like this," she said. "'You're a dead man, Haskell Blevins, and then, something something, something, I'm gonna kill you.' And then he hung up."

Something, something, *something?* Melba could forget the medal. I don't know, maybe I was being a real slave driver here, but it seemed to me that what Melba had left out might possibly have been a significant part of the message.

"Melba, for crying out loud—" I began, but she interrupted *me* this time.

"Now, Haskell, don't start. You know very well my shorthand's a little rusty, and that guy was yelling a mile a minute. I did the best I could do."

Melba must've heard me starting to hyperventilate, because she didn't give me a chance to say a word. "I got *all* of the second threat, though. *Every single word.*" She now sounded as if she expected praise. "The second guy said, 'Tell him, you ain't got long to live, asshole.'" Melba read the words just as if she were reciting a memorized verse in elementary school, and then she paused. "Even though this one didn't actually call you by name, I was pretty sure he meant you, don't you think?"

I decided that was one of those rhetorical-type questions I didn't really have to answer. "What about the third one?"

She cleared her throat. "Oh yeah. This one said, 'Tell

Haskell he don't deserve to live, so I'm going to kill him for what he did to Rigdon.' That's pretty much it. Maybe not word for word, but it's the gist."

Melba was giving me the *gist* of death threats?

On second thought, being the sole support of five kids might not be enough to keep me from killing her.

Of course, knowing the exact messages probably wouldn't help all that much. Lord knows, the one message I did know word for word wasn't exactly an eye-opener. In fact, all it did was narrow down the field to just those folks in the immediate area who had bad grammar. Which, as best as I could tell, probably encompassed most of Crayton County. Myself included, I'm ashamed to admit.

"Is there anything else in particular about the callers that you remember?"

Melba smacked her gum once again before she answered. "Yeah, there was one thing," she said. "They all sounded real mad."

Folks are calling up, threatening to kill me, and it struck her that they sounded *mad?*

I decided getting off the phone now would be a good idea. Not just because Melba was driving me crazy, but also because while I'd been talking to her, I'd come to the conclusion that I hadn't been paranoid earlier after all. The store really had gone quiet the second I walked in.

And stayed quiet.

Higgins's Stop 'n' Shop is not real big, so it's pretty easy to tell if the folks in it are talking or not. It's only about the size that a convenience store would be back in Louisville. In fact, from the outside, looking at the white aluminum siding and the flat, narrow, red roof, you might think you could actually be in Louisville, pulling up in front of a 7-Eleven.

Except, of course, for some of the signs on Higgins's windows.

One of these signs says, OFFICIAL DEER CHECK STATION. Another, OFFICIAL TURKEY CHECK STATION. I don't recall ever seeing either one of these signs in any store in Louisville.

Oddly enough.

Not being a hunter myself, I'm not quite sure what these signs mean. I've never asked anybody either, on account of there not being a doubt in my mind that just *hinting* that I didn't already know would probably cause whoever I asked to have a stroke.

From laughing so hard.

Both the deer sign and the turkey sign have the words "Kentucky Department of Fish and Wildlife" printed in real small type at the bottom, so I figure the signs must mean that Higgins's is the place where you check in what you've bagged, like a suitcase. Or where they count how many you've gunned down so far. So that, eventually, the folks at Higgins's can tell you whether or not you get to keep whatever you dragged in.

Either that, or else those signs mean that Old Man Higgins takes personal checks from both deer *and* turkeys.

There's one other sign in Higgins's that you also probably won't find in Louisville. The one that says "Live Bait" taped on the front of one of the refrigerators in the back. Right next to the one with the ice cream bars and frozen sandwiches.

Which sort of made looking for a treat real exciting.

Other than these notable exceptions, Higgins's is just your basic convenience store, I reckon, with four aisles lined with shelves that only go up to about shoulder height. So that when you're standing in the back where I was, you can still see everybody else in the store.

That's how come, when I turned to face the front as I hung up the phone, I could see Old Man Higgins himself standing behind the front counter next to the register, near the double door entrance.

I could also see the old woman in the flowered house-dress and straw bonnet standing right in front of Higgins, apparently waiting to have her fresh vegetables rung up.

I could also see the young couple standing right in back of the old woman, holding a couple of videos they obviously intended to rent. And the guy in his twenties in back of the couple, holding a six-pack of beer.

Not to mention, the old guy sitting at the only table in the store, next to one of the windows, leafing through the Louisville *Courier-Journal*.

And the young girl over in the candy aisle.

From where I was standing in the back, I could see every one of these folks. I could also see that every one of them, at that moment, was looking holes through me.

Oh yeah. I hadn't been paranoid earlier.

I can't say it was a relief to find that out.

I swallowed uneasily. A year ago this being stared at wouldn't have been all that big a thing. Right after I first got back into town, after being gone some eight years, I pretty much got used to getting the once-over every time I went anyplace.

To tell you the truth, I expected it. I knew very well that folks in Pigeon Fork, just like folks in every other small town in America, can't seem to resist staring at new faces.

I've tried to tell visitors from out-of-town that nobody really means any harm by staring. Folks, for the most part, are just trying to decide if they know you, or if they know any of your relatives, or if any of your relatives know any of their relatives. *Or* if you really are an honest-to-God stranger. That's pretty much all there is to this staring business.

And it's not as if it doesn't happen anywhere else in these United States. Back when I was in Louisville, I noticed that folks there stare at strangers every bit as much. The only difference is, Louisvillians peer at you from behind a newspaper, or a magazine, or they stare at your reflection in a store mirror.

In Pigeon Fork, folks are just a lot more open. If they want to look at you, they don't try to cover it up. They just outright gawk.

I had always thought this was kind of refreshing.

Up until now. Having been back in town for as long as I have, my being stared at has become pretty much a thing of the past. Here lately, whenever I walked in someplace, I'd been lucky if I rated a glance.

I believe, then, that I could now assume that none of these folks in Higgins's Stop 'n' Shop were staring at me because they didn't know me. In fact, they seemed to be looking at me because they knew *exactly* who I was. They knew, and they weren't happy about it.

Lord. The grapevine in Pigeon Fork must be even more efficient than I'd thought. Everybody had not only heard what had happened to poor Rigdon. They'd also obviously heard what had happened shortly before at Frank's.

It kind of made you wonder if everybody standing in line up front wasn't there to pick up some tar to melt and a few chickens to pluck.

My stomach started to hurt all over again.

I myself would've liked to have picked up a large bottle of industrial-strength Maalox before I left, but I suddenly didn't much feel like hanging around the Stop 'n' Shop any longer than absolutely necessary.

I was almost running by the time I cleared the front doors. That's how downright anxious I'd gotten to get myself home to what might easily be the only creature left in Pigeon Fork who still regarded me in a favorable light.

My dog, Rip.

Rip and I live about seven miles outside of Pigeon Fork in a small cedar A-frame smack dab in the middle of five acres of wooded hills. Which means that in order to get home, I have to travel up an unbelievably steep gravel driveway for about a quarter of a mile.

During winter months, and particularly after a good snow, I've actually complained about my hill. Tonight, though, I was feeling downright pleased that my house wasn't the sort of place you could get to real easy. Tonight I needed to get someplace where there would be no accusing eyes, and that long, steep driveway of mine pretty much guaranteed it. There wouldn't be any Avon ladies or Jehovah's Witnesses dropping by—or, say, anyone convinced that I'd recently caused somebody's death.

As soon as I started up my driveway, I could hear Rip at the top of the hill, barking his head off. Since Rip doesn't get to bark at very many trespassers, apparently he decided a long time ago that he'd put in his barking time whenever I showed up.

Usually I find this real irritating. I know very well this isn't normal canine behavior. I'd had two other dogs before Rip, and neither one of them ever barked at me. Of course, both my other two dogs died before they were even a year old. I never did figure out what the problem was. I got them both all their shots, took them both regularly to the vet, and still they up and died on me.

Fact is, that's why I named Rip what I did. I'd gotten so used to my dogs dying on me that right after I got this new puppy, I decided I might as well go ahead and write R.I.P. on his doghouse.

Rip, however, is six and a half now. I think he's going to live. If, of course, I don't kill him for barking at me all the time. Like I said, usually it's a real irritating thing to have your own dog acting as if he thinks you're Jesse James.

Tonight, however, just to show you what an emotional basket case the day's events had made me, I actually found Rip's barking sort of endearing.

Half German shepherd, half big black mutt, Rip kept right on with his endearing barks and growls even after I'd pulled up in front of our A-frame, hit the garage door opener, and drove my truck into the garage.

By then there was no way Rip couldn't have recognized me. In fact, he had to have recognized not only me, but also my truck. And yet, endearing old Rip kept right on. He'd calm down a bit, like maybe he'd finally made up his mind that he really did know me, but then he'd be at it all over again. Barking louder than ever. Snarling and growling and carrying on. As if maybe after a couple seconds he'd started questioning his own judgment.

I reckon, after living together for so long, Rip and I are like old married folks. We've settled into a routine. Every night, right after I get home, we pretty much do and say the same old things. Tonight was no different.

By the time I'd walked out of the garage, heading toward the steps leading to my deck, Rip's barking had gotten to be quite a bit less endearing. So I found myself saying, sure enough, exactly what I always say as soon as I get home. "Rip! Hey! RIP! Shut UP, for God's sake! It's ME! I *live* here!"

Rip followed the same old routine too.

He barked even louder.

Sometimes I think that dog is snickering in the back of his throat even as he's barking his head off.

It was only when I started walking up the steps to my front door that Rip finally quit carrying on. Standing there at the top of the steps, acting as if it had suddenly just hit him that I probably really had been speaking the truth—yes, by God, this did look *exactly* like the guy he'd been living with ever since he was eight weeks old—Rip started wagging his tail so hard, it almost knocked him off his feet a couple times.

Since he'd finally shut up, I had to praise him, of course. "Good boy, Rip," I said. Just like always. "Good boy."

This is something Rip apparently can't hear enough. Rip now started alternating wild tail wags with delirious leaps of joy in the air. This is also something he does every single night, and it's a feat which, I believe, should earn Rip extra points for degree of difficulty.

Rip's tail-wagging/joy-leaping routine probably would've been a lot more impressive if I hadn't known that part of the reason for his sheer ecstasy at seeing me was a real practical one.

As I neared the top step, Rip scooted as close as he dared to the edge of the steps.

Our A-frame is surrounded by a large deck, so you have to climb quite a few steps to get to my front door. That is, to be specific, *I* have to climb them. Rip, believe you me, has never made the trip. He's never gone up the stairs, and he's never gone down the stairs. He's been afraid to ever since he was a puppy. I've actually tried coaxing that fool dog downstairs with a thick, juicy porterhouse, and Rip still stubbornly refuses to budge.

I, of course, knew all this about Rip before I moved him and me out here to the woods. I reckon, though, I didn't quite think it through. All I saw was the privacy and the trees and the wonderful view off the deck. Something else should've crossed my mind.

Now, as I got to the top step, Rip calmed down. And waited.

For me, yes, to pick him up and carry him down all those steps to my yard. Since Rip doesn't get much exercise these days, being as how he spends the majority of his life snoozing, he's really been packing it on lately. That dog's got to weigh at least sixty pounds.

Picking him up is like lifting a sack of potatoes. A squirming sack of potatoes. A squirming sack of potatoes that's trying to lick your face.

Usually, having to haul Rip's butt out to the yard while he's slobbering all over me is even more irritating than having him bark at me. Tonight, though, as further proof of my basket case condition, I didn't even mind this. In fact, I actually thought it was kind of nice to have something warm acting so affectionate with me.

Obviously, I was rattled beyond belief.

Of course, carrying Rip down the steps is a real improvement over what I'd been doing a few weeks ago. Back then Rip was still recovering from, believe it or not, a bullet wound that he got in the line of duty. I felt real bad about it too, being as how Rip pretty much got shot on account of my stirring up a hornet's nest during the last case I worked on. I almost felt like it was poetic justice for a while there that I not only had to carry him up and downstairs, I also had to carry him out to the deck.

It wasn't so much that Rip was physically unable to go out on the deck on his own, mind you. Oh no, he pretty much recovered physically in record time. It was his mental recovery that took some time.

For a while there he'd added going out on the deck to his list of "Things I Couldn't Possibly Do." The times I carried him out there, Rip would howl piteously in my arms.

The deck, you see, was where Rip had been shot. It's taken him all this time to make up his mind that the shooter is not still out in the woods somewhere, waiting. In fact, it's only been this week that Rip has actually ventured out on the deck alone. He whimpers, of course, glancing around real nervouslike, but he does go out there.

Once Rip did his business, I picked him up and carried

him back up the stairs. Usually this is the part of Rip's and my daily routine when I begin to breathe heavily and to grunt with every step I take. It's also usually when I start to tell Rip for about the millionth time that he is going to *have* to learn to go up steps, that was all there was to it. I usually also follow this up with idle threats. Like, "Rip, if you don't learn to go up and down steps soon, you're going to be sorry. I mean it."

As you can imagine, this sort of thing generally strikes real terror into Rip.

Particularly after he's actually had somebody shoot him.

These days I can pick up a rolled-up newspaper, and Rip will just look at me real blank. As if to say, "You think *that* can scare me? Is this a joke?"

Tonight, however, this was where our usual routine varied. I hauled Rip up all those steps, breathing hard and grunting as usual, of course, but without making a single threat. When I reached the deck, I put him down and actually patted his head. Every bit as affectionately, I think, as he'd licked me earlier. "Rip, old fella," I said, "I have had one unbelievably rotten day. But tonight you and I are going to have us a nice steak dinner. Alone."

Of course, the only thing Rip understood of all that was the word "Rip." Still, I think he must've noticed the change in my usual demeanor. He was now eyeing me real suspicious as he followed me inside. Like maybe he thought I was pulling some kind of fast one.

Rip particularly looked at me funny when I gave him a dog biscuit as soon as we walked into the kitchen. In fact, that dumb dog was so suspicious he didn't even eat the biscuit right away. He put it down on the linoleum and sniffed it a few times before he wolfed it down.

And I'd thought *I* was getting paranoid.

As it turned out, what I'd told Rip about us having

dinner alone was a tad optimistic. Not ten minutes after those words were out of my mouth, he started barking again.

Rip and I were still in my kitchen at the time. I was standing by my sink, going through my mail, which, as usual, consisted mainly of bills, and Rip was lying in the doorway, head on his paws.

Apparently, Rip had decided that he was going to follow his usual routine no matter what I did. He always stretches out in the doorway of the kitchen. He has the entire room to choose from, but he always manages to select the one spot where I'll be most likely to trip over him when I go out.

That dog is always trying to be real helpful this way.

When Rip started barking, I knew right away he wasn't fooling around. He knows he's not allowed to bark in the house, so usually, if a deer bounds out of the woods, or a bird lands outside on the deck, Rip generally confines himself to mumble-barking.

Which is barking that sounds as if Rip has oatmeal in his mouth.

Tonight's barking, however, was clearly not mumble-barking. His first full-throated bark actually made me jump.

Rip, of course, was jumping too. He leaped to his feet and ran out of the kitchen, through the dining room, and into the living room toward one of the large picture windows facing the driveway. On the way, he pretty much threw himself into his barking routine, body and soul.

When Rip acts like this, I know somebody really is coming. I was particularly convinced when he actually growled a couple of times. Growling is something Rip reserves for really special occasions. Like when the UPS guy shows up with a delivery. Or when one of my neighbors' dogs takes his life into his paws and actually wanders up our hill.

Evidently, growling and barking was not making the statement Rip was aiming for. Now, to demonstrate just how disappointed he was that somebody was interrupting our solitary evening, he tried to claw his way through the picture window.

Rip, you can tell, loves doing this kind of thing. Slobbering and growling and barking his head off, he is pretty impressive. In fact, I believe if they ever do a remake of that Cujo movie, Rip has a real good chance at the lead.

"Okay, boy," I said, "okay." I'd followed Rip into the living room and was looking out the picture window, trying to figure out what in hell was making him do his Cujo impression. It was already pretty dark outside, but I spotted what it was, all right. Two headlights were making their way up my hill.

I stared at those lights for a long moment. Just to make sure, of course, that they really were headlights. And not the flickering lights of torches. Being carried by irate villagers.

Nope, those lights were definitely not flickering.

Thank God, I might add.

I watched the headlights for a moment longer, and then realized that whoever was coming my way had obviously never visited me before. Because Headlights didn't seem to realize just how steep my hill is. You won't make it to the top unless you have your car in low gear.

And sometimes, even then, you won't make it.

As I stood there and watched, and as Rip barked and growled and clawed at the window, Headlights traveled about a quarter of the way up my hill, going fairly fast. Then the lights began to slow down, and down, and down, until finally they came to a complete halt about halfway up.

Even with the door shut and my central air going, I could hear car wheels spinning.

Lord. I hadn't heard wheels spin that fast since the Indianapolis 500.

Have I mentioned that there are some pretty deep ravines on either side of my driveway? They're deep enough so that from the edge of my driveway, you can look down at the tops of trees. Whoever Headlights was, he'd better hope he didn't suddenly regain traction. As fast as his wheels were turning, if they ever caught hold, he was going to be starring in his own episode of *Lost in Space* in about a half second.

I needn't have worried. Headlights only spun his wheels for the next minute or so.

Then he just sat there, in the middle of my driveway, for maybe another minute.

After which the lights slowly began to back down. Very slowly.

I can't say I envied whoever it was. My driveway is one of those twisting, turning things that winds its way through dense trees. In the daylight it makes for a real scenic drive on the way up. In the dark, however, on the way down—particularly if you happen to be going down backward—it makes for a major pain in the neck.

Since I myself have a four-wheel-drive truck, I've only had the pleasure—or lack of it—of backing down my hill just once. It was during the day right after an ice storm had turned my hill into a ski slope. I didn't even get up my driveway as far as Headlights. Not to mention I must've sweated buckets by the time I made it all the way back down to the bottom.

After that one memorable experience, I learned my lesson. Now, if it looks at all as if I might have trouble making it all the way to the top, I don't even try.

I particularly don't try it in the dark.

I've had friends, however, who have. Notice I said, I've

had friends. Past tense. Oddly enough, those particular friends have never been back. One of them didn't even try to come up my hill a second time. He tried once, failed, backed down in the dark, and then turned around and left.

Forever.

I halfway expected Headlights to do the same now. But no, once whoever it was had finally made it back down to the beginning of my driveway, he sat down there for a minute or so, no doubt gathering courage, and then came roaring up my hill about five times as fast as he was moving before.

Lord.

You'd have thought bears were chasing him. *Rabid* bears.

By this time, of course, I was real curious who it could be that was this determined to see me. The car that finally crested my hill turned out to be a silver-gray Camry.

A car nobody I know drives.

I was by then, of course, curious as hell. Rip must've been curious too, because although I meant to shut him inside, he managed to snake through the door before I could get it latched. Rip was still, of course, barking and growling and carrying on.

I was kind of glad he was still doing his Cujo routine. Just in case the Camry was holding a lot of villagers.

The Camry braked in front of my garage. I moved down my deck toward the steps, trying to get a better look.

I could see now, with some relief, that there was only one person in the car.

I leaned forward off my deck, peering into the dark.

That's when I saw the door on the driver's side open and a shapely leg appear.

I blinked. If this turned out to be an Avon lady, I was probably going to have to let her sell me some makeup.

Just on account of her going to so much trouble to get up my hill.

Getting out of the Camry, however, was no Avon lady. In fact, as that old joke goes, it was no lady, period.

It was my ex-wife.

CHAPTER
10

Claudine was wearing a dress that made the nickname "Headlights" seem real appropriate. With long, see-through sleeves, it was a body-hugging, black and white polka-dot thing that had a square neckline even more low-cut than that of the red dress she'd been wearing at Frank's.

Which I wouldn't have thought possible.

This dress might've also been tighter than the red one. As best as I could tell as dark as it was, quite a few of Claudzilla's polka dots were no longer round, but stretched into long, thin ovals. These misshapen polka dots, oddly enough, seemed to be clustered across Claudzilla's chest.

To put it mildly, Claudzilla certainly had a brand new look these days. Well, no, not exactly a *new* look. Matter of fact, this was precisely how Claudzilla had looked when I'd first met her. She'd been working as a salesgirl in one of the men's stores in the Galleria in downtown

Louisville, and I have to admit, she sure caught your eye the second you walked in.

Now that I thought about it, this particular look was new only in comparison to the one Claudzilla had been wearing during the last few months of our marriage. As I recall, back then Claudzilla had almost always worn a shapeless navy-blue sweat suit. Covering her from head to toe. She also wore furry blue house shoes, not a bit of makeup, and as likely as not when I got home, she'd have just finished smearing something on her face that was the consistency of transmission fluid.

Now, watching Claudzilla wiggle her way toward me on black and white polka-dot shoes with spiked heels at least five inches tall, I reckon if I hadn't known Claudine so well, I might've enjoyed the view. She was bouncing quite smart as she made her way across my gravel driveway.

Knowing Claudzilla, however, as well as I did, I wasn't enjoying anything. I was too busy bracing myself.

Claudzilla, you see, has never been one to go through something unpleasant without immediately assigning blame. She usually does this blame-assigning in a voice that could solder steel.

Moreover, Claudzilla has never, in my experience, ever assigned blame to herself. She has, however, made a career of blaming me.

When she overcharged our MasterCard, she blamed me. For not having a higher credit limit.

When she bounced a check, she blamed me. For not making more money.

When she rear-ended somebody at a stop sign, she blamed me. I hadn't even been in the *car*. She'd actually told me later, "I was thinking about you, Haskell, and how mad you always make me, and it made me lose concentration." She'd asked the cop who wrote up the accident to put that down on the accident report as the cause.

Lord. They'd kidded me about that one for months down at the station.

And now, tonight, even though it was obvious that Claudzilla had started up my hill in the wrong gear, there wasn't a doubt in my mind that she was about to once again lay the blame at my feet.

Claudzilla was now climbing the steps of my deck.

Rip, of course, was still barking. It had been over a year since he'd seen Claudzilla, so maybe after all this time he really didn't remember her. To hear him carrying on, though, you would've thought he'd gotten her mixed up with Ma Barker.

Of course, I reckon that could be a real easy mistake to make.

"Haskell!" Claudzilla said. Now halfway up the stairs, she lifted her hand in a wave. "HI!"

With Rip barking and carrying on, I wasn't sure if I'd heard Claudzilla right, but she might've actually sounded *pleasant*.

"Claudine," I said, trying not to sound as uneasy as I felt.

She had reached the top of my deck and was now tottering toward me on those polka-dot heels. Her progress was hampered some by the way her spike heels kept getting themselves stuck between the boards of my redwood deck, but even though she had to keep stopping to unstick one shoe or the other, she didn't stop talking. "Well, Haskell, I heard what happened, and I knew you'd be upset. So I just thought I'd better come right out here and make sure you're okay."

At this point I tried real hard not to stare at Claudzilla, but I couldn't help it. Let me see now. Her eyes were round as saucers, her face was chalky white, and her hands were shaking. Obviously she'd just gone through a harrowing experience getting up my hill.

And yet, she actually sounded *in a good mood*.

This was such an unexpected turn of events that I almost stammered when I said, "Well, uh—well, my goodness, it's right nice of you to come out here like this, Claudine."

She waved her hand in the air again. "I just wanted to make sure that you knew that I was on your side two hundred percent."

I blinked. There was every chance that Claudine really did think you could be something two hundred percent.

I was by then, of course, looking Claudine over real good. Maybe this wasn't my ex-wife at all. Maybe this was some nice stranger, and I had been married all that time to her evil twin sister.

Claudine was making it real easy for me to look her over. She'd moved so that she was within inches of me. "I, for one," she said, "don't believe for a minute that you drove that guy to suicide."

I sort of wished she hadn't said that "for one" part. It sounded as if there was not another soul in Pigeon Fork who believed I wasn't responsible. It also sounded as if the only person now on my side was Claudine herself.

If this were true, judging from past experience, I was in real trouble.

Claudzilla was now standing close enough for me to catch the scent of Joy. I'm not familiar with a lot of perfumes, but I sure know that one. The entire time we were married, Claudzilla wouldn't wear anything else. Would you believe, this stuff actually costs over a hundred dollars an ounce? Oh yeah, it was a Joy, all right. At least, it was a Joy for Claudzilla. To stick me with the cost.

"Haskell, you're okay, aren't you?" Claudzilla was

now leaning even closer, looking up at me up through her eyelashes as she spoke.

I blinked again. Claudzilla has told me about a million times that I don't know the first thing about women, but if I didn't know better, I could almost get the idea that she was making a move on me.

As soon as the thought crossed my mind, though, I almost laughed. Let's face it—I did know better. This was, mind you, the very same woman who, the day she and I got our final divorce decree, had sashayed her way out of the courthouse and done a little jig on the courthouse steps.

As I recall, that little performance had turned the heads of several men strolling by.

I also couldn't help but remember what Claudzilla had said when the judge asked her on what grounds she was divorcing me. She'd looked him straight in the eye and said, without a second's hesitation, "Why, I hate his guts."

Oh, yeah, I'd say I knew better, all right. I'd say the chances of Claudine making a move on me were about as likely as aliens landing in my yard.

In fact, I believe aliens landing and *them* making a move on me was a *lot* more likely.

Claudzilla had now moved even closer and was saying, as she tapped me in the chest with a manicured finger, "I want you to know too, you big lug, that I went to a lot of trouble coming all the way out here."

Uh-oh. I braced myself again. She was going to start carrying on about my driveway, sure enough.

Claudzilla was still tapping me. "I had to ask for directions and everything, just so I could drive over here especially to tell you that I was standing by you."

I can't say I was all that impressed. While my house isn't exactly easy to find, she made it sound as if she'd made her way through the frontier or something. As I mentioned earlier, I do live in a fairly dense wooded area, but you don't exactly need Lewis and Clark to show you the way.

"But I *wanted* to do it," Claudine was now saying. "I wanted you to know that you could count on me in your time of need."

Okay, okay. By this time I was getting suspicious. I may be dumb when it comes to women, just like Claudzilla says, but I'd have to be a Gunterman twin not to be wondering exactly what was she was up to by then. I halfway expected Claudzilla to break into a stirring rendition of "Stand By Your Man" any second now.

Instead she started fawning over Rip.

Rip had been barking at Claudzilla off and on the entire time she was talking. A thing which, unbelievably, Claudzilla actually ignored. In the past, I've seen her take off one of her shoes and throw it at Rip for doing a lot less.

Every time Rip revved up his barking again, I'd taken a quick, uneasy look at Claudine's shoes. Those spiked things looked as if they could put an eye out.

Hell, they could possibly get him afraid to come out on the deck again.

Rip was still barking right smart, but Claudzilla actually smiled when she looked his way. "Oh, Rip, how are you, boy?" Glancing back over at me, she said, "Isn't he the cutest thing? I've sure missed him."

I couldn't help it. This time my mouth dropped open. Was she kidding? The last time she'd seen Rip, she'd called him "a mangy mutt."

Not to mention, while we were married, she'd actually called up the dog pound and had them pick Rip up. *Twice.*

I don't want to dwell on the negative or anything, but as I recall, it had cost me sixty-three dollars a throw to bail Rip out.

And now, suddenly, Rip was *cute?* A thing like this could make a person suspicious.

Apparently, it could even make a dog suspicious. When Claudine came toward Rip, hand extended, ready to pet him, he broke off in mid-bark.

And backed away.

Tail between his legs.

It looked as if he finally remembered where he'd seen her before.

"Rip, you sweet thing," Claudine was saying. "Come here, baby."

Oh yeah, Rip recognized her, all right. His ears went flat to his head, and he dropped to a crouch. Actually quivering a little, he began to back toward the house, his eyes never leaving Claudine for a second.

"Rip," she said. "Come here, boy, come on now, sweetheart."

Sweetheart?

That did it.

"All right, Claudine," I said. "What's up?"

Claudine gave up on petting Rip and actually looked taken aback. "Why, Haskell Blevins, I'm sure I don't know what you mean." She took a step toward me then, twisting a platinum curl around a fingertip. "Why, all I wanted to do was come out here and let you know I was on your side, and look—just look at the way you act."

What was it that Humphrey Bogart said about Lauren Bacall? She was good. She was very, very good.

But I didn't believe this performance for a second. I particularly didn't believe it when Claudine hurried on. "I also thought maybe I could make you dinner. Or—Or something."

Remembering Claudzilla's cooking skills, I believe I would opt for the "or something."

I didn't have a chance to opt for anything, though. Claudzilla stepped deftly around me and Rip, went right through my front door, and actually headed for my kitchen.

Rip and I both went through the door after her.

She slowed down about a half second right after she went through the front door.

That was when she got a load of my living room.

I braced myself again. When we were married, Claudzilla had always insisted that I keep things picked up. She also complained real loud if I took food into her pristine living room. Now I could see her eyes focus on the crumpled bag of Tostitos that I'd left on my couch from the night before. And the half-empty glass of Coke that had been sitting so long on my end table that it looked as if it had grown hair. And the tattered, multicolored afghan that Rip has chewed two corners off.

What can I say? I hadn't known I was expecting company.

Even Rip, I believe, expected Claudzilla to react the way she always did. He ran straight across the room and disappeared under one of my end tables. At least, most of him disappeared.

You could still see his tail sticking out.

Quivering.

Amazingly enough, Claudzilla only paused for a fraction of a second. Then, squaring her shoulders, she took a deep breath and sailed right through the living room. Not looking left nor right. As if maybe she couldn't stand seeing any more than she had already.

I stood there and stared after her.

My God. Either Claudine was not the person I'd thought she was, or else, when it came to major personality changes, she could give Sybil lessons.

Claudine had headed into my dining room without slowing down, and from there she moved straight into my kitchen.

By now I was slack-jawed. Not only had Claudzilla

passed up a terrific opportunity to point out what a complete pig I was, she'd also actually located the *kitchen.*

During the four years we were married, I'd never had any reason to believe Claudine even knew what a kitchen looked like. In fact, I'd finally come to the conclusion that Claudine thought a kitchen mainly consisted of a phone and a list of takeout and pizza delivery phone numbers.

From the sounds she was making in there, I could tell she was now pulling pots and pans out of my kitchen cupboards. Lord knows what she intended to do with those.

Frankly, I was a little afraid to find out. I turned to head toward the kitchen, fully intending to tell Claudine that her making dinner would not be necessary.

The second I moved, however, Rip started mumble-barking. He alternated his mumble-barks with whimpers.

I stopped and just stared at that dumb dog. Rip was under my end table, facing the wall, for God's sake. What could he be barking at under there? A trespassing fly?

Or was this Rip's way of cursing me out for bringing Claudzilla back into his life?

As it turned out, I was wrong on both counts. When Rip paused for breath, I heard the light tap on my screen door.

I hadn't heard anybody come up my driveway, what with Claudzilla banging around pots and pans. But apparently what Rip had been trying to tell me was that we had ourselves another visitor.

When I looked over and saw who it was, I considered running over and joining Rip under the end table.

And maybe doing a little whimpering myself.

It was Imogene.

Having tapped on my door, she was now opening it and walking on in. "Hi, Haskell," she said, smiling at me. Her smile, however, looked a little uncertain, and as she spoke, her eyes traveled around the room. Obviously, Imogene had seen the silver Camry parked out front and was wondering who it belonged to. "I was afraid you might be feeling kind of bad, Haskell, considering what happened and all, so I thought I'd come over and make you a nice, home-cooked meal." Imogene paused here and added, "Unless, of course, you're busy."

For a long moment I just stared at her. "Busy? Well, uh—"

That's about all I had time to say before Claudine appeared right in back of me. Carrying a pan in one hand and a ladle in the other. Claudine apparently had heard somebody come to the door, and had come out to see who it was. "Why, Emma Jane!" Claudine said. "I was just making Haskell some dinner. How nice to see you again!"

"Nice" was obviously not the word Imogene would've used. She took one look at Claudine and turned almost as white as my refrigerator.

"My name is NOT Emma Jane." That's all Imogene said, but her voice was shaking real bad when she said it.

Then Imogene turned on her heel and walked very fast back the way she'd come.

I, of course, followed her outside. Stammering like a total fool. "Imogene, come on now, listen to me—"

Imogene came to an abrupt halt just as she got to the top of the stairs leading off my deck. She turned to face me, her eyes unnaturally bright.

I swallowed. "I know this looks bad, but—"

"Bad?" Imogene said, shaking her head. "Oh, no, Haskell, this doesn't look *bad.*"

For a split second I actually felt relieved that Imogene

was being so understanding. Unfortunately, however, Imogene hurried on. "What this looks like to me is *familiar*."

My throat tightened.

I knew, of course, exactly what Imogene meant. She'd told me all about how her last boyfriend had run around on her. Apparently, her ex could've made Don Juan seem bashful.

"Imogene," I said, "you've got to believe me. Nothing is going on between Claudine and me. I'm telling you the truth."

Imogene gave me a tight-lipped smile. "You know," she said, "what you just said sounds familiar too." Her voice was getting real ragged.

It was almost a physical pain to see Imogene this upset. I took a step toward her. "Imogene," I said, "listen to me. Claudine just came by tonight because—"

Imogene took an even faster step away from me. "Haskell," she said, "I don't even want to hear it."

I probably should've taken her at her word, but I went right on. "Claudine heard about what happened with Rigdon, and she just came by to say she was on my side, that's all."

Oh yeah, I should've taken Imogene at her word, all right. She obviously knew what she was talking about. "*I said* I didn't want to hear it," Imogene said. Two bright spots of color had appeared on each cheek. "But I do have something more to say to you! If you still believe that your ex-wife is not making a play for you, you're a MORON!"

After which Imogene stomped down my steps, got in her car, and pretty much broke every speed record in the book going down my hill.

I stood, motionless, out there on my deck, watching Imogene go, and feeling pretty much like what she'd just called me.

A moron.

When I finally turned to go inside, I was surprised to find Claudine standing at my front door, looking my way.

"I guess Emma Jane won't be staying to dinner?" she asked.

I blinked. *"Nobody's* staying to dinner," I said.

It was Claudine's turn to blink this time. "Nobody? Are you telling me you want me to *go?"*

I took a deep breath. "Look, Claudine, I don't know what kind of games you're playing here, but you're really messing up my life. I've got a good relationship going, and I'm not about to stand by and let you—"

Claudine at this point pulled out her secret weapon. It's the weapon she always used on me during our marriage, and I don't think it ever failed her.

She burst into tears.

And flung herself into my arms.

There didn't seem anything else for me to do but pat her on the back until she got herself under control again.

And, while I was doing all this patting, thank the Good Lord that Imogene had already left.

When Claudine finally got down to just whimpers, she looked up at me through wet lashes. It was a look I couldn't help remembering that, at one time, had made my knees actually feel weak.

Now I just stared right back at her, my knees feeling sturdier than ever.

Claudine batted her damp lashes a couple times before she spoke. "Okay, Haskell, I—I guess I'll have to tell you the truth, I do have an ulterior motive for wanting to see you again. But Haskell, it—it's not a game!" She sobbed outright for a full minute, and then she looked back up at me. Again, through the damp lashes. "I'm scared, Haskell, I—I'm really scared!"

I just looked at her. Now this was a switch. In my

experience, Claudzilla had been the one that was scary. Not the other way around.

Claudine was now going through her pockets, finally coming up with a lace handkerchief. She's the only person I've ever met who still uses cloth handkerchiefs instead of a good old Kleenex. Now, of course, I realize that I should've known the second I saw that first hanky years ago that we were going to be incompatible.

Claudine dabbed her eyes a couple times, making heavy black smudges on the lace, before she hurried on. "I—I guess I was just real dumb," she said.

I didn't say a word. Even though the phrase *Tell me something I don't already know* immediately sprang to mind.

"I recently broke up with a guy, and, well, this guy wouldn't take no for an answer. He's started to scare me, Haskell," Claudine said. *"Really."*

If I'd just met Claudine, I probably would've taken her story at face value. Unfortunately, however, mine and Claudine's meeting had been a long, long time ago. "So," I said, "what's this guy's name?"

She wiped her eyes before she answered. The smudges were getting worse. "It's, um, Buck. Buck Harrison."

I just looked at her. Now *this* had the ring of truth. Matter of fact, I didn't find it at all hard to believe that a woman who loves money as much as Claudine would have been wildly attracted to somebody named Buck.

"Buck's been threatening me, Haskell," Claudine said. "That's why I'm here in Pigeon Fork. I—I'm hiding out. The police in Louisville can't help me because Buck hasn't actually done anything yet." She took a long, shaky breath. "Oh, Haskell, I want your help if Buck tracks me here."

What had Imogene called me? A moron? I knew, of course, that I was at that moment proving Imogene right, but what could I do? If Claudine really was in some kind of danger, and I didn't help, and then if something happened—well, I could end up feeling every bit as bad as I now felt about Rigdon. "All right, Claudine," I finally said, "I'll—"

That was all I got out. The rest was pretty much cut off by Claudine kissing me very hard right on the mouth, her arms tight around my neck.

For a moment there it was almost like old times. Claudine warm and yielding in my arms, and me actually beginning to return her kiss with enthusiasm.

Then, of course, I had a sudden burst of lucidity. My God. What in hell was I doing? It was Imogene I cared about these days. Not Claudine. Right?

Right?

I pulled away with a jerk and just stared at Claudine.

Claudine, I thought, was looking a tad pleased with herself. She gave me a little smile, and leaning close, whispered, "You know, Haskell, maybe I should stay the night." Twisting a platinum curl around a forefinger, she looked up at me through her lashes again. "For, um, protection purposes, of course. In case Buck shows up here in Pigeon Fork."

Okay. Okay. I may be every bit as dumb as the Gunterman twins, but I did have some brain waves left. "I think that would be a bad idea, Claudine," I said.

I reckon it was the first time I'd ever said no to Claudine. If, of course, you didn't count the times I'd had to tell her she couldn't charge any more on our credit cards. In those cases, though, it had not been me saying no, though, so much as the banks and the department stores.

Claudine actually looked at me as if I was speaking a foreign language. "What?"

"I don't think there's much likelihood that this guy has followed you all the way here to Pigeon Fork, do you?"

Claudine's neck turns red when she's mad. Right now

her neck looked like a salami. "Well, uh, yes, Haskell, as a matter of fact, I think he might've followed me all the way here," she said, her voice hurt. "I think he could very well be right here in—"

I interrupted. "Have you heard from him?"

"Well, no, but—"

"Have you seen him around town?"

"Well, um, no, but—"

"Then I think you'll be fine in town," I said.

Claudine obviously did not agree, but she did go ahead and get her purse.

The only real bad part was when she turned and looked at me right before she went out my front door. It sort of reminded me of the expression on Rigdon's face right after he heard me say what I'd said at Frank's.

Claudine didn't say anything, though. She just walked out, head high, bouncing as she went.

Oddly enough, I didn't sleep well that night. All night long I kept tossing and turning. Dreaming of Rigdon and Claudine.

Both of them looking at me as if I'd let them down.

It didn't help any to have Rip start barking real loud at about three in the morning.

It wasn't mumble-barking either. It was full-throated barking that woke me with a start.

Rip sleeps at the foot of my bed, but when I opened my eyes right after he barked, he was already gone. Running toward the living room.

I found him standing once again in front of one of the picture windows in my living room. Snarling and drooling and clawing all over again.

This time, though, there were no headlights coming up my hill. There was, in fact, nothing outside that I could see that would've warranted Rip's little performance.

I finally decided he must've been having nightmares too—Claudzilla had apparently rattled Rip as much as she'd rattled me—and I went back to bed.

The next morning I headed out bright and early, intending to investigate the Rigdon case in earnest. I was planning on talking with Rigdon's aunt Agnes first, to try to get her to tell me a little more about what she'd mentioned to me yesterday. I particularly wanted to hear all about Rigdon having a lot to be depressed about lately.

When I got into my truck, however, I noticed something strange.

There were tiny animal footprints all across my hood.

I got out and looked at the prints real close. These prints looked to me to be a lot like those I'd seen around Rigdon's cereal bowl.

Of course, not being an Indian scout or anything, I'd say one tiny footprint looks pretty much like another.

Not to mention, having footprints on my truck wasn't all that difficult to explain. Mind you, I *do* live in the woods. Occasionally, animals do wander into my garage. For a while, in fact, they'd been coming in on a regular basis, until I realized it was a big sack of Rip's dog food in there that was attracting them.

When I moved the dog food inside some months ago, that seemed to have cleared up the problem. And yet, maybe whatever animal had crawled across my hood had not yet gotten the news. Or maybe he was just checking to make sure I hadn't changed my mind and started storing Rip's dog food outside again.

The footprints, once I thought about it, weren't really strange at all.

What *was* strange was what I discovered as I was driving down my hill.

I no longer had brakes.

I found this out as I was going around the first turn.

And as I was sailing off my driveway into the ravine.

And as I was flipping over and landing in the creek.

CHAPTER
11

The creek was almost dried up, and I was wearing my seat belt.

Otherwise, I probably would've ended up in one of Horace Merryman's funeral parlors, no doubt right next door to Rigdon.

Instead, I ended up at Crayton County Memorial. Right next door, in a manner of speaking, to a deeply tanned, extremely wrinkled old geezer who had to be at least a hundred if he was a day.

Looking like an overgrown raisin in his white hospital gown, this old guy was the first thing I saw when I opened my eyes. Lying in the bed next to me—the one closest to the window—he was snoring loud enough to wake up everybody (and I do mean, every *body*) at Merryman's some twenty-five miles down the road. The window wasn't even open, and this old guy probably could've still waked them all up.

Lord knows, he'd waked me up, and I was still feeling real groggy from whatever the folks in the emergency room had pumped me full of. It must've taken me a full minute to get my eyes to focus on the old guy. Unfortunately, when I did finally have a clear look at him, I noticed that he had a tube running into his arm and a tube running out of someplace hidden by his sheets. I wasn't absolutely sure where this last someplace was, but I had my suspicions.

Particularly since a golden liquid appeared to be flowing through that tube and into a kind of plastic pouch hanging off the old guy's bed.

You know how I said at the beginning that we detectives suspect things, and then we check our suspicions out?

This right here was a notable exception.

You could pretty much count on my never checking this particular suspicion out.

Right after I noticed the tubes running in and out of the Old Raisin next to me, I noticed something a lot worse.

The tube running into *me*.

I had a tube taped to the middle of my left hand, and a bottle of clear liquid suspended above my bed, dripping into the tube.

Having spotted one tube just like one of Old Raisin's, I immediately did a quick search for the other one, my heart starting to beat a little faster.

Thank God I didn't find it.

What I did find was a cast on my left arm, covering every bit of skin from my wrist to almost under my armpit. I also found that my cast-covered arm was now bent pretty much permanently at the elbow, and that it was hurting real bad.

Right after I noticed the pain and the cast, I noticed the bandage covering my ribs. I also noticed how tight that bandage was. And, oh yes, incidentally, that my ribs—like my arm—were hurting real bad.

After that, moving right along, I noticed the bandage covering the entire top of my head, from the forehead up, and that my head was—you guessed it—hurting real bad.

In fact, it was almost as if I were attending a symphony of pain, with my arm doing a throbbing, pulsing beat, my ribs doing crescendoes whenever I shifted position even slightly, and my head more or less maintaining a continuing refrain in the background.

I can't say I felt the least bit inclined to applaud.

This little symphony, however, was nothing compared to the pain of what happened not ten minutes later.

Both Imogene and Claudine showed up in the doorway to my hospital room at exactly the same moment.

For a split second I just stared at them both. I couldn't believe it. Had they phoned each other just so the two of them would be sure they didn't miss each other?

Or did I have the worst luck of any man in Pigeon Fork?

If, of course, you didn't count Rigdon.

Imogene and Claudine must not have phoned each other, because each of them looked distinctly unhappy to see the other one. Imogene, in fact, looked as if, had she been given the choice between running into Claudine or running into Jack the Ripper, she'd have picked Jack in a heartbeat.

Jack, no doubt, would've been a lot more appropriately dressed than Claudine.

Claudine was wearing a hot pink puff-sleeved shirt tied in a big knot right under her breasts. This little number left Claudine's tanned midriff bare and about two inches of cleavage showing. That wasn't all that was showing either. Evidently to coordinate with her shirt, Claudine was also wearing hot pink, hip-hugging spandex biker shorts with lace around the legs. These shorts didn't quite cover her belly button.

It must've occurred to Claudine that somebody might possibly get the idea that she hadn't dressed up enough to go visiting at a hospital, because she'd also put on pale pink lace-edged socks and hot pink patent leather high heels.

Imogene's eyes were doing that shrinking thing again as they traveled rapidly over Claudine's outfit. When Imogene's eyes got to Claudine's cleavage, they stopped shrinking and popped out a little.

Claudine was giving Imogene the once-over too. In fact, Claudine seemed to be looking holes through Imogene's conservative black linen suit and low-heeled pumps as Imogene beat her through my hospital door and hurried toward my bedside. "Haskell," Imogene said, "you're awake!" You could actually hear the relief in her voice.

I smiled at her, feeling downright touched.

"I've been up here three times already today," she said, "and I tell you, Haskell, you scared me. You really did."

"Don't worry, I'm fine," I lied. "I'm just fine."

Claudine, evidently, wasn't about to be outdone. She hurried to stand just on the other side of Imogene, saying as she went, "Well, *I* was terribly worried about you too, Haskell. I really was. In fact, I called up this hospital more than once today, checking to see just how you were." Her tone implied that this had required extraordinary effort on her part.

Lord knows, picking up a phone could be exhausting.

Claudine was hurrying on. "And I knew you wouldn't be feeling very good when you woke up, Haskell, so that's why I decided to wear something that would really cheer you up."

So that was her thinking behind that getup. She was a sort of walking, talking get-well card. I hoped that the Old Raisin in the next bed didn't wake up and see this particular get-well card. It might be more than his heart could take.

Claudine now turned to Imogene. Giving one of her platinum curls a little flip, she said, "Don't you think this outfit could really cheer up a man, Emma Jane?"

Imogene did a quick intake of breath. "You know," she said, "I think you're right, Clau*dette.*" Imogene put a little extra emphasis on that last syllable. "In fact, I bet that's the kind of outfit Florence Nightingale probably wore, don't you think?"

Claudine's face had gotten a tad pinched-looking the second Imogene called *her* by the wrong name, but when Imogene mentioned Florence Nightingale, Claudine's face went totally blank for a split second. "Oh, uh, *sure,*" she said uncertainly.

I believe we can assume that on the days they were teaching all about Florence in World History, Claudine had not exactly been hanging on every word.

Turning toward me, Claudine now abruptly changed the subject. "Haskell, how in the world did a thing like this happen? I always told you that you drove too fast. Why, I remember when you and I took that little weekend trip to that cute bread-and-breakfast right after we first started dating, why, you just sailed right around curves like they weren't even there . . ."

Just like that, Claudine was off and running. With another quaint story of our life together back in Louisville.

I idly considered ringing the nurse for a painkiller. Something that would really dope a person up.

Not for me, of course. For Claudine.

She was still going on, but evidently Imogene had decided to pretend that Claudine was actually talking to the Old Raisin in the next bed.

This was a bit of a stretch, being as how the old guy was still snoring. With his mouth hanging open.

"How are you feeling, Haskell?" Imogene said, right over Claudine.

This, of course, put me in a real precarious spot. I could either answer Imogene, and make Claudine real mad for siding with Imogene and pretty much ignoring that she herself was still speaking. Or I could *not* answer Imogene, and pretty much guarantee that Imogene's and my dating days had just come to an abrupt halt.

I have to hand it to myself. Even injured the way I was, and doped up the way I was, I was still a damn fast thinker.

In fact, it was being injured that pretty much gave me a way out.

I looked Imogene straight in the eye.

And moaned.

Grabbing my ribs as if caught by a sudden spasm of pain.

The thing, I believe, that made this little performance so convincing was that the second I moved, I really was hurting pretty bad.

Imogene's eyes narrowed, but what could she do?

Especially since Claudine abruptly cut off her bed-and-breakfast story and was now saying, "Oh you poor baby, does it hurt?"

As Claudine spoke, she started to move even closer to me. It also looked as if she might actually be reaching for my hand.

Imogene must've played a little basketball at one time, or else she was a natural. She cut off Claudine's drive toward me much as she might've cut off an open lane to the basket. Deftly stepping right in front of Claudine, she grabbed up my right hand off the bed in one smooth motion.

If that move had been seen by a referee, I'm pretty sure Imogene would've been called for a foul.

Having made this little maneuver, however, Imogene

acted just like every other basketball player I've ever seen do it. She acted as if it had never happened. Hell, I'm pretty sure if she had been called for the foul, she would've, no doubt, even argued with the ref.

Imogene didn't even look toward Claudine as she said, "Is there anything I can do, Haskell? Do you want me to get the nurse?"

I shook my head. I didn't, however, let go of her hand.

"You know, I think you're right," Claudine put in, tapping a manicured finger against her chin as she peered at me, "I think Haskell does need a nurse. Why don't you go get him one?"

Imogene had now evidently decided to pretend that Claudine no longer existed. While her fingers squeezed mine, Imogene went right ahead talking just as if Claudine hadn't said a word. She told me how I'd been found by my neighbors right after I'd gone into the creek, and how they'd pulled me and my truck out with a tractor, and how it was now almost five in the afternoon. "You were out an awful long time, honey."

It was the first time Imogene had ever called me that. I don't think she'd really meant to either, being as how Claudine was standing right there, gawking at the two of us. The word must've just sort of slipped out, because Imogene abruptly cleared her throat and said, "You're going to be in here for a little while, Haskell." Her voice had turned almost businesslike. "Do you want me to feed Rip for you? I'd be glad to do it."

Claudine now looked like somebody whose game-winning shot had been blocked. "Well, now, *I* was going to offer to do that," she said. Her voice was almost a whine. Turning to me, she added, "Haskell, don't you think it would be better for me to take care of Rip? I mean, I'm the one that's on vacation—"

I didn't want to say anything, but as best as I could recall, Claudine had always been on vacation.

Even when she'd been working.

So what was her point?

"—and I've got a lot more time on my hands than you do," Claudine went on, turning back to Imogene.

From the look Imogene shot her, I started being real glad we were in a hospital. Just in case one of them needed emergency care. "Why, that's really nice of you," Imogene said. Her voice was no longer businesslike. It was saccharine-sweet. "But I think Rip knows me better than you, and he'll feel a lot more comfortable if I take care of him, Clau*dette.*" Imogene gave Claudine a chilly smile.

Claudine stiffened. "Claudine," she said. "Not Claudette. Clau*dine*. And that's terribly kind of you to offer, but I really think Rip would prefer being with somebody he lived with for *years.*"

Imogene blinked. "Rip doesn't even know you anymore."

Claudine blinked back. "Nonsense, that dog ADORES me."

I stared at Claudine. Apparently she had the two verbs "abhor" and "adore" mixed up.

Imogene must've thought so too. She gave Claudine another chilly smile. "You must be mistaken, Clau*dette,*" she said.

"Oh no, it's you who's mistaken, *Emma Jane,*" Claudine said.

I, of course, was just lying there, getting more and more uneasy by the minute.

What Claudine didn't know was that Imogene was not anywhere near as prim and proper as she looked in that business suit. In fact, the first time I'd ever laid eyes on her, Imogene had been kicking both Gunterman twins in the ankles. It had been the day her sister had died, and the twins had actually tried to keep her from entering her sister's house.

The twins had eventually given up.

And what Imogene didn't know about Claudine was that Claudine had never been one to back down from a fight. Not to mention, Claudine had a real talent, as I recalled, in the going-for-a-person's-throat department.

Watching the two of them practically sparring with each other was turning up the volume on my pain symphony. My head was getting to be no longer just a continuing refrain. I believe a drum solo had been added.

Claudine was now turning to me. "All right, Haskell, you decide. Rip would definitely want me to take care of him, don't you think?"

I just stared at her. Maybe instead of having them give a painkiller to Claudine, I'd take it myself, after all. A double dose.

Hell, I'd even take whatever they were giving the old guy in the next bed.

As it turned out, I never did have to answer Claudine, being as how my brother Elmo got me off the hook. Bless his heart. Elmo came walking into my hospital room at that exact moment, saying, "Haskell, Haskell, Haskell, didn't I tell you something like this was a-going to happen?"

Elmo is only four years older than me, but they were apparently real hard years. While he has red hair like mine, he doesn't have much of it left. In fact, he's only got an orangy red border around his ears and the back of his head. On top, he's just got nineteen hairs left. I counted them once when Elmo fell asleep on my couch, watching a football game.

It's my considered opinion that Elmo's hair fell out because he worries so much—all that extra energy coming out of his brain has burned up his roots.

"You got to find yourself a safer line of work, Haskell," Elmo was going on, "or else you're a-going to end up—"

Elmo broke off here as he caught sight of Claudine

standing beside my bed. "Why, why, it—it's—I mean, it's—"

Elmo apparently had not yet heard that Claudine was in town. Or else he couldn't quite get complete sentences out because a significant portion of his attention seemed now to be focused on the outfit Claudine was wearing. Elmo's eyes particularly seemed to keep gravitating toward Claudine's cleavage.

It was like watching two blue billiard balls that kept rolling toward the same side pocket.

"Elmo!" Claudine squealed. "Elmo Blevins! Why, isn't it wonderful to see FAMILY again!"

Imogene evidently didn't agree. The second Claudine said the word "family," a muscle began to jump in Imogene's jaw.

Claudine hurried across the room and threw herself into Elmo's arms.

I would've said "waiting arms," except that Elmo's arms were far from waiting. In fact, the second Claudine made contact with him, Elmo turned every bit as hot pink as Claudine's outfit. It looked to me as if even the skin under Elmo's nineteen hairs was now the exact shade of Claudine's spandex shorts.

It took Elmo a couple of minutes to extricate himself from Claudine, but when he did, I could tell he was taking real pains to not even look in her direction again. Elmo, I believe, has always been under the impression that his wife Glenda has supernatural powers. He's convinced that if he even glances at another woman, Glenda will somehow know. "Uh, nice to, uh, see you again, uh, Claudine."

As Elmo said this, he was looking at the floor and moving to stand real close to my side. You might've thought Elmo was looking to me—a man with a cast on one arm, a few bruised ribs, and a concussion—to protect him from Claudine. While he stood there, staring at the floor, Elmo told me once again what he has told me only about a hundred times before.

How I should join him in the thrill-packed world of drugstore management.

Uh-huh.

Good idea, Elmo.

An even better idea was the one he came up with when Claudine and Imogene began discussing the Rip dilemma all over again.

"Why don't you just take turns?" Elmo said.

I wasn't sure if Claudine and Imogene agreed to this because they couldn't think of a reason not to, or if they really thought it was a good idea.

From the way Claudine reacted, though, you might've thought Elmo had just thought up tearing down the Iron Curtain. "Oh, Elmo," she said breathily, "what a WONDERFUL idea." She batted her eyes at him. "Leave it to a *man* to come up with the perfect solution. Why, us girls might've been arguing all night *long* if it weren't for you."

Imogene was giving Claudine a look that clearly questioned her sanity. Elmo, however, was obviously trying to look humble but lovable. "It weren't nothing, really," Elmo said.

I couldn't argue with that.

"I always thought your brother was every bit as smart as you are, Haskell," Claudine was now saying. "And every bit as good-looking."

Elmo had passed hot pink by then, and was now working on flaming crimson.

At my elbow Imogene was taking the kind of breaths I think they make you practice for childbirth. I stared at her, wondering if maybe she might need a hospital bed worse than the Old Raisin.

I also idly wondered if the hospital could possibly give me a shot of anaesthetic that would put me out for the entire length of time Claudine was going to be in town.

Elmo left a half hour later, and once he left, I sort of hoped that Imogene would hang around until after Claudine was gone. So we'd have some time alone. It got to be real clear, however, that this wasn't going to happen. Particularly after I said, "You know, Claudine, I bet Rip is probably hungry right now. Maybe you could take your first turn now?"

Claudine just stared at me for a moment. "Okay," she finally said, and then she turned to Imogene. "I'll need you to come with me for my first time, though. So you can show me where everything is."

Oh, yeah. That pretty much killed any possibility of me and Imogene having any time alone.

I had a moment of real trepidation handing over my front door key to Claudine. Watching her manicured fingers close over it made my drum solo start up all over again.

I don't think Imogene liked seeing my house key going into Claudine's hand any better than I did. She seemed to stare at it for an awful long moment.

It wasn't long after the women left that Vergil came by. I don't think the sheriff cottons to being around sick people any more than he does being around upset people. He stood for a while in the doorway of my hospital room, as if he didn't really want to come in. Finally, though, he walked on in, looking as if invisible forces were pulling him in against his will.

Vergil also definitely looked disconcerted by the Old Raisin, who was at that moment breaking his own record for Loudest Snore By a Man Over a Hundred. Vergil glanced that way, focused for a split second on the tube running out from under Old Raisin's sheet, and then didn't look in that direction ever again.

"How are you doing, Haskell?" Vergil asked.

It's my opinion that if you got your arm in a cast, a large bandage on your head, and your chest wrapped up like something you just took out of the freezer, the answer to a question like that is pretty obvious. "Peachy," I said.

Vergil just stared at me, his eyes as sad as I've ever seen them. "Well," he said, "your truck's totaled."

For once, Vergil made something sound like tragic news, and it really was. I liked that truck. I really did. I also particularly liked the nice paint job I'd paid extra for. Midnight-blue with a metallic flake.

And the brand new muffler and heavy-duty shocks that I'd gotten installed just two weeks ago.

A shot of anaesthetic would've been a real help at this point.

Vergil was droning on. "You know, it sure looks as if somebody jimmied with your brakes."

I just looked at him. No kidding. Tell me something I *didn't* know.

"I think it's clear," I said, "that my looking into the Rigdon Bewley case is making somebody real nervous."

Apparently, it wasn't as clear as I thought.

Vergil sighed. "Or else, you'd *already* made somebody real mad at you," he said, sighing again. I believe I've mentioned how good he is at this. "In fact, from what I've heard, there's quite a few folks around town that are real mad at you. On account of what happened at Frank's—"

I held up my hand. He didn't have to remind me.

Apparently, Vergil's point was that my assailant could've been any one of a vast quantity of people who'd all been pretty much standing around, more or less waiting for their number to be called, so that they could do me in.

"Thanks so much, Vergil. This is the sort of cheery conversation you need to hear when you're flat on your back in a hospital bed. You really ought to do volunteer work as a candy-striper."

Vergil evidently chose to ignore my remarks. "You didn't happen to notice anything odd before you got into your truck, did you?"

I really hated to answer that one, but I thought I probably should let him know all the pertinent facts. "Matter of fact," I said, "when I pulled out of my garage, I saw a lot of footprints on my hood."

Vergil blinked. "Footprints? Like somebody walked across the hood of your truck?"

I started to shake my head, but the motion made the pain symphony reach a crescendo. "No," I said, now trying real hard to hold my head absolutely still. "Like some *animal* walked across the hood of my truck."

Vergil could've had a better reaction to what I'd just said. He just stared at me for about a half second, and then his mouth started twitching. Like maybe for the first time since I'd known him, he was on the verge of actually smiling. "Do you think the animals in the woods are now after *you?*"

My head was really pounding. "No, Vergil," I said through my teeth. "I just thought I ought to mention it, that's all."

Vergil cleared his throat. "I didn't notice any footprints on your truck."

"I reckon they were washed off when my truck ended up in the creek."

"Uh-huh." That's all Vergil said.

Just before he left, however, he reached over and gave me a self-conscious pat on my arm. "Take care of yourself, boy," he said.

It's times like these that make me remember that Vergil was my dad's best friend, and that with my mom and dad gone, he's the closest I've got to parents.

Lord. Old Vergil actually looked a tad upset that I'd gotten myself hurt.

Would wonders never cease.

They insisted on keeping me in the hospital for a few days observation.

What I believe they were observing most closely, however, was how rapidly they were removing money from my bank account. I figure that little hospital stay cost me somewhere in the neighborhood of eight hundred dollars a day.

Eight hundred dollars a day to have Claudine and Imogene dropping in on me at almost the exact same time almost every single day. It got to be where I actually started suspecting that Claudine was following Imogene around.

That woman, no doubt, hated to pass up the opportunity to make my life miserable.

The one time Imogene actually walked in without Claudine shadowing her was late Wednesday afternoon, and I didn't waste any time. I reached over, pulled Imogene close, and gave her a kiss that I do believe made me feel significantly better almost immediately.

It was too good to last, of course. Right in the middle of that kiss, Claudine walked in. I was pretty much occupied at the time so I really didn't notice her until Claudine cleared her throat and said, "Afternoon, you two."

I reckon by then I must've gotten real accustomed to having Claudine around when I was with Imogene because I didn't even feel self-conscious at her having caught us smooching.

Imogene immediately pulled away, of course, and I turned to stare at Claudine.

She was wearing another one of her get-well-card outfits—a bright yellow halter top and skintight white jeans with little hearts cut out all down each side. It looked as if somebody had stamped her jeans with a heart-shaped cookie cutter. "I—I'm sorry to interrupt," Claudine said, "but—"

By now I was really staring at her. Her voice was actually shaking.

Lord. Could she sound this upset because she'd found me kissing Imogene?

Surely not. This *was* the woman who'd done the courthouse jig. The woman who'd told a judge that guts-hating was grounds for divorce.

Imogene, however, didn't have the benefit of my touching memories. She obviously was convinced that it had been our kiss that was rattling Claudine. Imogene flashed me a pointed look the second Claudine started talking.

Claudine took a couple of steps closer to my bed and said, "Haskell, I—I came by to tell you that now I know for sure that Buck Harrison really has followed me here! I—I found a note from him stuck under my door at that rooming house I'm staying in!"

So it hadn't been the kiss that had upset Claudine. Just as I'd thought.

Imogene's eyes were no longer flashing me pointed looks. In fact, they appeared to have narrowed some.

I took a deep breath. As much for Imogene's benefit as anything else, I said, holding out my hand, "Okay, Claudine, let me see the note."

Claudine blinked and took a step backward. "Well, uh, I don't exactly have it with me."

It was at this point Imogene rolled her eyes.

Claudine hurried on. "I—I was so upset when I first read the note that I forgot to put it in my purse. I must've left it back at the rooming house."

Imogene was really rolling her eyes now, but once again, mind you, I had the benefit of memories that Imogene did not share. I couldn't help but remember what a real flake Claudine had been during our marriage.

It wasn't beyond her to forget something real important.

Hell, quite a few times it had even slipped her mind that she was married.

"Haskell, I'm afraid to go back to that rooming house now, I really am," Claudine was saying. "Will you let me stay at your house until you get home from the hospital? Please? That way I can be there to take care of Rip, and Lord knows, Haskell, I'd feel a whole lot safer."

I didn't have to even glance toward Imogene to see what she thought of this little arrangement. In fact, I could hear Imogene's heavy breathing right beside me. She sounded like a vacuum cleaner with something caught in the hose.

"I don't know, Claudine . . ." I hedged.

"Look, I'll move out the second you get home from the hospital! I will," Claudine said. "I mean it! Please, Haskell, I—I'm really scared." She was now clasping her hands in front of my face. *"Please,* Haskell?"

I reckon I don't have to tell you who Claudine suddenly reminded me of.

CHAPTER
12

Please, Haskell?" Claudine was saying. "I just want to stay at your place until you're out of the hospital. That's all. I would feel SO much safer there."

I couldn't help myself. I found myself saying before I even had a chance to think about it, "Okay, you can stay there. But only until I get out of here."

Imogene's reaction was a lot better than what I might've expected.

"WHA-A-AT?" she yelled.

Imogene's yell actually woke up Old Raisin. For a second anyway. He sat bolt upright in bed, looked our way foggily, flopped back down and went promptly back to sleep.

Claudine stared at Old Raisin, then turned back to me. "Thank you, Haskell, thank you, THANK YOU, you sweet, sweet, SWEET thing," she said. "You won't be sorry."

I just looked at her. I was sorry already.

Claudine was heading out the door even as she was

saying her thank-yous to me. I knew, of course, why she was leaving so quickly. She didn't want to give me a chance to change my mind.

Claudine might've also been a little afraid to stick around once she got a good look at Imogene's face. Lord knows, I was a little afraid myself.

"I can't believe you've let that woman move in with you!" Imogene looked as if somebody had just set off dynamite behind her eyes.

I tried to remain calm, hoping Imogene would follow suit. "Now, Imogene," I said, "Claudine is not moving in with me. I'm not even there!"

I thought this was a perfectly valid point.

Imogene apparently wasn't impressed. "Look, Haskell, I'm not going to argue with you, but if you can't see that Claudine wants you back, then you're BLIND!"

I shook my head. I had evidently recovered some, because I could shake my head here lately and the symphony didn't start up. "Believe me, you're wrong, Imogene," I said. I told her then all about Claudine's little jig on the courthouse steps. All about Claudine running around on me. And all about what Claudine considered grounds for divorce.

"So, see?" I said cheerfully. "Claudine really can't *stand* me!"

Imogene just stared at me. "Haskell, I said I wasn't going to argue about it, and I'm not. I just don't want to fight. Particularly with you hurt and all." She drew a long, ragged breath. "BUT if you don't see that your letting your ex-wife move into your house plays right into her hands, well, then, all I can say is that you're a blithering idiot!" Imogene was now pacing in front of my bed, waving her hands in the air. "You're a moron! A complete imbecile! A total nincompoop!"

Having said all this, Imogene turned and walked abruptly out of my room without looking back.

I laid there in my hospital bed, watching her go. Thank God she didn't want to fight.

I spent three days in all at Crayton Memorial, and the day they finally let me go home was the day of Rigdon's funeral. It was scheduled for two o'clock that afternoon, and frankly, I can't say I was all that glad I was going to be able to attend.

I might as well admit that staying that long in the hospital had not done wonders for my mood. By the time they finally let me go home, in fact, I was pretty much madder than a hornet. Mainly because, by then, I'd had quite a lot of time to think about what all had happened to me.

Let me see now. I'd been in a lot of pain. I had me a broken arm. And my truck was totaled.

Not to mention, my girlfriend was not dropping by to visit me anymore. Or even taking my phone calls.

All on account of my ex-wife moving in with me when I wasn't even there.

It did cross my mind that *if* whoever it was who'd messed with my brakes had *not* tried to kill me, I would never have been in any position to let Claudine stay at my house in the first place, and none of this would've happened.

If you follow what I'm saying.

Oh yeah, I'd say I was mad all right when I finally got myself discharged. And I was getting real determined to find out who was behind all this.

It also didn't help any to know full well that at any given moment Claudine was probably walking around my place, acting as if she belonged there.

Just picturing such a thing was enough to give me the willies.

The first place I headed after getting out of the hospital, however, was not directly home to tell Claudine to start packing. It was to Rigdon's aunt Agnes's. Mind you, I headed there because I really did want to talk with Agnes, and not at all because I was avoiding going home to face Claudine.

My unfortunate trip into the creek might've slowed me down some, but I still was real interested in hearing what Agnes might have to tell me about "Rigdon having a lot to be depressed about lately."

Transportation might've been a problem, but good old Elmo had come through, lending me the car his wife Glenda usually drives. It was a 1983 Ford Thunderbird in a neon-blue that made it real easy to spot in the hospital parking lot. The Thunderbird wasn't exactly the kind of car that made my heart beat faster or anything, but beggars can't be choosers. I was real happy to get it. I was also happy that the thing had an automatic transmission so that I could still drive, even with one arm in a cast.

Elmo's car also had power door locks and power windows, so that once I was inside, I didn't have to do much moving around. This last gets to be real important if you happen to be lugging around a few extra pounds of plaster.

I drove to Agnes's as fast as possible under the circumstances. Which meant, of course, that I all but crept down the road, following Rigdon's signs once again.

It was kind of sad now seeing those signs appear, one by one, on the side of the road.

I pulled up in front of the yellow house directly across the street from Rigdon's place, and Agnes answered her door after only one knock. She didn't look a bit surprised to see me with a cast on my arm, so I reckon once again the Pigeon Fork grapevine had worked with its usual efficiency. "Haskell," Agnes said, folding her pillow arms across her massive chest, "I'm afraid we're not receiving company until *after* the funeral. I appreciate your coming by and all, but you really ought to come back then."

"Agnes, this isn't a social call," I said. "I need some answers. About Rigdon."

Agnes immediately started shaking her Gibson-girl head. "Oh, no, I don't think so. I don't like to spread gossip, you know."

I, of course, just looked at her. If Agnes didn't like to gossip, fish didn't like to swim.

"Nope, Ernal don't like me telling tales." Agnes was saying all this in an awful loud voice, and I immediately saw why. In back of her, Ernal was standing in the far door of the living room, looking our way.

Leaning toward me, Agnes said, "Look, Haskell, I know you mean well, but Ernal and Rigdon were real close, and Ernal don't want me betraying any of Rigdon's confidences." Agnes was practically shouting now. "Why, I couldn't possibly tell you a *thing!*"

I could see now that Ernal had turned and moved out of the doorway.

There didn't seem to be anything else for me to do but leave. I turned to do just that, and Agnes took a step toward me, grabbing my arm. "Haskell?" she whispered. "The person you ought to be talking to ain't me. It's *Bertie Lee.*"

I blinked at that one.

Bertie Lee Strait, the wife of Rigdon's best friend, Curtis?

Agnes patted her Gibson-girl hair. "As far as I'm concerned, it's mostly Bertie Lee's fault that Rigdon is dead!"

It didn't take any time at all to get into the Tunderbird, back it out of Agnes and Ernal's driveway, and pull it into the driveway of the green house next door.

Bertie Lee started looking wary the second she opened

her door and saw me standing there. Still apparently making her wardrobe choices based on *Hee Haw* reruns, she had on a yellow gingham sleeveless shirt and a pair of white shorts with yellow gingham patches for pockets.

I believe I've mentioned before that Bertie Lee isn't real pretty in the face. She has no eyelashes to speak of, and her eyes are set too close together. Of course, it doesn't much matter how close together her eyes are, being as how you can only see one of them anyway. She peered at me from behind her curtain of straight, black hair.

"Haskell." That's all Bertie Lee said. Then she just stood there, glaring at me out of her one good eye.

If she thought that Phantom of the Opera look was going to intimidate me, she had another think coming. I decided to save some time and cut to the chase. "Bertie Lee," I said real quietlike, "you might as well talk to me, because Agnes just told me all about it."

Bertie Lee's mouth dropped open. At least, the half I could see did.

She swallowed a couple times, took a quick, nervous look in back of her, carefully closed her front door and came out to stand with me on her stoop. "Okay," she finally said, "so Rigdon and I did have an affair? So what? It's not exactly all my fault, you know. I mean, what with Curtis being a truck driver and all, he's not home all the time, and I got my needs, you know—"

Matter of fact, I did not know about her needs, and I wasn't particularly interested in finding out about them. I interrupted. "Agnes seems to think that your affair could've contributed to Rigdon's suicide."

Bertie Lee's good eye looked alarmed. "Baloney! That old biddy doesn't know what she's talking about. Our affair only lasted three weeks, for Christ's sake. That's all. It wasn't as if we'd been carrying on for *years* or anything."

196

I swallowed, staring at her. Toward the last of our marriage, Claudine had said much the same thing. Apparently, Bertie Lee and Claudine would agree that infidelity was something that could be measured by the clock. Both women seemed to believe that if you played around on your husband for a few short hours, then you should also get full credit for all the many other hours in which you'd somehow managed to remain faithful.

I never did quite understand the logic here. I was pretty sure Curtis probably wouldn't get it either.

"And then one day it was over," Bertie Lee was now saying with a shrug. "Rigdon had gotten to feeling real guilty about, you know, carrying on with his best friend's wife and all that, so he just broke it off." Bertie Lee was shaking her head. "I told him too. I said, hey, Rigdon, you're not the one who stood up in front of everybody and promised to be faithful, so what in the world is your problem?" She ran her hand through her hair, and I glimpsed her second eye for a moment. It looked sullen. "I mean, if anybody was letting Curtis down, it was me. Not Rigdon."

I just looked at Bertie Lee. She did seem to have everything figured out nicely. "But, no," she hurried on, "would you believe I went over there one day, and Rigdon actually looked surprised to see me. He teared up and shut the door in my face. Saying that he still loved me, but it was over. And he meant it."

"How long ago was that?"

Bertie Lee's good eye was now starting to blink real bad. "Two weeks ago, that was all. It was just two weeks ago. And—And now he's gone! He's really gone! I'll never get him back now!"

I had to admit, her odds were real slim.

Bertie Lee had taken a step toward me and was now grabbing at my arm. Fortunately, the arm closest to her was not the one in the cast. "You're not going to tell

Curtis, are you? I mean, I'm just telling *you,* is all. So's you'll stop poking around, asking a lot of questions. It ain't really nobody else's business. I mean, it—it's not going to go any further, is it?"

I wasn't going to lie to her. "Bertie Lee, I can't rightly say—"

That was all I got out before Bertie Lee actually screamed, "NO-O-O! You can't tell Curtis. You *can't!*" Bertie Lee's good eye was now sparkling with unshed tears. "For one thing, Curtis is delivering Rigdon's eulogy this afternoon, and he might not do all that good a job if he knows the truth."

Rigdon's eulogy seemed to be the least of her problems, but Bertie Lee did have a point.

"Bertie Lee," I said, "I'll try to keep what you told me to myself. Okay? And I'll for sure keep it to myself until Rigdon's funeral is over."

I could tell that wasn't exactly what she wanted to hear, but it was the best I could do.

I got back in the Thunderbird and drove on home. On the way, of course, I pretty much went over in my mind what all I'd just found out. And tried not to think of what I faced at home.

And by that, I don't mean Rip, of course.

Although Rip did carry on something awful when he found out it was really me heading up his stairs. Evidently, having Claudine stay with him for the last couple of days had scared Rip badly.

He only barked at me once as I got out of the Thunderbird, and then that dumb dog went straight into the most frenzied display of tail-wagging and joy-leaping that I'd ever been embarrassed to witness.

Lord. For a second there I actually thought Rip could be weeping.

He was certainly whimpering as he jumped into my arms.

I, of course, tried too late to stop him. "No, boy, NO, no, RIP, no, down, NO! DOWN!"

I might as well have saved my breath. Rip crashed head first into my cast, and immediately after that both of us stumbled around my deck for the next few seconds, pretty much whimpering in pain.

"Oh, for crying out loud."

This was Claudine. She'd gotten up off a lounge I'd forgotten I had and was now walking toward where I was still holding my cast and wincing.

At Claudine's approach, Rip looked as if he'd gotten hit in the face all over again. He dropped to a crouch and ran around in back of me, looking at Claudine through my legs.

What a watch dog.

Claudine, I suppose, was something to watch.

She was wearing the tiniest string bikini I think I've ever seen. It looked a little like what you might end up with if you recycled postage stamps.

"You okay?" she said. "I guess I should've tied Rip up."

I just looked at her. The casual way she said that sort of made you wonder just how much she'd kept Rip tied up while I'd been gone.

"I sure hope he didn't hurt you, Haskell," Claudine was saying. She stood there, facing me, hands on her hips, all but glowing with suntan oil. Goodness me, she did have herself a nice tan.

"Oh no, I'm fine," I said. Oddly enough, my voice came out as a croak.

Claudine smiled and stretched lazily. "You really should've called me, you big lug. You know I would've come out and picked you up at the hospital if you'd wanted me to."

She was just standing there in that little bikini, smiling at me. I knew, of course, that she was probably just being real nice and all. And yet, what flashed through my mind real quick was a single thought. What if Imogene should show up right now?

At this moment?

With Claudine prancing around my house half dressed?

Lord. And I thought Imogene was mad *now*.

I made myself return Claudine's smile. "You know," I said brightly, "I've got some real good news for you. Elmo has offered to let you stay with him and Glenda for the rest of your vacation out here."

This, of course, was an outright lie. Elmo didn't exactly offer. What he exactly did was finally give in after I begged him off and on for about an hour.

In fact, Elmo's wife Glenda was still not speaking to me. I believe, in fact, Glenda's response to this little idea had been: "Oh, SURE, what woman wouldn't want the SEX POT from HELL staying a few nights at her house? WHAT a terrific idea!"

Glenda can be real understanding this way.

Glenda, however, apparently had Claudine beat out real bad in the understanding department. Claudine was now looking at me with huge, hurt eyes. *"Me?* You want me to go stay with your brother?" Her lower lip was noticeably trembling. "I am in real danger here from some sadistic nut who's stalking me, and you're passing me off to your *brother?"*

I believe I could put Claudine down as not being all that grateful for the chance to reacquaint herself with her old in-laws.

In fact, I don't believe she said thank you once as she stormed around my house, tearing clothes out of closets, and grabbing stuff out of dresser drawers, and packing up her suitcases. Claudine didn't even bother to change out of her bikini. She just pulled a skintight T-shirt over the top and a pair of short shorts over the bottom.

"Now, Claudine, don't be like that," I said. Lord. If I'd had a dollar for every time I'd asked Claudine not to be like that—whatever that means—I'd be a rich man today.

When she was finally ready to go, Claudine stopped for a second in my doorway. "Oh, by the way," she said, her voice cold as ice, "not that you *care,* but here's the note I found under my door a couple of days ago."

With that, she threw a piece of paper in my direction, stomped off to her silver Camry, and sped off down my hill.

I noticed that Rip did not look the least bit distressed to see her go.

In fact, he sat at my feet, tongue lolling happily, wagging his tail to beat the band.

So much for tearful good-byes.

Claudine's note, I thought, made for snappy reading.

Written in ballpoint pen, with an extreme backhand slant, it said: "Claudine, you are so gorgeous. I must have you. If I can't have you, nobody else can. I mean it."

I swallowed and actually felt chilled. My goodness, if this guy meant what he'd written, then he really was a psycho.

Or else he didn't know Claudine at all.

The paper was crumpled badly, so Claudine must've been carrying it around for a while. It sure didn't look as if there'd be much use in having the thing dusted for fingerprints.

It was getting close to one-thirty by then. I put the note in my pocket, went into my bedroom, and changed as quickly as I could. After which I took a deep breath, got into the Thunderbird, and headed for Rigdon's funeral.

Funerals are real strange things. It's just about the only event you could ever attend where everybody's talking except the guy you all came to see.

Merryman's Funeral Home was packed. As I got out of

the Thunderbird and looked at all the trucks and cars crowded into the funeral home parking lot, I was amazed. Either Rigdon Bewley had been one popular son of a gun or else his funeral had gotten to be the social event of the year in Crayton County.

Folks did seem to be all decked out for Rigdon's send-off. You might've thought it was Easter, except for the preponderance of black as a wardrobe color choice.

I myself was wearing my only black pair of slacks. I didn't have a black coat, so I'd settled for gray blazer.

I couldn't help but notice that quite a few of the folks that I passed on my way into the small chapel Horace Merryman makes available for this kind of occasion seemed to be outright frowning in my direction.

I was pretty sure it wasn't just because they didn't approve of my gray coat.

One of these folks was Imogene. She was sitting about two pews from the back, and when I walked in, she turned and looked straight at me. When I glanced her way real nonchalantly, she looked away.

So much for making up.

Rigdon's funeral was pretty much run-of-the-mill until it was time for Rigdon's best friend to come forward to say a few words.

Wearing a black suit, a string tie, and black cowboy boots that made him look a lot more like Johnny Cash than Jimmy Dean, Curtis Strait didn't look any too steady on his feet. As he went by me, I was pretty sure the smell of whiskey followed him. That probably accounted for the way Curtis weaved a little as he headed up to the pulpit.

Curtis did make for a wretched figure up there, hands trembling, tears streaming down his face, the toothpick in the corner of his mouth bobbling up and down pitifully. You couldn't help but feel sort of emotional just looking at him.

Poor Curtis's voice cracked a few times as he said, "We're here to say good-bye to Rigdon Bewley, and I've been asked to tell you what kind of man he was." He cleared his throat and gripped the edge of the pulpit. "Well, I'll tell you, all right. I'll even show you. Here's what I think of Rigdon Bewley!" He leaned to one side and spit out his toothpick. "Rigdon was a lying, cheating asshole! That son of a bitch was sneaking around with Bertie Lee right under my nose! I don't care if he'd gone crazy or not, it weren't no excuse! If he hadn't kilt himself, I'da been glad to do it for him!"

I can't say it was the finest eulogy I'd ever heard.

CHAPTER
13

If it weren't for Horace Merryman, Curtis's eulogy probably would've lasted a lot longer. Curtis did seem to have quite a lot of material he wanted to cover. In fact, Curtis had just draped himself over the pulpit, more or less making himself comfortable up there, when Horace came hurrying down the aisle.

Horace was fidgeting up a storm as he all but dragged Curtis off.

Curtis was, of course, pretty much kicking and screaming the entire way. "Let go of me, you old coot! LET GO OF ME!"

You could tell Horace was trying to remove Curtis in a way that was still in keeping with the solemnity of the occasion, but it's pretty hard to maintain a dignified manner when somebody is screaming at the top of his lungs. And trying to break your grip on his arm. And kicking at your ankles.

"DAMMIT! Let go! I got a lot more to say! LET ME GO!"

Horace's face was beet-red by the time he'd gotten Curtis out of the chapel.

When Horace and Curtis went by me, I got up and followed them.

Out in the vestibule Horace immediately released Curtis pretty much the way you might drop off a particularly odorous sack of garbage at the curb.

Curtis wrenched away, rubbing his arm, and stumbled out of the funeral home into the parking lot outside. Out there, Curtis was evidently determined to have the final word. "ASSHOLE!" he yelled.

Horace's mouth pinched up some when he heard that, but he dusted off the front of his black suit, fidgeted with his tie, and hurried back into the chapel. Without once even acknowledging I was there.

Horace had to have seen me. I was standing right there, practically at his elbow. Apparently, however, Horace had decided that the best thing to do was pretend as if none of this had ever happened.

I hurried out into the parking lot where Curtis was now pacing up and down, up and down, flinging his arms around.

I went up to him real calmlike, and I made my voice as soothing as I knew how. "Okay, Curtis, now, calm down."

"Calm down?" Curtis said. "How can I calm down? I got me an anonymous phone call not even an hour ago, telling me all about Rigdon and Bertie Lee!"

Curtis actually looked as if he were going to start blubbering again. I believe I've already mentioned how I'm not real good around crying women, so you can imagine how I am around a crying *man*. Hell, I wouldn't even know whether I should offer him a Kleenex or not. That's why I jumped right in, to head off any possible water works. "Curtis, did you ever think maybe it isn't true? Maybe that phone call was just some kind of sick prank?"

I knew, of course, that if Curtis believed this, I could probably sell him a few bridges, but what I was trying to do here was divert Curtis's attention some. So I didn't have to start looking for Kleenex.

Apparently, however, Curtis being in the bridge market was wishful thinking on my part.

"Are you NUTS?" he said.

Now, this was the *third* time somebody had said this to me in the last week. I really was starting to feel as if somebody was trying to tell me something.

"Don't you think the first thing I'd do would be to ask Bertie Lee?" Curtis was rubbing his chin distractedly. He already had a five o'clock shadow, and it wasn't even two-thirty. "I was hoping—GOD, I was hoping—that she'd just deny everything."

I cleared my throat. "I take it she didn't?"

Curtis was now running his hand through his black hair. "She *confessed!* Can you believe it? Bertie Lee didn't even have the decency to lie to me!"

I blinked at that one. That was one way to look at it. If, indeed, it were the right way, then all those times I'd been angry at Claudine for lying to me after I'd caught her being unfaithful, I'd been real wrong. What I should've been was grateful to her for sparing my feelings.

Curtis was blinking now too. "That's what really hurts. If Bertie Lee hadn't told me all about her and Rigdon, I probably would've thought that damn phone call was a prank, just like you said. But no-o-o, she had to be honest!"

I just looked at him. The nerve of that woman.

Curtis was now blinking real fast. "That's what's so hard to take. If Bertie Lee hadn't told me, I never would've known for sure. Hell, it wasn't as if *Rigdon* would've ever told me!"

I had to admit Rigdon's lips were pretty much sealed.

Curtis made a quick swipe at his eyes, and then abruptly clapped me on the back. "Dammit, Haskell, I'm glad now that you called Rigdon a lunatic in front of the whole town!"

I hated to burst his balloon, but I thought I should set the record straight. "Uh, Curtis, I didn't exactly call—"

Curtis went right on as if I hadn't even spoken. "Hell, the son of a bitch deserved it!" He swiped at his eyes once more, and when he spoke again, his voice sounded as if he were trying to talk with crackers in his mouth. "Dammit, Haskell, you can't imagine how a thing like this feels."

I stared at him. I wasn't about to tell him, but he was, of course, mistaken. I knew *exactly* how it felt. Imagining, in fact, would not be necessary.

"Dammit! Dammit! DAMMIT!" Curtis was now punctuating what he had to say by pounding one fist against his leg.

I couldn't help staring at him some more. Curtis was carrying on so much, I actually wondered if he might not be overdoing it some.

Maybe Curtis was just *acting* as if he were this upset so that everybody would believe that he'd only just found out about Bertie Lee's infidelity. Maybe Curtis had found out, oh, say, two weeks ago, and had immediately started trying to kill Rigdon. Leaving behind footprints of animals so that if his attempts failed, nobody would believe Rigdon if Rigdon told anybody what was happening.

It could also be that, when his other attempts had not done the trick, Curtis had finally settled on a surefire way to get rid of Rigdon. Curtis had decided to string Rigdon up and make it look like a suicide.

Oh, yeah, that could work.

I was also wondering something else. It was obvious that Curtis had not been at Frank's, or he would've known that I had not called Rigdon a lunatic. And yet, what if Louise had told Curtis what all had gone on at Frank's, and Curtis had immediately seen this as a golden opportunity to kill Rigdon and make it look as if *I* had driven Rigdon to take his own life?

Curtis was now squatting in the middle of the parking lot, holding his head between his hands. In that black suit, he looked like an old-time preacher, praying. There was really no use asking Curtis if Rigdon's sister, Louise, had told him what had happened at Frank's. Anybody with the brain of a chicken would surely know to lie about such a thing. Particularly if he really had staged Rigdon's death.

I peered at Curtis a little closer. Admittedly, Curtis *had* spent a good portion of his life trying to look like a man who was trying to look like James Dean. Moreover, Curtis had done this even though he himself had black hair and a five o'clock shadow. Which some might say should've probably encouraged him to try to look like a man who was trying to look like, oh, say, *Al Pacino,* for example.

I took a deep breath. Bearing all this in mind, I was still, however, pretty sure that Curtis Strait did have the IQ of poultry.

No doubt about it, he'd know to lie to me, all right.

There was, in fact, only one way to find out if Louise had told Curtis about the incident at Frank's. I left Curtis still holding his head in his hands, and headed back inside Merryman's Funeral Home to find Louise.

As soon as I walked in the front door, I realized that the funeral service must've just ended. Folks were pouring out of the little chapel and were more or less milling around the vestibule.

I spotted Louise right away. Wearing an ankle-length black dress that made her look a little like the Wicked Witch of the West, she was standing over to my left, getting herself hugged and kissed by just about everybody that went by. Everybody appeared to be following Horace Merryman's lead and trying real hard to act as if they hadn't even heard Curtis's unique eulogy.

In fact, it was as if—since no one knew exactly what the proper way was to behave under such unfortunate circumstances, being as how they were pretty much on uncharted territory here—everybody had decided just to pretend it never happened. In fact, I even heard one woman say in a simpering tone to Louise, "It was a lovely service, dear. Just *lovely.*"

Even Louise looked a little surprised at that one.

Most everybody else didn't even mention the service. Instead, as best as I could tell, the folks who spoke to Louise mainly concentrated on just saying a few words about Rigdon. "We're all going to miss him," seemed to be the most popular sentiment. Once, however, right after this was said, somebody in the back of the crowd added, "Particularly Bertie Lee," but Louise either didn't hear the comment or chose to ignore it.

Louise did not choose to ignore me. The minute she saw me heading her way, she said, in a voice I thought was much louder than necessary, "Well, Haskell, I guess *you* were real glad to hear Curtis's eulogy, now weren't you?" Louise was carrying what looked to be a black cloth dinner napkin, and she waved it in my direction as she spoke.

It seemed to me as if every single person in the vestibule turned to look at me. I swallowed uneasily. "Well, uh, no, Louise, I can't rightly say that I—"

That was all Louise let me get out. "I guess you think Rigdon did what he did because he was feeling so guilty about everything. Well, if you think this lets you off the hook, Haskell Blevins, it doesn't! I still blame you. As far as I'm concerned, you're still a damn murderer!"

I don't know. Maybe I was just too thin-skinned, but this being called a murderer in front of a crowd of people was getting real old. I tried to remind myself that Louise was a bereaved person, and that I probably shouldn't want to punch her lights out, but it was getting harder and harder to remember.

"Louise," I said, biting out the word, "I *am* real sorry about Rigdon. I believe I've already told you, I had no idea my voice was going to carry all over that—"

Louise glared at me and interrupted. "But it did, didn't it?" Her eyes were tearing up. "You ought to be ashamed of yourself, holding up to ridicule a poor, crazy man like Rigdon!" She dabbed at her eyes with the dinner napkin.

I was all but swallowing my own anger now. "I can't blame you for being mad," I said. I took a deep breath, staring straight at Louise. "In fact," I went on, "I wouldn't blame you if, as soon as you found out about it, you told everybody you knew what I did . . ."

Louise took the bait. "You're darned tootin' I told everybody! I told Curtis and Agnes and—"

I interrupted. "You called Curtis?"

Louise nodded, now looking at me a little funny. "Well, sure I did! When I saw how upset you'd made Rigdon, why, I knew to be worried about him. I knew! That's why I called up Curtis and told him that maybe he ought to look in on Rigdon. Besides, I wanted Curtis to know what you did!" Louise's voice got even louder. "I wanted *everybody* to know!"

This wasn't exactly earthshaking news. Now that I thought about it, I'm surprised she didn't put it in the paper. Maybe tacked it on to Rigdon's obituary. Something along the lines of, "The family requests that memorial gifts be made by hiring a hit man to knock off Haskell Blevins."

"I reckon that's why you called up Agnes too," I said.

Louise looked spiteful as she waved her napkin at me again. "I called Agnes up because I knew that she'd spread the story a lot better than I could!"

I swallowed again, staring at Louise. Between Louise and Agnes, they'd probably told most of Pigeon Fork just how I had been making fun of poor Rigdon's infirmities. No wonder everybody in town had heard the story so quick.

No *wonder* every time I'd walked into any place in this town, I'd felt as if everybody expected me to be ringing a bell and yelling the word "Unclean!"

"I want you to know something else too," Louise said. "It had to be you, *and nobody else,* who caused Rigdon to do what he did, because Rigdon wasn't feeling all that bad over Bertie Lee."

I just stared right back at her. This was not exactly what Agnes had told me.

"That's right," Louise said, now giving me a self-satisfied little sneer. "Rigdon didn't care two cents about Bertie Lee! She was just a little fling to him, that's all." Louise was now jabbing her finger in my direction. Have I mentioned how much I hate that? "You just got to understand the way Rigdon was. He was an *artist,* understand? That's just the way artists are."

I was still staring at Louise. Lord. She made Rigdon sound like maybe he was Van Gogh or something. The next minute she'd be telling me Rigdon had intended to cut off his ear and mail it to Bertie Lee.

"Oh, yeah, Rigdon told me all about his and Bertie Lee's affair," Louise was now saying, dabbing at her eyes still again with the napkin. "He also told me that he'd realized that the whole thing was a big mistake. And so he ended it. Just like that."

Louise snapped her fingers.

Floyd, Louise's husband, had come into the vestibule right about then, and walked over to where Louise and I were standing. Like me, he must not have had a black coat, because Floyd was wearing a white shirt and black trousers. He looked as if he were dressed to sing in a school choir.

Floyd evidently had heard every word of what Louise had just told me, because he immediately started nodding his head. "That's right," he put in. "Rigdon couldn't possibly have cared all that much about Bertie Lee." Floyd said the name with something like scorn. "He didn't even care enough to break up with her in person. He just sent Bertie Lee a note one day. I reckon you'd say it was a 'Dear Bertie Lee' letter." Floyd smirked at his little joke. "Anyways, that was that. End of story. El finito." Floyd gave his black trousers a little hitch and snorted. "Yep," he said, "that's how Rigdon handled his women."

I just looked at him. Old Floyd sounded as if he certainly admired Rigdon's way with the ladies.

Well, it looked as if this conversation was pretty much over. I cleared my throat. "Louise. Floyd," I said, nodding my head toward both of them, "I'm real sorry about your loss."

Their response was less than cordial, I thought. They both sneered.

I turned and headed toward the door. As I went, I tried to recall the exact words of Rigdon's suicide note. How did it go? "I guess it's pretty clear by now how bad I feel about what happened. It's no use going on. I'm ending it once and for all. Good-bye forever." And then there had been Rigdon's signature.

Which Louise herself had said was genuine.

I also remembered what Bertie Lee had told me about

the break-up. She'd said that Rigdon had talked to her face-to-face. In fact, she hadn't mentioned a note at all.

So what exactly did all this mean?

I took still another deep breath, and went over it all again in my mind. Assuming what Bertie Lee had told me was the truth—and this, I knew, was a big assumption—then it sounded to me as if Bertie Lee had never gotten the note Rigdon had written her.

It might be a reach, but it seemed to me as if somebody could've read the note, realized that it could possibly be read to have another meaning, and then could've taken the note to use at a later date.

Which meant, then, that somebody could've been planning to murder Rigdon and make it look like a suicide for quite some time.

I swallowed uneasily. Poor Rigdon. He'd done the right thing and ended an affair, and the very words he'd used to end it had apparently made it easy for somebody to end his life.

It was just like my daddy used to say: Sometimes you can't win for losing.

I stepped outside into the parking lot and found that Bertie Lee had joined Curtis out there.

Bertie Lee had apparently dressed to the hilt for the occasion. She was wearing a black sleeveless dress, black shoes, black hose, and a tiny black feathered hat with a veil pulled down over her face. That is, the veil had been pulled down over the half of her face you could see.

Bertie Lee may have been dressed appropriately, but what she had to say to Curtis was anything but comforting. "You ruined the whole damn thing, that's what you did!" she was yelling. "You ruined poor Rigdon's beautiful funeral!"

Curtis did not look contrite. "Well, I sure hope I did! Rigdon don't deserve no beautiful funeral. Not after what he done!"

Curtis apparently had not paid a whole lot of attention during grammar lessons back in elementary school. I couldn't help staring at him as I headed across the parking lot in his and Bertie Lee's direction. No doubt about it, old Curtis certainly sounded as if he were capable of phoning in at least one of my death threats.

By the time I'd gotten to them, Bertie Lee had taken off her hat with the black veil and she was shaking it in Curtis's face. "You humiliated me in front of the whole town!"

Curtis's answer to that was a snort. "I humiliated *you?* Are you kiddin' me? You humiliated me! Carrying on with my best friend, for God's sake! Why, you ain't nothing but a tramp!"

Bertie Lee glared right back at her husband. For a split second I thought she was briefly considering ramming her hat down Curtis's throat. "And you're nothing but an asshole! Ruining a dead man's reputation like that!"

Curtis's eyes looked as if somebody had just lit a fire right behind them. "Oh yeah? Well, I might be an asshole, but I'm real glad everybody inside knows now exactly what kind of man they're about to bury today!" He took a step toward Bertie Lee, sticking his face right up next to hers. "You hear that? I'm glad! GLAD, do you hear?"

I don't see how Bertie Lee could've failed to hear him. Hell, there were probably folks in Tennessee who could make him out clear as anything.

I don't mind telling you that listening to Curtis and Bertie Lee yell at each other was a real unpleasant thing to have to do. Not only because it was a real ugly scene, but because it also reminded me of the kind of arguments that Claudine and I had indulged in toward the last of our marriage. Only, unlike Curtis, I hadn't known for sure at the time that Claudine was really running around on me. I'd only suspected.

And, unlike Bertie Lee, Claudine had lied her head off right up to the end.

Matter of fact, Claudine didn't admit she'd even had an affair until she was walking out the door. Then, of course, she was kind enough to let me know that she'd not only had one, she'd had several.

One had been with my own partner in homicide.

Which, I have to say, I was just about as happy to hear about as Curtis here.

Curtis was pretty much demonstrating his good mood when I walked up. "Yeah, what do YOU want NOW?"

The answer to that one was, of course: to be any place but here.

I didn't say that, though. I just said, "I want to ask Bertie Lee a question, if you don't mind."

"Well, yeah, I DO mind. You get what I'm saying? I MIND A LOT."

Curtis was now taking a step toward me, doubling up his fists. I got the feeling Curtis wanted to hit somebody real bad and he didn't much care who it turned out to be.

Bertie Lee, however, moved between us. "Well, *I* don't mind answering some questions." She threw Curtis an angry glare. "In fact, I'd LOVE to!"

Obviously, Bertie Lee was just saying this to enrage Curtis.

Which, I have to hand it to her, certainly worked.

Curtis's face turned blood red, and he started clenching and unclenching his fists.

His obvious fury made me wonder all over again if he might not have been the one who killed Rigdon and made it look like a suicide. I mean, I could sure sympathize with him being so mad and all, but Curtis seemed almost totally out of control, he was so angry.

With Curtis looking as if any minute he was going to do an impression of Mount Vesuvius, I, of course, did what I think any detective would've done under the circumstances. I started talking as fast as I could. In fact, I was talking so fast, what came out almost sounded like one word.

"AllIwanttoknowBertieLeeisifyouevergotanotefrom Rigdonbreakingupwithyou?"

I probably should've slowed down a tad. Bertie Lee was now staring at me, a puzzled frown on her face. "Huh?" she said.

So I had to repeat the entire thing. With Curtis still clenching and unclenching his fists right next to me. "All I want to know," I said to Bertie Lee, "is if you ever got a note from Rigdon. A note saying he was breaking up with you?"

This time Bertie Lee immediately shook her head. "Nope, can't say that I did." Her one good eye looked to be perfectly guileless.

"Are you sure? Because I've had more than one person tell me that Rigdon did write you a note like that."

Bertie Lee was still shaking her head. "No he didn't," she said. "I didn't get no note."

It was at this point that I began to seriously doubt what I'd just been suspecting. Curtis could very well be innocent after all. Because now he sure acted genuinely surprised to hear what I'd just said.

"You mean to tell me," he said, his eyes getting real round, "that Rigdon was supposed to have written a *note* to say good-bye to Bertie Lee?"

He was looking straight at me, fiddling now with his string tie.

I stared right back at him and nodded. "That's what I was told."

Curtis now not only acted surprised, he acted down-right amused. "You mean to tell me that Rigdon thought so much of Bertie Lee that he just wrote her a 'Dear John' letter?"

This time Curtis didn't wait for me to answer. He slapped his thigh, threw back his head and laughed.

I have not met too many folks who can convincingly fake a laugh.

Curtis's laugh sure sounded genuine to me.

"Why, that's a hoot!" he said, wiping his eyes. "That's a damn hoot!"

I just looked at him, feeling kind of let down. Once I eliminated Curtis, who was left? Who might've known about the note—and also had the opportunity to take the thing?

Not to mention, of all the people who might've known about the note, who of them would've also known about the scene at Frank's in order to take advantage of the opportunity it suddenly presented?

Bertie Lee was now glaring at Curtis. Evidently she didn't find the idea of a "Dear John" letter anywhere near as amusing as her husband. "What the hell are you cackling about? You sound like a chicken that's just laid an egg!"

Curtis apparently didn't care. He kept right on cackling.

I stared at Bertie Lee. From what I could remember, she definitely knew about the scene at Frank's. And she could be lying about never getting the note.

Maybe Bertie Lee *had* gotten the note, and saved it to pay Rigdon back permanently for dumping her.

Then again, Agnes and Louise also both knew about what had happened at Frank's. Whether they'd known about the note, however, was anybody's guess. If Rigdon had been as close to Ernal as Agnes said, then Rigdon might've told Ernal about the note he'd written Bertie Lee. And Ernal might've shared what he knew with Agnes.

"You're the chicken!" Curtis was now saying, pointing his finger at Bertie Lee. "In fact, you're a dumb cluck!"

This last evidently really struck his funny bone, because he all but collapsed, laughing and pointing at his wife.

I was still going over possible suspects.

Floyd, Louise's husband, for example, had by his own admission also known about the note. But had he known about the scene at Frank's? Had Louise told Floyd what Rigdon had told her?

With all these questions running through my mind, my head was beginning to rerun the pain symphony once again. I rubbed my temples. If the note had been saved to make Rigdon's death look like a suicide, then one of these people had been planning to murder Rigdon for a good two weeks. But why? Even more telling, why *now?* What had Rigdon been doing lately that would suddenly make him a target for murder?

The only thing I could possibly think of was Rigdon's plan to put on the addition to his house. That seemed to be the only thing that had apparently been new in Rigdon's life.

Folks were now beginning to leave the funeral home, to get in their cars to go to the grave site. As they went, quite a few of them openly stared at Bertie Lee and Curtis. Bertie Lee was doing her best to give them something to stare at. She was now screaming in Curtis's face, "Shut up! SHUT UP THAT LAUGHING!"

I headed straight for Agnes again.

She'd just walked out of Merryman's and was standing just outside the funeral home entrance, obviously waiting for somebody. I was pretty sure she was standing there waiting for Ernal, so I started talking real fast. "Look, I know this is a bad time and all, but could you answer a couple more questions?"

Agnes was staring at Bertie Lee and Curtis, her thin mouth pinched with distaste.

"Agnes?" I said. "I need your help. I really am trying to find out who murdered Rigdon."

Agnes's eyes got quite a bit bigger. "I thought you were just saying that on account of what Louise was saying about you."

"No, Agnes, I really do think Rigdon was murdered."

Agnes's only reaction was to press her thin lips together even tighter. "I can't believe that," she said, shaking her Gibson-girl head from side to side. "Of course," she added with a shrug, "I can't believe he kilt himself neither."

Agnes had started blinking real bad, so I started talking even faster. "How long have you lived across the street from Rigdon's house?"

Agnes looked surprised that I was even asking such a thing. "Why, ever since that house was built twenty-two years ago."

"Do you recall if there's ever been any construction on the house?"

Agnes was no longer looking surprised. She was looking as if maybe I was nuttier than Rigdon had been. "Nobody has ever done anything to that house, Haskell, except paint it." She cocked her head in my direction. "The first owners were Rigdon's parents, you know."

As a matter of fact, I didn't know, but I nodded anyway.

"When Rigdon's mother died and his father took off, the property naturally went to Rigdon, being as how he was the oldest child." Agnes blinked some more and then she hurried on, her ragged voice the only thing that betrayed any emotion. "The house was rented for a while, up until Rigdon was old enough himself to move in." Agnes drew a long, shaky breath.

I swallowed and asked, "You don't know where I could get the keys to Rigdon's house, do you?"

Agnes's eyes were getting real round again, so I hurried to add, "I just want to do a little looking around, that's all."

"Why, I got the keys right here," Agnes said. Then she just stood there, staring at me for a long moment. As if she were making up her mind. Finally she opened her purse, rummaged around in it for a second, and then handed me a set of keys.

The key ring had a rabbit's foot dangling from it.

I might've guessed it.

Agnes had evidently not been waiting for Ernal after all. It was Louise and Floyd who walked out of the funeral home and joined her. Agnes was still watching me, as a matter of fact, as I headed across the parking lot toward Elmo's Thunderbird and as she headed toward Louise and Floyd's truck. As she went, her eyes looked downright puzzled. And more than a little worried.

I hadn't taken two steps when I was intercepted by Imogene.

For a second there I actually thought she'd come over to make up.

"Haskell," Imogene said, "I just want to tell you one thing. You're a damn fool if you don't realize that Claudine is trying to get back together with you."

She went out of her way to tell me this? This wasn't exactly news. In fact, I believe she'd already pretty much covered this subject at length.

"Imogene," I said, "I just want to tell *you* one thing. You don't know what you're talking about. Claudine is no more interested in me than the man in the moon."

Okay, so that was more than one thing. I got carried away.

Imogene just looked at me. Real level-like.

I gathered from her look that she apparently thought that Claudine and the man in the moon might make a real attractive couple.

"Imogene, I mean it," I said, "Claudine is only interested in me in a purely professional way."

Imogene actually rolled her eyes when I said this.

"I mean it," I said again. To back up my argument, I showed her the note Claudine had thrown at me this morning.

Imogene stared at that note in much the same way she'd stared at me moments before. I wasn't sure, but I didn't think she looked impressed. She fingered the edge of the paper. "Hm," she said, "this is not exactly the kind of paper you'd think a macho-type ex-boyfriend would pen a few threatening words on, is it?"

My eyes followed hers. The paper *was* a fine linen. With a watermark. "Maybe it was all the guy had on hand?" I said.

Even I had to admit that sounded a little lame.

Imogene must've thought so too. She threw up her hands in disgust and walked off.

Without looking back.

I would've gone right after her, except—to tell you the truth—I couldn't think of a thing to tell her that I hadn't already.

Instead I turned and headed toward Elmo's Thunderbird. Most everybody was gone by now, having headed out to the Pigeon Fork Cemetery for Rigdon's burial. I, on the other hand, intended to head in the opposite direction—to Rigdon's house. Maybe this time if I poked around in there long enough, I'd find out what Rigdon was up to that might've led to his death.

I'd reached the Thunderbird by now, so I unlocked the door on the driver's side and got inside.

At which point I discovered a real disadvantage to having power door locks.

When I turned the key to unlock the door on the driver's side, I, of course, unlocked all the other doors too. That made it real easy for Ernal Bewley to jerk open the door on the passenger side and get in beside me.

For a second I just stared at him. "Ernal?" I said.

Ernal's heavy Lincoln eyebrows were almost meeting in the middle. "Drive, Haskell," he said. "Drive to your house."

It was then, of course, that I noticed the gun.

And the way Ernal's bony hand was shaking a little as he pointed the thing in my direction.

I could be wrong, but suddenly it seemed to me as if Ernal was looking less and less like Lincoln.

And more and more like John Wilkes Booth.

CHAPTER
14

It has been my experience that a gun pointed in your direction looms unbelievably large in your mind. At that moment, for example, Ernal's gun looked to me to be just about the size of Mount McKinley. It was a wonder, in fact, that he had been able to get a thing that huge inside Elmo's Thunderbird.

Moreover, it was actually awe-inspiring the way Ernal managed to hold that enormous thing pointed at my side. "I said, DRIVE!" he said. "Get this thing started, and drive to your house."

I wasn't trying to be difficult, but with Mount McKinley pointed at me, it was real hard to follow what Ernal was saying. "Huh?" I said. I couldn't seem to focus on anything other than that mountainous weapon.

Ernal thoughtfully offered encouragement by poking me in the ribs with the barrel of the thing. "Move! NOW!"

Encouragement like that was definitely all I needed.

I put the car in Drive, and Ernal and I sailed out of Merryman's parking lot.

"Why are we going to my house?" We were now headed down the state road at about forty-five miles an hour, and the speedometer was still climbing.

My question seemed like a pretty obvious thing to ask, but Ernal didn't seem to appreciate my curiosity one bit. He sneered at me. With that big Lincoln lower lip, it did not make for a pretty picture. "We're going there because that happens to be the place where, unfortunately, you're about to be overcome with remorse."

I blinked. "Remorse?" I said. If Ernal really wanted to know, I was pretty much overcome with remorse right now. I was feeling damn sorry I'd ever borrowed Elmo's car with the power door locks. A rental car with ordinary manual door locks would've done just as well.

Ernal sneered again. The man evidently had a real sneering talent. It appeared to be something that came naturally to him. "Yeah, Haskell," he said, "you're about to become so broke up over causing poor Rigdon's suicide that you're going to take your own life."

I blinked again. "No kidding," I said. I eased up a little on the accelerator. If I was driving to my own death, I didn't particularly want to speed.

Ernal was so intent on what he was saying, he didn't seem to notice that we'd slowed down a little. "Yep, Haskell, you're gonna hang yourself—exactly like Rigdon done."

When you're a private detective, even one who's being held at gunpoint, you don't really want to look as if everything you're hearing is a surprise. It pretty much ruins your credibility if your mouth keeps dropping open from shock. I couldn't help it, though. Finding out that it had been Ernal who'd staged Rigdon's suicide caught me pretty much off guard. I turned to stare at my passenger. "You? It was *you?*" I could barely choke out the words.

Ernal returned my stare. Almost defiantly. "Yeah, it was me." He snorted. "And you were going to find out about it soon enough. Oh, yeah, you were going to put it together. You were going to keep on snooping and snooping and snooping until you knew everything."

Oddly enough, Ernal did not sound as if I should take his comments as a compliment.

"I saw Agnes give you those keys, you know. I saw," Ernal said. "But now none of that matters. On accounta you're not going to live long enough to tell anybody what I done."

I done? Ernal's bad grammar sounded kind of familiar.

"I reckon it was you, then, who called my office, threatening my life."

He nodded. "Yep, that was me, all right." He actually sounded proud. "Matter of fact, I called three different times, disguising my voice each time I called so's your secretary wouldn't know it was the same person every time." Ernal drew a long breath. "Yep, that's how hard I tried to warn you off."

I don't know. Somehow, I didn't feel like thanking him for his effort.

Particularly after Ernal drew yet another long breath and said, "But you wouldn't listen, would you? You just wouldn't pay me no never mind."

The man clearly needed real help with his grammar.

Still, I had no trouble whatsoever understanding exactly what he was saying when he went on and added, "So, Haskell, how's hanging sound to you?"

I kind of wished I hadn't understood him, because now that Ernal mentioned it, I couldn't exactly say that hanging sounded all that great. In fact, I couldn't help but get a quick flashback of the way poor Rigdon had looked the afternoon I'd found him. I don't consider myself particularly vain or anything, but the thought of exiting this earth with a purple face pretty much left me cold.

I cleared my throat. "You know, Ernal," I said, "you don't suppose I could just shoot myself while I'm at it?"

Ernal, well, you know what he did then. The man, no doubt about it, *was* a sneering natural. "No, you can't shoot yourself," he said. He sounded as if the subject was not open to discussion. "I know damn well that there's ways the law can test to find out if you were really the one that pulled the trigger. So, in order for it to look right, I'd have to just hand you over my gun for you to do it yourself."

I just looked at him. So? There certainly didn't seem to be any problem in *my* mind with his handing me his gun.

Not surprisingly, there did seem to be a problem with it in Ernal's mind. "I mean, what do you think I am, *stupid?*" he said.

I decided it was probably best if I didn't answer that one. After all, did he really expect me to think that somebody who intended to kill me in the next few minutes or so was *smart?*

Ernal was now poking Mount McKinley in my side again. "You know, this whole situation is really all your fault."

I gave him a quick sideways glance. If *that* was true, I really was going to be overcome with remorse.

"If you'd just done things like you were supposed to," Ernal went on, "*I* wouldn't have to do this." He punctuated that last sentence with another poke in my side.

I was getting real tired of Ernal poking me. My ribs were still bruised some, so it really didn't feel any too great. I also couldn't help but idly wonder if Ernal had Mount McKinley's safety on. I realize, of course, that this might sound like a real dumb thing to worry about under the circumstances. Being as how I was supposed to be dead real soon anyway. Still, I did prefer to put off dying until the last possible moment.

"You're *making* me do this, you know," Ernal was going on.

His voice was getting almost as shaky as his gun hand. Like maybe old Ernal was working himself up into some kind of anger frenzy.

This is not the sort of thing you want to see in a person pointing a gun at you. In fact, seeing just how nervous and agitated Ernal was becoming was making *me* feel downright nervous and agitated too.

To calm him down some, I forced myself to sound real nonchalant. "Oh? How do you figure I'm making you do this?"

I could've been asking how he figured his income tax, my tone was that casual. And yet, to tell you the truth, I was a lot more than casually interested in finding out what I was doing to encourage him. Lord knows, I'd be more than happy to stop doing whatever it happened to be. Hell, I think I was pretty safe in saying I'd never do it again.

Ernal's sneer this time was one of his best. It curled the entire left side of his mouth. An even less pretty picture than before. "You're supposed to be suspecting Curtis now," he said. For emphasis, apparently, he poked my side again. *"That's* who I wanted you to think killed Rigdon."

I tried not to wince, but Ernal was poking the exact same place time and time again. I was pretty sure if I pointed this out to him, however, and asked him maybe to choose another place to poke, he would not oblige. Matter of fact, just judging from his repetitive sneers, I'd say if I called this little matter to his attention, he'd particularly enjoy poking me a whole lot harder. And even more often.

I don't know. For a man who looked like Lincoln, Ernal seemed to be singularly lacking in compassion.

I decided I'd just skip bringing up the side-poking issue.

Tomorrow, though, my side was going to be real sore.

On the other hand, to look on the bright side, there looked to be a real good chance I wouldn't be here tomorrow to feel it.

I gripped the steering wheel a little tighter. What a cheery thought.

Speaking of cheery, Ernal's tone now was not. In fact, it seemed to have taken a definite turn for the worse. He sounded downright testy. "That's why I went to all the trouble of phoning Curtis this morning and telling him all about Rigdon and Bertie Lee. So's you would end up suspecting *Curtis.*"

I blinked again at that one. Then it had been *Ernal* who'd made the anonymous phone call? My goodness, he did seem to enjoy reaching out and touching someone.

Anonymously, of course.

"You know, Haskell," Ernal was now saying, "you're just like Rigdon." His tone had turned contemptuous. "You just won't do what's best for you."

I wasn't sure what he was getting at, but I wasn't about to argue. As far as I'm concerned, if a man with a gun tells me something, it's the gospel truth.

"I reckon you're right," I said, keeping my eyes on the road ahead.

"I didn't want to kill Rigdon, you know, any more than I want to kill you," he added.

Now what do you say to that? Then, *don't? Break* my heart?

"I really never wanted to hurt anybody." Ernal's tone was now no longer contemptuous. In fact, he actually sounded as if he might be getting a little weepy on me. If he did, I knew what to do this time. I was *not* giving him a Kleenex. "I considered that boy my own son, I really did. But Rigdon made me do it, you know, he *made* me."

I nodded and tried my best to look sympathetic.

Ernal returned my nod, his voice almost eager now. "I tried, you know, I really tried to talk Rigdon out of building that addition to his house, but he just wouldn't listen."

I was still nodding. Sympathetic as ever, I hoped.

My thinking here was to try to encourage Ernal to keep talking. Back when I was a cop in Louisville, I'd been taught that this is the thing you're supposed to do in situations like this. Keep the gunman talking.

Until you see a chance to go for his weapon.

It didn't look like keeping Ernal talking was going to be hard. He was talking faster and faster now, as if it were almost a relief to finally get to tell somebody all about what he'd done.

"Can you believe," he was saying, "I actually stole dismembered animal paws out of Rigdon's workshop, and I dipped them in mud, and I faked footprints all over the place. *That's* the kind of trouble I went to."

I dropped the sympathetic look, and now tried to look impressed.

"Oh yeah," Ernal said, "I really tried. I did everything I could to save that boy."

Ernal's eagerness to talk was not exactly a surprise. This is another thing I'd learned back in Louisville when I was working homicide. It's not all that uncommon for killers to actually *want* to talk about their crime. In detail. I reckon the main reason for this is that a major down side to committing the perfect murder is that you never really get the opportunity to tell folks just how brilliant you've been. For a lot of killers, would you believe, it isn't so much guilt over the crime that starts eating them up inside, it's that they just start hankering for a chance to brag.

Ernal was pretty much behaving typically. He was talking up a storm now, his tone more and more eager. "I even put friggin' *razor blades* in the tomatoes in Rigdon's garden to throw a scare into the boy," he said.

I nodded, doing sympathy again. As I nodded, I took a quick look at Mount McKinley. There didn't seem to be any way in hell that I could take that thing away from Ernal without catching a few bullets myself.

Not to mention, now actually being in the situation that had only been discussed in class when I was a cop, I could see a real problem with the Keep the Gunman Talking Plan. Just because a guy was talking didn't necessarily mean that he was too preoccupied to shoot you. It wasn't exactly like walking and chewing gum.

We were now approaching on the left the one-lane gravel road that, after about a mile of winding past several fenced pastures and over a small bridge, leads directly to my driveway. As I slowed down and made the turn, I gave Ernal a quick sideways glance.

Oh yeah, I'd say Ernal looked as if he were perfectly capable of walking, chewing gum, talking, and shooting me, all at the same time. Without it being any kind of a stretch in the least.

He was sounding testy again. "I did all these things trying to get Rigdon to forget about his damn museum, but Rigdon kept right on."

I gave Ernal yet another sideways glance. "Well, you tried your best," I said.

Ernal's eyes actually looked pleading. "I did, didn't I?"

I nodded again. "Kids today. They just won't listen."

Ernal, unbelievably, nodded his head. "Now that's the truth," he said.

While he was lamenting the state of the younger generation, I was trying real hard not to let what I was suddenly feeling show in my face. Because something had finally sunk in. If, as he'd just admitted, he had put the baneberries in Rigdon's cereal and footprinted the table around the bowl, then he had also jimmied my brakes and stamped animal footprints on the hood of my truck.

You remember, that truck that I liked. That Ford truck with the great paint job. Midnight-blue with a metallic flake.

Ernal had also given me this here broken arm. And he'd helped me make Imogene real mad at me.

What a guy.

For a second I could hardly breathe, I was so furious. I found myself gripping the steering wheel so tight, my knuckles went white.

Beside me, Ernal's mood had not improved either. He was sneering again. He followed his sneer up with another poke with Mount McKinley.

Have I mentioned how REALLY tired I was of him doing this?

"I reckon," Ernal said, "you know why I did all that stuff with the footprints, don't you?"

The answer to that question, of course, was, *Sure, because you're an asshole,* but I knew that wasn't what Ernal wanted to hear. "I got me a guess," I said.

Ernal actually grinned at me then. He sat there with that huge gun pointed in my direction and grinned as if he were proud of himself.

You know how you never see a picture of Abraham Lincoln with a big grin on his face? Up to that moment I'd always thought Lincoln never smiled because of all his sorrow over the Civil War and all. Now I realized there was another real good reason. A grinning Lincoln looked a little scary.

"I was trying to make Rigdon sound like a nut, so that if he told anybody what was happening, they'd never believe him." This time Ernal not only sneered, he snickered.

I was now feeling real cold. Ernal's plan had worked, all right. It had even worked with me. Poor Rigdon had come to me for help, and I'd let him down.

Fury was now washing over me in waves.

Ernal and I had traveled by now a good three-quarters of the way down the gravel road. A lot of the times when I travel this road, one of my neighbor's cows gets out and blocks my way. Or one of my other neighbor's suicidal chickens flies toward my car. Or runs across the road directly under my wheels.

All of which causes me to have to slow down. At the very least. And, occasionally, to come to a complete stop. For several minutes. And, in the case of the cow, as much as an hour.

Today not a single cow was blocking the road. And when I passed the kamikaze chickens, they actually had the nerve to just stand there and watch me go by.

Wouldn't you know it?

Ernal poked me with that damn gun yet AGAIN. "Actually, I wouldn't have minded if folks thought you were a nut, too, Haskell," he said. "Particularly the way you were nosing around, looking into Rigdon's museum plans and all."

At this point I really wanted to ask why Rigdon's addition would've been such a bad idea, but I sure didn't want to ask anything that would make Ernal any more agitated than he already was.

And he seemed to be getting real agitated again. "Can you believe," Ernal said, "Rigdon was so dumb, he actually told me about the affair he was having with Bertie Lee?" With his left hand—not the one holding Mount McKinley—he scratched at the sideburns on that side of his craggy face. "Rigdon talked the whole thing over with me, and he even took my advice about ending it. I told him the best way was a clean break. That he ought to just write Bertie Lee a note. That there was no use in him seeing her ever again."

I swallowed. Poor Rigdon. He'd walked right into his own death, with his eyes wide open.

Ernal obviously did not look at it quite the same way I did. His voice was now almost gleeful as he said, "I even told Rigdon what he ought to say, can you believe it?"

Oh yeah, I could believe it, all right.

Ernal was shaking his head and grinning again. "And *then,* to top it off, Rigdon even gave me the note he'd written, to *deliver* to Bertie Lee for him! God, what an idiot!"

I didn't say it, of course, but I thought it. *Yeah, Rigdon was an idiot, all right, to ever trust a scumbag like you.*

Obviously Rigdon had never once suspected that the note had not been delivered. Even when Bertie Lee had showed up at his door, just as if she'd never read it. Rigdon had, no doubt, just thought that Bertie Lee was refusing to accept what he'd written to her. He must've thought Bertie Lee had come by his house to try to lure him back.

Ernal and I had finally arrived at the bottom of my driveway. I can't rightly say I was real glad to be there.

I put the Thunderbird in its lowest gear and we started up my hill. Already I could hear Rip trying out a few tentative barks. More or less just tuning up.

Ernal heard Rip too. He gave my side still another goddamned poke and said, "If you don't want that animal shot, you'd better tie him up the second we get out of this here car."

Ernal didn't have to tell me twice.

I was expecting Rip to start doing his psychodog routine as soon as I got out of the Thunderbird and he realized it was me. Rip, however, surprised me. He only barked a couple times, and then he just sat there at the top of the steps, whimpering a little.

Ernal, of course, was following me up the stairs. With the gun pointed at my back.

I decided Rip must've recognized the thing in Ernal's hand. After all, Rip had seen a thing like that not too long ago. Maybe old Rip was remembering just how this gray thing had spit at him once before.

That must've been it, because that fool dog was whimpering real bad by the time I reached the top step where he was sitting. "Hey, boy, it's okay," I said.

It wasn't okay, of course, but I didn't think Rip would know the difference. Apparently, though, he did. He kept right on whimpering the entire time I was leading him by his collar over to the chain I keep looped around one of the posts on my deck. I always keep the chain there just in case Rip gets too frisky in the presence of company.

Of course, he certainly wasn't frisky now.

In fact, that fool dog barely seemed to notice that we even had company. He hardly gave Ernal a glance. Rip appeared, in fact, to be far too busy whimpering.

Rip may not have been staring at Ernal, but Ernal was sure staring at him. "Nice watch dog you got there," he said.

Oh yeah, that was a smirk on Ernal's face.

I decided that didn't exactly deserve a reply.

Not that I could've thought of anything to say. Clearly, Rip had had better days. I wasn't sure what had gotten into him.

I hooked the end of the chain to Rip's collar, and he didn't howl like he usually does or anything. He just sat there staring at me, an expression in his brown eyes I couldn't decipher.

That's when it occurred to me that maybe Rip was picking up on just exactly how much trouble I was in.

Maybe *that's* why he kept on whimpering. And quivering all over. And doing a nervous little dance with his front feet.

On the other hand, maybe he was just upset because I wasn't immediately carrying him down the steps to the yard.

I was pretty sure, though, that there wasn't much use in asking Ernal if he'd put off murdering me until Rip had done his business. Ernal was clearly getting impatient. "All right, all right," he said, gesturing toward my front door with his gun. "Let's go."

When Ernal spoke, Rip's whimpering went up a couple of decibels.

Ernal smirked again. "My, my," he said, staring at Rip. "You could easily get that dog confused with Rin Tin Tin, couldn't you?"

I took a deep breath. It was bad enough that the guy intended to kill me, but did he have to insult my dog too?

As it turned out, I found out the second I walked through my front door what it was that was making Rip act so odd. Even for him.

I'd taken no more than three steps into my living room, with Ernal right in back of me, when—directly ahead of me, framed by the door leading into my dining room—Claudine sprang into view.

"Surprise!" she yelled. "SUR-pri-i-ize!"

Now, *that* was pretty much of an understatement.

I was surprised. And Ernal was surprised. And even Claudine herself was surprised.

Standing there in the doorway, arms spread wide, Claudine was wearing a big red bow around her waist.

And red spike heels.

And nothing else.

CHAPTER
15

For a moment it seemed as if all three of us were frozen in time.

First, there was Claudine, standing over there in my dining room doorway, without a stitch on.

If you didn't count her red bow and her red shoes.

I was pretty sure, though, that most folks wouldn't count them.

I certainly didn't think Claudine herself was counting them. She appeared to be looking past me, directly at Ernal. Her large blue eyes seemed to have grown about three sizes bigger, and her lipsticked mouth was making an almost perfect ruby-red O.

Next, of course, there was me, standing motionless in the middle of my living room and thinking: *Well, what do you know, Imogene might actually be right, after all. Claudine really could be making a move on me.*

And finally, of course, there was Ernal, right in back of me. Holding the gun still pointed at my back.

Oddly enough, Ernal didn't look so much like Lincoln

anymore, being as how his eyes didn't appear to be anywhere near as deep-set as usual. In fact, I'd say Ernal's eyes appeared to be popping pretty much right out of his head. I reckon if he was still looking anything at all like Lincoln, it would've had to have been Lincoln having a fit of apoplexy.

Not only were Ernal's eyes popping, but his mouth was hanging open. And every bit of air in his lungs appeared to be rushing right out of him.

Lord. Old Ernal sounded like a worn-out tire deflating.

Our mutual frozen moment seemed to go on and on, but in reality it probably only lasted a split second.

And then every one of us started moving again.

Claudine was the first to spring into action. She let out this little horrified squeal as her own huge eyes darted from Ernal's face back to mine.

After which she immediately started trying to cover herself with her hands.

Unfortunately—or maybe *fortunately,* depending on how you looked at it—there was an awful lot of Claudine that needed covering, and Claudine has never exactly been a real fast thinker on her feet. Now she couldn't seem to make up her mind which parts of her needed covering the most.

First she covered her bottom half with both hands, which, of course, left both breasts in full view. Next, she covered her breasts, which, of course, left her bottom half exposed. Then she covered her bottom half all over again.

She went on like this for some time.

It was quite a show. If you could judge from Ernal's appreciative wheezing in back of me.

I was, of course, at a distinct advantage. I'd pretty much seen this show before.

Ernal, however, was seeing it for the first time. His eyes

were bobbing up and down, up and down, like two Ping-Pong balls.

Oh yeah, I'd say Old Ernal did appear to be downright distracted. For a few moments, anyway.

"Lord have mercy," he managed to say, his voice ragged.

The Lord might've had mercy on him, but I sure didn't.

I saw my chance.

And I took it.

While Ernal's eyes were still playing Ping-Pong, I wheeled around. At the same time, I stepped to one side so that his gun was no longer pointing my way.

And I hit him.

As a matter of fact, I took great pleasure in clobbering Ernal as hard as I could. Right in the sideburns. I hit him with the only weapon I had handy. The cast on my left arm.

Ernal's Ping-Pong eyes were still bouncing when I connected.

After that, of course, I'm not exactly sure what happened. Being as how the excruciating pain from this little maneuver caused everything around me to suddenly go black.

I got the impression, however, as I immediately started heading rapidly for the floor, that Ernal was falling too, right next to me. It even seemed as if I heard his gun hitting the floor and skidding away. I couldn't be sure, though. By the time my face hit the hardwood, *everything* seemed as if it were skidding away.

And then, suddenly, everything was gone and the world went solid black. Like a television program I'd just snapped off.

When I came to, I was lying flat on my stomach on my living room floor, with my jaw aching.

A groan to my left made me turn in that direction. That's when I realized that I must've been right about Ernal falling after all. There he was, lying on his back. Moaning to beat the band.

I couldn't help it. I lay there for a moment, fervently hoping I'd hurt Ernal real bad.

Hell, it was the least I could do for Rigdon.

Ernal appeared to be just coming to, much as I was. In fact, the only difference between us seemed to be that he was moaning and holding his head. And I was moaning and holding my arm.

I don't mind telling you, my arm was hurting so bad, it actually brought tears to my eyes.

Not that I was crying, mind you. It was like the way your eyes water when they get something in them. That's all it was.

Actually, there was one good thing about my arm hurting so bad. It definitely took my mind off how bad my jaw was hurting.

I was in such pain, in fact, that I had a passing worry about Ernal, starting to move beside me. If he managed to get to his feet and tried to take me on, I couldn't say for sure I'd win that one. In fact, I'd say the odds might've been in Ernal's favor.

As it turned out, though, I didn't have to find out.

I'd been right about the gun falling out of Ernal's hand. It had evidently skidded across the floor in Claudine's direction, because she now had Ernal's gun in her hand and was pointing it directly at him.

This was a first. The first time I'd ever seen Claudine with a weapon in her hand and been downright delighted to see it there.

Of course, it might've been the first time she'd had a weapon and not been intending to use it on me.

When I noticed the gun, I also noticed something else.

Evidently Ernal and I had been out for only moments because Claudine was still wearing exactly what she'd been wearing when I hit the floor.

Not a thing.

If, of course, you didn't count the bow and the shoes.

"Haskell?" Claudine said. "Are you okay? Answer me. Are you okay? Haskell, come on now, speak to me. . . ."

I started to nod my head, but that made me feel a little sick to my stomach. "I'm fine," I said, and to prove it I started to get to my feet.

It took me a couple of tries, but I made it.

"Oh, thank God!" Claudine said. She was still holding the gun on Ernal, but she moved to my side and wrapped one arm around me. "Thank God you're okay!"

Ernal had scrambled to a sitting position by then, and when Claudine hugged me, Ernal actually threw me an envious look.

I think he might've let Claudine shoot him if she would just agree to hug him first.

"Thank God, thank God, thank God," Claudine was saying. "Oh, Haskell, you had me worried for a second there!"

I probably would've been more impressed with how relieved Claudine was that I wasn't bad hurt if she hadn't immediately gone on to say, "Now *you* can hold this damn thing on him!" Claudine stuck the gun in my hand, shaking her blond head with distaste.

"Haskell, you *know* how I hate guns!" she added as she turned to walk across the living room. I could see where she was headed. She was intending to get the afghan off my couch. The tattered multicolored one, you remember, with the two corners missing that Rip had chewed off. The one that a few days earlier Claudine had stared at with obvious distaste.

Apparently, she no longer cared what kind of condition that afghan was in. In fact, she seemed almost anxious to get hold of the thing and wrap herself up in it.

Claudine, however, definitely could've moved faster. I reckon since everybody in the room had already gotten a good look at her, though, she didn't particularly see the need to hurry.

Or maybe she just wanted to take advantage of one last opportunity to impress upon me exactly what I'd been missing since our divorce.

She really didn't have to remind me. I knew. Lord knows, right after our divorce, I'd laid awake nights on end, remembering.

I sort of wished that Claudine would've hurried it up, though.

Mainly because right about then somebody new appeared at my front door.

I had no warning at all. I hadn't even heard Rip bark.

Of course, I had been a tad distracted.

It was Imogene. Apparently she didn't see Claudine right away. I don't think she even saw Ernal, or that she even really focused on what I was now holding in my right hand.

One reason for this was that when Imogene opened my front door, her eyes were on the floor. Another reason was that she was obviously concentrating on what she wanted to tell me.

"Haskell," Imogene was saying as she opened my door and walked through, "I've been thinking it over, and I realize I—I've been acting like a fool. I want you to know I'm real sorry, and—"

It was right about then that Imogene's eyes fell on Ernal. Sitting on the floor to her left.

Imogene lifted her eyes to mine, and then, of course, immediately saw Claudine. In fact, Imogene saw quite a bit of Claudine since Claudine hadn't quite gotten around to completely covering herself with the afghan.

Matter of fact, all Claudine had managed to do by then was just to pick it up.

"Hi, Emma Jane," Claudine said.

Imogene just stood there, right inside my door, her eyes getting real, real round.

First, Imogene stared at Claudine.

Then she stared at Claudine's red bow.

And finally she turned her head and stared at me.

Imogene's stare seemed to be saying, loud and clear, "I told you so."

I took a deep breath. What I was thinking, of course, was that it would probably have been best if I'd just stayed unconscious.

In fact, going into a coma right about now sounded like an awful good idea.

CHAPTER
16

Once Ernal was arrested and pretty much permanently housed behind bars, he started spilling his guts. Vergil, believe it or not, actually phoned me at home one night and told me everything Ernal had said. "I reckon you deserve to know," he said, "being as how you brought him to justice and all."

I didn't argue.

Matter of fact, I knew this was just about as close as Vergil would ever come to telling me I'd done a good job.

According to Vergil, Ernal finally admitted that twenty-two years ago, during the time he was building what turned out to be Rigdon's house, he'd had himself an affair with Margaret Bewley, Rigdon's mom and Ernal's own brother's wife. "Ernal was planning to leave Agnes, and he'd wanted Margaret to leave George, but Margaret wouldn't do it. She told Ernal that she never had any intention of breaking up her marriage." Once Vergil started telling me all this, I knew why he'd decided to phone me at home instead of telling me face-to-face.

What he had to tell me had too much sex in it. He'd have been too embarrassed to tell me in person.

In fact, I could almost feel Vergil reddening over the phone.

"So Ernal decided that if George was only out of the picture, Margaret would be his, and his alone," Vergil said. His voice was pretty much a monotone. He may have been talking about some real juicy goings-on, but he sure wasn't going to sound the least bit excited by it. "So Ernal up and killed George," Vergil went on, "and he wrapped the body in plastic, and he sealed it in the outside wall of the house he was building."

Vergil had gone on to tell me that Ernal had started the rumor that George had run off with some woman in another town, and everybody around Crayton County had believed it. "Except, of course, for Margaret," Vergil said. His voice was still a monotone, but it was starting to sound real sad. "Margaret suspected what Ernal had done to George, and she couldn't stand knowing that she'd been the cause of her own husband's murder, so she up and hung herself."

According to what Vergil told me, it had taken several men—including the Guntermans, who, no doubt, enjoyed themselves tremendously—to rip out the wall in Rigdon's house. Where, of course, the remains of poor George Bewley had been found. The only way to identify him was from the contents of his pocket and his dental records.

Vergil didn't tell me this part, but I heard it around town. Vergil hadn't thought to tell either Gunterman twin why it was they were tearing down that wall in Rigdon's house. Maybe it had slipped Vergil's mind, or maybe he'd pretty much suspected that the twins might not be all that willing to help if they knew.

From what I'd been told, when they discovered George

Bewley's body wrapped in that plastic, you could hear the twins' identical shrieks a mile away.

I listened to Vergil tell me all this, and I realized even as he was still talking exactly why Ernal had suddenly found it necessary to do what he did. Ernal had known that if Rigdon built his museum, Rigdon would've had to tear down that wall and George's body would've been found.

It gave me a kind of creepy feeling to know that Rigdon had been hanging mooseheads and the like on the very wall his own father had been hidden behind all these years.

Vergil also told me that Ernal knew there were folks still around town who would remember that Ernal had insisted on putting up that wall all by himself. "Ernal knew he'd be arrested for murder," Vergil said sadly, "so he killed Rigdon to protect his secret."

Speaking of secrets, Claudine also admitted a few. None so horrible as Ernal's, of course. She showed up at my house the day after Ernal was arrested, and said, "Okay, Haskell, I guess I might as well make a clean breast of it."

I, of course, didn't say anything, but to tell you the truth, after what she'd had on the day before, I probably wouldn't have used those particular words.

"I—I did invent the story about Buck Harrison stalking me, okay? I wrote that note myself that I gave you. I knew you'd recognize my handwriting and all, so I disguised it by using a real backward slant."

She actually looked as if I should admire her ingenuity.

"Claudine, why in the world would you lie about—"

Claudine held up her hand. "Now, I didn't completely lie," she insisted. "I did once have a boyfriend by that name."

I just looked at her. Oh well, *that* certainly made all the difference in the world.

Moving to my side, she linked her arm through mine —the one without the cast—and she said, "I just did it so you'd realize that you—well, that you wanted me back." Claudine looked away and started talking real fast. "That's why I did what I did yesterday too. I went to a lot of trouble to surprise you. I hid my car in the bushes down at the bottom of the hill, and I walked all the way to the top. In high heels!" Her tone was aggrieved. "Just so you'd be surprised to see me!"

I tried not to smile as I said, "Well, Claudine, I was surprised, all right." I couldn't help wondering if Claudine had walked all the way up my hill in the exact same outfit she'd been wearing yesterday, or if she'd disrobed after she got to my house. I decided it probably wasn't prudent to ask.

Claudine had moved on to other topics anyway. "I wanted you to realize that you still wanted me, because I want you, Haskell, I really do!" she was now saying. "I've been on my own for almost two years now, and—and I know now that *you're* the only man for me, Haskell."

I just looked at her some more. "I am?"

She nodded eagerly. "You're a lot nicer guy than any guy I've ever met. Before or after we were married."

Mentally, of course, I added the words, Or even *during*.

Claudine was tightening her hold on my arm. "Oh, Haskell, sweetheart, I didn't know what I'd had, or I'd never have let you go!"

I couldn't help remembering that Claudine's "letting me go" had included a little jig on the courthouse steps.

Claudine was doing this wriggling thing, like a puppy quivering with joy. "Oh, Haskell, remember how wonderful it was, you going to work, and me keeping house for you? It was so great, my keeping our little apartment spick-and-span! I just loved it—I just loved taking care of my man!"

I was, of course, by this time practically gaping at her. *Claudine,* going on and on about how much she enjoyed housework? Maybe this really was her twin sister.

I took a deep breath. "Claudine, didn't you use to tell me that what you really wanted was a career? Which is what you're doing now?"

Claudine was shaking her blond head. "Career, schmeer," she said, "I know now that my career should be in the home. Making my man happy."

I cleared my throat. "You want to quit your job?"

Claudine's eyes lit up. "Oh, my goodness, YES!"

So that was it. Claudine didn't like having to work for a living.

I stared at her. Well, join the club.

No wonder I was suddenly looking so good to her.

I stepped away, turned, and put my hands on both her shoulders, looking her straight in the eye. "Claudine," I said, "listen to me—"

I put it as gently as I could. I certainly didn't say what I was really thinking. Which was that reviving my marriage to Claudine would be a lot like what Rigdon had tried to do with all those furry creatures in his living room.

There wasn't any getting around it. Once something was dead, it was dead. And although you could work with it and work with it and work with it, there was no way it was ever really going to be alive again.

Claudine, I believe, took the news real well. For her, anyway. As soon as she pretty much got the gist of what I was trying to say, she shrugged off my hands and glared at me.

"You're turning *me* down?" she said. "YOU are turning ME down? Who the hell do you think you are? I'm willing to get back together with somebody like *you,* and you say no? Is this a joke?"

I knew I wasn't laughing.

In fact, you could almost get the idea that the woman looked down on me. Like maybe she actually thought that coming back into my life would've been a gigantic favor on her part.

As I recalled, that was pretty much the attitude she'd had during the entire four years of our marriage.

"Well, you better think it over, bub, because this is your last chance."

I didn't even hesitate before I answered. "I've thought it over, Claudzi—" I caught myself just in time. "Clau*dine,*" I finished.

"Hmmph," Claudine said.

On second thought, I probably should've hesitated before I answered, after all. I should've stood there and acted as if I were really pondering all the pros and cons of the thing.

Mainly because, even though Claudine had immediately headed for the door, she seemed to think better of it. She turned, walked back to where I was standing, and gave my cast a sharp rap with her knuckles.

I actually saw stars for a second.

I heard that Claudine left town that very afternoon. I reckon I'd worry about her, but I'm pretty sure if she tries that little stunt with the red bow again, the next guy will fall for it, hook, line, and sinker.

Speaking of being hooked, I reckon that describes me regarding Imogene these days. She also showed up at my house the day after Ernal was arrested, thank God, some time after Claudine had bid me a less-than-fond farewell.

I, of course, could tell that Imogene was nearly as hopping mad as Claudine had been. She slammed the door of her Mustang and came stomping up to my front door.

I, of course, was pretty much getting ready to block any further knuckle-raps.

Imogene came running straight toward me. "Okay,

Haskell," she said, "I've thought it over, and I'm going to have to do something I hate to do. I'm going to have to give you an ultimatum. It's either Claudine or me. Which is it?"

"You."

It was a real short conversation, but I sure like the way it ended. With Imogene in my arms. The good one and the one in the cast.

These days Imogene and I have been getting along even better than before. One reason for this, I believe, is that I now realize that Imogene genuinely does care about me. She's even told me more than once how angry she was that Claudine was obviously making a move on her man.

I kind of like the sound of that. *Her* man.

I was also real glad to hear something else. Just last night, as a matter of fact. Imogene and I were driving up to the Stop 'n' Shop, just to pick up some Cokes and a rental movie, when we started passing Rigdon's signs.

I couldn't help sighing a little when I saw them.

"Old Rigdon was an artist," I said.

Imogene gave me a sidelong glance. "Come on now, Haskell," she said. "I feel real bad about what happened to him, too, but Rigdon Bewley was no artist. Why, that turkey head is the worst thing I've ever seen."

I turned to stare first at her, and then back over at the Rigdon sign we were passing right that minute.

Turkey head? Now that I looked, I realized that Imogene was right. That furry thumb-looking thing *was* a turkey head. What I'd mistook for a thumbnail was the thing's beak.

"How in hell did you know what that was?" I said.

Imogene just gave me one of her soft smiles. "Why, it's pretty obvious, isn't it?" She took a deep breath and added, "What did you think it was—a thumb?"

I decided right then I wouldn't answer. Instead, all I did was return her smile with a real big grin of my own.

You know how I said at the beginning that detectives are supposed to suspect things and all? These days I've been suspecting that Imogene would look right fetching wearing nothing but a big red bow.

Being the detective professional that I am, I reckon I'm going to have to check that one out.